CARBONATE HILL

D0950325

XENIA STREET

SOUTH STREET

4TH STREET

SECOND STREET

SOUTH FIRST STREET

AVENUE

Praise for *What You Said to Me*

"As her Tree of Life series continues, Oliva Newport once again delivers complex characters and cross-generational storylines that show us how words can wound...and yet can also heal. In *What You Said to Me*, Newport examines the depth of human frailties at any age, reminding us that truth has a way of coming to the surface and that what we choose to do with it will make all the difference. Add the fascinating historical threads of the nineteenth century collapse of the US silver market, and readers will enjoy this well-crafted story."

–Julie Cantrell, *New York Times* and *USA TODAY*
bestselling author of *Perennials*

"So few of us truly know our ancestors—their dreams, their challenges, their disappointments, their secrets. In fact, we often don't know those important things about the living because we are experts at hiding, deflecting, and stoically carrying on. In *What You Said to Me*, Olivia Newport unfolds the story of a family nearly lost to the ravages of time and forgetfulness. The result is a tender tale of a troubled girl discovering her unique past and finding hope for a better future. Perfect for fans of historical fiction, genealogy buffs, and anyone who wishes they knew who the people in all those old family photos were."

–Erin Bartels, award-winning author of *We Hope for Better Things*

"Olivia Newport's storytelling is smart, smooth, and sassy in *What You Said to Me*. A cast of endearing characters, a small-town setting, and perfectly woven contemporary and historical threads make for a fast-paced read that ties time and family together. Thank you, Olivia! I couldn't put *What You Said to Me* down!"

–Leslie Gould, Christy–award winning and #1 bestselling author

TREE OF LIFE · BOOK 4

WHAT YOU SAID TO ME

Olivia Newport

SHILOH RUN PRESS

An Imprint of Barbour Publishing, Inc.

© 2020 by Olivia Newport

Print ISBN 978-1-68322-997-1

eBook Editions:
Adobe Digital Edition (.epub) 978-1-64352-820-5
Kindle and MobiPocket Edition (.prc) 978-1-64352-821-2

All Scripture quotations are taken from the King James Version of the Bible.

This book is a work of fiction. Names, characters, places, and incidents are either products of the author's imagination or used fictitiously. Any similarity to actual people, organizations, and/or events is purely coincidental.

Cover design: Faceout Studio, www.faceoutstudio.com

Published by Shiloh Run Press, an imprint of Barbour Publishing, Inc., 1810 Barbour Drive, Uhrichsville, Ohio 44683, www.shilohrunpress.com

Our mission is to inspire the world with the life-changing message of the Bible.

Printed in Canada.

DEDICATION

For Tracy, who takes me to surgeries, calls me after surgeries,
and generally cares about all the parts of life that
go into knowing you matter.

CHAPTER ONE

Wile slightly on the monochromatic end of the culinary spectrum, the dish would pass for edible—more than edible in most family kitchens that wouldn't have Jillian Parisi-Duffy's father coming through the door before it was due to come out of the oven. Every food he prepared was better than everything she made, but she tried to hold up her end of the household balance of chores. Nolan had been arriving home late more and more evenings recently with a bulging briefcase, reminiscent of her childhood when it was her mother who fed the family and her father either missed the evening meal or ate hastily so he could work again in his home office.

That was before Nolan discovered his inner-chef self when circumstances thrust upon him the responsibility of feeding a motherless child.

Jillian was fairly certain she had no inner-chef self awaiting discovery. She simply plodded along, following recipes the way most people did.

This one had been successful enough to repeat every now and then. The casserole dish held cubed chicken with peas, carrots, celery, and onions covered in a roux. Jillian stabbed at a lump in the sauce with a fork and sighed, wondering how many other clots had gotten past her effort this time. In a mixing bowl, she had biscuit dough ready to drop on top. A cheater's chicken pot pie, she called it. No real crust from scratch, which she would have failed at miserably, but plenty of hearty satisfaction, reasonable nutrition, and leftovers for easy lunches.

Jillian had a year and a few days before her thirtieth birthday. Maybe if she didn't share a home with a widowed father who had become such an enthusiast in the kitchen, her own efforts would be more impressive by now.

Doubtful. She was one of those people who enjoyed partaking of interesting meals but found less pleasure in creating them.

She turned on the oven to preheat and dropped rounds of biscuits at carefully calculated intervals. The refrigerator held arugula, avocado, and plum tomatoes for a salad she could throw together at the last minute.

While she waited for her dad, Jillian cleaned up after herself, rinsing the pans and utensils she'd used before loading the dishwasher and wiping down the gray-speckled granite counter and breakfast bar. By then the oven was just about ready. Nolan's pickup rumbled into the driveway, and a couple of minutes later he ambled through the back door.

"You cooked?" Nolan's keys clanked into the copper bowl on the counter.

"I sent a text telling you I would."

He plopped his briefcase onto the breakfast bar and dug for his phone in a pocket. "I see that now. Sorry. It's been a hairy day."

"The mediation isn't going well?"

"I can't seem to get the parties in the same library, much less reading the same book or on the same page."

"You'll do it, Dad. I know you can."

"Thanks for the vote of confidence, Jilly. And for dinner." He inspected her offering. "Have we run out of magical little black flecks?"

Jillian rolled her eyes. "Pepper is your department. Just don't overdo it, all right?"

"I don't conceive that as a possibility in the existing universe."

"Your taste buds live on steroids." Jillian tossed her sponge in the sink. "Do you feel up to making the dressing for the arugula?"

"Happy to." Nolan sprinkled pepper on the main dish and put it in the oven. "I arranged some help for you today."

Jillian cocked her head. "I wasn't aware I needed help." A maid? A counselor? A spiritual director? A running coach?

Nolan spun her around by the shoulders and marched her into the dining room. "Has it occurred to you that we have been unable to dine in this room for quite some time? That in fact it is becoming increasingly difficult even to traverse safely through on the way to the living room?"

"You can always go by way of the hall. I have it under control, Dad."

"I beg to differ."

Jillian scowled. Usually she kept her work contained to her office, which was a few steps down a short hall right off the kitchen. Overflow files might temporarily occupy the two side chairs across from her desk but not often for long. Many of her genealogical research projects required no physical files at all.

The St. Louis project was different. It involved hundreds of papers from the client, dating back long before the internet was in everyone's house, supplemented by auxiliary information she was already dredging from assorted research sources that might or might not prove relevant. It would take time to sort through what she had to work with and find credible starting points for all the genealogical trails the work demanded. Files from decades ago rambled over the dining table and onto half the chairs. Well, all except the one Jillian sat on. Several stacks on the floor converged in a trail leading into the living room. But Jillian knew generally what everything was and what she intended to do with it. Eventually.

"I have a system," Jillian said. "I know how to do my job. This contract is just larger than most."

"Monstrously," Nolan said. "I know you plan to subcontract some of it out to other genealogists once you get a better grasp of what all is here, but don't you think you could use a teeny bit of administrative help on the front end?"

"Maybe." She wasn't persuaded. "I don't even know how I'd figure out what to pay someone. I'm still getting my head around the project."

"The beauty of my plan," Nolan said, "is you don't have to pay a penny."

"Oh no."

"What does that mean?"

"It means—*Dad*!"

"Aren't you getting a little old to use that suspicious tone?"

Jillian cleared her throat. "Would you like to explain?"

The doorbell rang.

"No time." Nolan headed for the front door. "She's here."

"Who's here?"

"Just give her a chance."

"Dad!"

He wagged a finger at her.

Nolan opened the door on one side of the spacious Victorian home that served as its main entrance. Jillian hung back, but she could see the figure on the porch.

A waif of a teenage girl with bright pink hair, ripped cut-off shorts, and twigs for legs met Nolan's exuberant greeting with the deadpan expression of a comedic straight man.

This was help?

Surely she had a crate at her feet and was about to launch into a canned speech about how buying candy or magazine subscriptions would help underprivileged youth such as herself go to camp and develop leadership skills. Someone else would come to the door in response to Nolan's arrangement.

Instead, Nolan welcomed the girl in.

No crate of items to sell.

"Jillian, this is Tisha Crowder."

"Hello." Jillian knew who she was—at least by sight, and who her mother was. Brittany Crowder was three years ahead of Jillian in school. Everyone knew her. She'd always been popular. Then the rumors started flying that she was pregnant even though she'd never had a steady boyfriend in Canyon Mines—that anyone knew about—and she was tight-lipped about who the baby's father was. But Jillian was a freshman and Brittany a senior, or would have been, when the baby was born. She'd dropped out. The rumors shifted to saying that she never told a single person who the child's father was. Not her mother. Not her best friend. Not her doctor. No one. Jillian didn't care. By the time Brittany had her baby, Jillian was mourning her mother. Speculating about another student she barely knew was the last thing on her mind.

Brittany kept the baby and continued living with her mother and grandmother. Over the years, the three women rotated through working in one Main Street shop or another, so their faces were familiar to everyone. Jillian tried to ignore the gossip about why there were never any men in that family. Tisha's hair had been blue and then green before this summer's pink. Once it had even been half and half. Then there was the year she'd cut the hair on the sides of her head two different lengths.

It would be hard not to notice Tisha Crowder.

Jillian eyed Nolan. Her father could strike up a conversation with every stranger he met, but even for him it seemed a stretch to propose Tisha as an answer to Jillian's need for help.

Help she did not actually need and had not asked for and did not want.

"Tisha is in a bit of a pickle," Nolan said. "She needs to do some volunteer hours between now and when school starts again in a few weeks."

"Oh?" Jillian looked from her father to the girl. "A school project of some sort?"

"No." Tisha blew a bubble with her gum and popped it, staring at Jillian all the while. It was as if she were reading off a script about how to fail a job interview.

Look like a punk. Check.

Wear inappropriate clothes. Check.

Seem disinterested. Check.

Display annoying habits. Check.

"Not school," Nolan said. "A legal matter."

Jillian returned her gaze to Nolan, feeling her eyebrows lift involuntarily.

"Why don't we sit down?" Nolan cleared a stack of yellow file folders from the purple chair where Jillian liked to sit. While she settled in, he sat beside Tisha on the navy sofa.

"Tisha pleaded guilty to shoplifting at a downtown Denver department store," Nolan said.

Tisha shrugged and muttered, "They had me on camera."

Undeterred, Nolan proceeded. "It was her first time in court, and the value of the item was low enough that she qualified for alternative sentencing. No one is interested in ruining a young person's life over one overpriced silk scarf."

The mental image of a silk scarf from a department store around the neck of Tisha Crowder lacked coherence. Wouldn't a designer shirt or even a handbag make more sense? Or electronics?

"Her lawyer was someone whose services her mother once used, a long time ago."

"I see."

"I know him from family court connections. It's pro bono all around. When he saw Tisha had a legal address in Canyon Mines," Nolan said, "he reached out to me to see if I would be willing to supervise something."

"I'm sorry, I don't follow," Jillian said. "Supervise?"

"Tisha needs some sort of structured community service or volunteer work experience over the summer to meet the terms of her alternative sentencing. Doing it in Denver isn't practical. We're already past the Fourth of July. Half the summer is gone. The rest will go fast. If she completes her hours successfully and stays out of serious trouble for the next twelve months, the incident will be taken off her record. Happily, I knew somebody who could use an extra pair of eyes and hands for a few weeks."

Oh Dad, oh Dad, oh Dad. You've got to be kidding.

"Tisha," Jillian said, "do you have any work experience?"

"Nah." She smacked her gum and crossed her bare legs, letting a yellow flip-flop dangle from one big toe.

"Tisha just turned fifteen," Nolan said, "so she would have needed a work permit. But we had quite a lengthy conversation with her caseworker, and she is confident of Tisha's abilities."

And what abilities are those?

In response to a buzz, Tisha pulled an iPhone several models newer than Jillian's from her back pocket and began texting. Where did she get the money for that? Or had she bypassed cash in the manner in which she acquired it?

Monosyllabic responses. Check.

No prior experience. Check.

Text during interview. Check.

"What kinds of things are you interested in?" Jillian asked. "Do you like history?"

"History?" Tisha didn't look up from her phone. "Not really."

"Do you have computer skills?"

"Duh. Internet-native generation."

Tisha didn't look up. Jillian glared at Nolan.

"Are you good at sorting information into files?"

"Don't know. Never tried."

"Tisha needs about fifteen hours a week for the rest of the summer," Nolan said. "That sounds right, doesn't it, Tisha?"

"I guess." Tisha finally shoved her phone back in her pocket.

"We can make up some kind of a time sheet. It doesn't have to be the same three hours a day, as long as it comes out to fifteen every week. And this week we need to make up for missing today."

"So you're thinking we'd start tomorrow?" Jillian forced thin words past the choking sensation.

"Can you think why not? It's only Tuesday."

"Kris might need some extra help down at the ice cream shop. She hires teenagers," Jillian said. "And summer housekeeping is always busy for Nia at the Inn. She takes on extra people for the season. We could check around for something we're sure is the best fit for Tisha's skills."

"Every plan should always be open to adjustments, of course," Nolan said, "but I'd like to see us give this a chance before we reevaluate. You could really use some help in an immediate way."

He pointed toward the dining room, and Jillian's gaze followed his finger.

So you brought me a juvenile delinquent who clearly doesn't want to be here?

CHAPTER TWO

I'll leave it to the two of you to work out the details," Nolan said. "Take a few minutes to get to know each other while I work on dinner."

Pressure lurched through Jillian's chest. He wasn't going to invite Tisha to eat with them, was he?

"Would you like to stay for dinner, Tisha?" Nolan said. "We'd love to have you."

Jillian clenched her teeth.

Tisha narrowed her eyes. "What are you having?"

Well, that's rude.

"Jillian made a delicious version of chicken pot pie," Nolan said, "and I'm going to throw together an arugula salad with homemade dressing."

"Arugawhat? I think I'll just go home to eat. See what Grandma Ora cooked."

Jillian eased out a breath of relief.

"We'll try again another day," Nolan said. "Take your time, Jillian. We probably still have at least thirty minutes."

The blanch of boredom that trundled through Tisha's face said she didn't intend to be at the Duffy residence in thirty minutes. Jillian certainly wouldn't argue the point.

Humming, Nolan picked his way through the cluttered dining room and into the kitchen.

"Okay," Jillian said, "maybe we should have a look at my project."

"We could just do it tomorrow."

The thought was tempting.

"If I explain a few things now," Jillian said, "maybe we can hit the ground running in the morning."

"Morning?"

"Will that work for you?"

"Well, I guess I don't want to wreck my whole day hanging out here."

Yep, this was going to work out just swell.

"It doesn't have to be first thing," Jillian said. "Nine o'clock would be fine. You'd be finished by lunchtime."

"Yeah, we could try that."

Tisha's response hardly sounded like a commitment.

"In here." Jillian gestured toward the dining room. "How much did my dad say about the work?"

"Not much. Just piles of papers."

Jillian suspected Nolan had said more than that and Tisha hadn't been listening because she'd been looking at her phone.

"Well, there are piles, as you can see," Jillian said.

"So, alphabetizing or something?"

"It's more complicated than that. The files have to do with children who were stolen from their parents anywhere from the early 1930s to the late 1950s. They were adopted by other families who thought they were paying large fees to legitimate adoption agencies. The truth only came out a few months ago."

Tisha glanced at Jillian, slightly puzzled, but her hand was on the back of her hip, where her phone had been buzzing intermittently the whole time Jillian was speaking.

Jillian plowed ahead. "I'm a genealogist. I trace family lines and help people put the pieces together. My client has hired me to see if it's possible to trace accurate information about the real identity of any of these children and find relatives in the families they were taken from. Make sense?"

"I guess. It looks like a lot of papers." Tisha's phone started buzzing again.

"It is. But these children were stolen, so it's important. What happened was criminal."

Tisha was texting. *Tap tap tap tap tap tap tap.*

Pause.

Tap tap tap tap tap tap tap.

"Anyway," Jillian said.

"Yeah?"

"So far I've been trying to look at the documents and decide which ones are the best leads, the ones most likely to yield information we could actually do something with. At some point I'll scan as much as I can so I can work electronically the way I usually do, but some of the documents may be too fragile. There's always photographing. In any event, for now there is a lot of basic sorting to do, and we have to be careful not to mix up anything or tear anything."

We. Jillian could hardly believe she was using that word with an uninterested teenager she'd never spoken to before tonight. There were so many opportunities for error. How could she be sure she could trust Tisha?

She couldn't.

"I've developed a system for the documents," Jillian said. "Color-coded file folders to represent different stages of the project. I'll explain more tomorrow."

"I'm not going to know what to do with all these papers," Tisha said.

"I'll try to make it as clear as I can," Jillian said. "But I think you'll be able to help with making file labels easily enough. I also bought some boxes made to hold file folders, and you can put those together. Eventually everything will be stored on shelves in a spare bedroom upstairs, but I don't have the shelves yet."

"Yeah." Tisha looked around. "How many kids?"

"I haven't actually counted. I guess you could help with that. Some have folders, but some were only listed in record books we found in the bottom of a file cabinet. In the hundreds, which is why things seem a bit out of hand."

"You could say that again."

"It's not actually out of hand," Jillian said. "It just seems like it. I know where everything is while I'm getting organized, but apparently my father would like the dining room back sometime before Christmas. He can be so picky."

Jillian attempted a smile, but Tisha didn't respond. Still gripping her phone, the girl was surveying the dining room. Dismay pulsed through her features with every blink.

"It's not as bad as it looks." Jillian straightened one pile.

"So you keep saying."

"Does nine o'clock sound good for a regular time?"

"Can we be flexible about that?"

"Do you have conflicts?"

"I might. I never know."

"Well, some days I have appointments or errands too, so I suppose we can be flexible," Jillian said. How busy could a fifteen-year-old in trouble be? "Maybe we can set the schedule a day or two in advance so we can both plan."

"Yeah. Sure."

"But nine o'clock tomorrow?"

"Okay. Fine."

"Do you live far?" Buried in Jillian's mind was the notion that Tisha's family lived across Eastbridge, on the other side of Cutter Creek, the small river that ran through Canyon Mines. The homes there were modest, some even tiny. The one Jillian shared with her father, which had once been two mirrored homes sharing a wall that was later removed, must have seemed lavish to the girl.

"It's okay," Tisha said. "I have my bike."

"All right, then." Jillian mustered another smile. "I'll see you out and look forward to the morning." *See you out?* Why was she talking like an English butler?

"Yeah."

If Nolan had not already made the hiring decision, Tisha Crowder would not be in the running—for a nonexistent vacancy.

Jillian closed the heavy front door behind the departing guest and padded toward the kitchen.

"Nolan Duffy, what have you gotten me into?"

"A chance to help." Nolan looked up from the bowl of arugula. "Don't you recognize the opportunity?"

"I recognize that she needs help more than I do," Jillian said. "Why didn't you talk to me before signing me up for this?"

Nolan tossed the greens and popped a plum tomato into his mouth.

"You were afraid I'd say no," Jillian said.

"The risk crossed my mind. Mostly I forgot. The afternoon got away from me—the same reason I never read your text about dinner. I'm sorry, Silly Jilly."

Jillian eased into a stool at the breakfast bar. "You must be working even harder than I realized."

"I got a call from the caseworker asking if I could squeeze in a meeting this afternoon." Nolan whisked the salad dressing. "I had to think on the spot and tell her something. I was sitting there in her office with Tisha—whose mother dropped her off for a court-mandated meeting and didn't even come in, so I'll have to have a word with her first thing tomorrow—and I had to give her some proposed description to put on her form. It had to be something that demonstrated I could give reasonable assurance I had this under control. We can finalize it in a few days."

"So you told Tisha to show up here."

"Then I dashed off to that befuddling mediation, and I was practically home before I remembered I'd never called you."

"I can understand why you want to help her, but I'm having trouble seeing how this is going to work."

"Please try, Jilly. You do need the help."

"That is a matter of opinion."

"I won't leave you stranded. My name and reputation are on the paperwork. I promise we're in this together."

"I'm not like you, Dad. You make friends with everybody. I tend to step in it and make a mess."

"You chronically undersell yourself on that question. And you need the help."

"You keep saying that! Even if I thought I needed help, Tisha doesn't want to help."

"Well, she has to. I'm working at home tomorrow, so I'll be here when she arrives to remind her."

"In the most affable way."

"Of course."

"I'm hungry." Jillian slid off the stool and went to a cupboard for plates. "Get my creation out of the oven, will you?"

CHAPTER THREE

Denver, Colorado
Wednesday, June 28, 1893

If his black fountain pen stained another white dress shirt cuff, Clifford Brandt would have no credible excuse to offer Georgina. Her patience over twenty-two years of marriage with his inability to be more careful with ink and clothing was saintly. Left-handedness put shirtsleeves at particular risk if he neglected to don a sleeve garter or roll up the cuff before working on Mr. Tabor's books during the daytime hours or writing in his journal at home, and his wrist moved over freshly scrawled lettering not yet dried.

"Papa?"

Clifford looked up from the desk in the smallest room in his home northeast of downtown Denver to see his eldest daughter standing in the doorframe. With a wife and three daughters, whose wardrobes alone seemed to take up more space than he could comprehend, Clifford was content with a modest space on the ground floor where he could occasionally withdraw.

"Good morning, Missouri." Clifford found pleasure in speaking her full given name these days. He and Georgina had always called her Missy and perhaps always would sentimentally, but she was twenty-one now, a woman—and named for the state he hailed from. Sometimes, after all these years, Clifford liked to hear that name spoken as well.

"Are you writing in your journal?" Missouri smoothed her skirt as she entered the room. "You don't usually do that in the morning."

Clifford blew on the ink and then dabbed at the last word he'd written to test its dryness. Satisfied, he closed the journal.

"I may not have time to write for a few days," he said. "I have to make a trip."

"To the mines?"

He nodded.

"My mine? The Missouri Rise?"

Clifford nodded again as he placed the brown leather journal on a shelf between the journal that had preceded his current volume and a thick dictionary. Missy had been a lifelong early riser, so how to name the mine for her had been no puzzle.

"May I come?"

"Not this time, Missy."

"Please, Papa."

"It's not the right trip."

She stepped toward the desk. "I read the newspaper, Papa. Mama may have her head in the sand, but I don't."

Clifford motioned for her to close the door, and she did.

"I know what's at stake," Missouri said. "Silver has been at risk ever since President Cleveland was elected and promised to end the Sherman Silver Purchase Act."

"It's more than that," Clifford said. "The international markets are falling apart too. India—the news has not been good for a long time. The price is down to seventy-three cents an ounce."

Missouri paled. "That's a dime less than two days ago."

"And a quarter less than a few months ago. We don't know where the bottom will be."

Missouri leaned against the closed door. "You're going up there to close the Missouri Rise."

"And the Decorah Runner and the Fidelity Wink." His other two daughters had mines named for them also—their first names and nicknames from their youngest years. Decorah had begged to race him through the house daily until Georgina put her foot down about encouraging a bad habit, and Fidelity still hadn't mastered winking only one eye but had amused him to no end trying. "And several for Mr. Tabor. His others are getting word to close as well. Nobody in the state will be mining silver anytime soon. There's no profit in it anymore."

Her charcoal eyes widened.

"You're strong," Clifford said. "I can tell you. We cannot afford to operate another day. We've been losing money hand over fist for weeks as it is. But don't tell Corah or Lity yet."

"And Mama?"

"I'll have to figure that out when I get back. For now she thinks I'm going to do inspections as I usually do." Clifford's three mines were small, his own modest investments made by carefully saving from wages paid by Mr. Tabor over the years. After sinking money into men, equipment, and dynamite, they'd finally begun to produce ore he could take to market.

And then the winds of the market shifted. Clifford didn't know if they would ever be worth anything again. And Horace Tabor? He was heavily invested in silver mining all over the state. Despite his lavish lifestyle, he was overextended. Once the debt collectors came—Clifford shook off the thought.

He hadn't told Georgina, and he didn't tell Missouri now, that Mr. Tabor hadn't paid his salary in weeks, not since every mine in the state began bleeding faster than the wounds could be stanched.

"I could still change clothes and ride up with you, Papa," Missouri said. "You know I'm good on a horse."

"As fine as any man I know." Clifford capped his fountain pen and stowed it in his desk drawer. "But not this time."

"Will you stay in Canyon Mines?"

He nodded. The thirty-year-old town served as a focal point for many mines in the area. It was a reliable channel for supplies, a town where married miners could send their children to school, and a place where ore could be assayed to determine the strength of a vein before investing too heavily in the wrong place. Nearby narrow-gauge railroad tracks ensured cars of ore could get down to Denver for markets and supplies up to town to keep shops well stocked.

Missouri's eyes clouded even as her face held its composure.

"I know you want to see him," Clifford said softly.

"What will he do?"

"I don't know. There will be many men in his position. But he has you."

"Will that be enough?"

"One day at a time, Missy. Right now that's all we can do."

Clifford kissed his daughter's cheek and went to find his wife to bid her as cheerful a farewell as he could manage. The day had adequate light remaining to get to the Missouri Rise, do what he had to do, and bunk in for the night in Canyon Mines. He let Georgina pack one of his saddlebags with food for the journey, as she always did. The pit in his stomach likely would not allow him to partake of her provisions, and Canyon Mines offered hearty fare at reasonable prices, but to decline Georgina's offer would only have made her fret, and his sweet Georgina found too much to fuss over as it was. She'd brooded over this property when they first considered it. The house was large, the yard longer than most in the vicinity, the stable out of place in a neighborhood built for access to streetcars or cabs. Yet she had liked the idea of a carriage, and they would grow into feeling at home in the house. So they'd bought it, and they kept horses that were temperate enough to pull the carriage but also take a saddle when called upon.

Through the years, after Horace Tabor discovered Clifford Brandt working one of his mines, made him a manager, and assigned him progressive responsibility in Denver, Clifford had enjoyed the inspection tours between bookkeeping duties and hiring decisions. He could have taken a train to Canyon Mines, but once there he preferred to have his own horse to travel between the various locations he visited. The hours spent on his mare winding into the mountains, eyes bursting at the expanse of forest before him and sky above him, soothed whatever worried him. If only Georgina would let the mountains speak to her the way they did to him, she might find balm for her anxiety, at least in the moment.

He reached the Missouri Rise, some miles west of Canyon Mines, before the crew was finished with their ten-hour shift. With the first vein of silver that paid off, Clifford had gone straight home from selling the load of milled ore and handed Georgina a wad of bills to use to redecorate the front rooms of the house. This had given her great pleasure, and while choosing fabrics and designs generated some fretfulness, the final result made her proud. It made him proud too to see her happy. She had done well. Every guest to their home complimented her tasteful choices.

Outside the mine, beside the pile of rocks that had been blasted out of the mountain, one firing of dynamite at a time, and hefted away from the tunnel's entrance, Loren Wade swung his pickax into the ground and raised a hand to wave at Clifford. "This is unexpected."

Clifford swung off his horse. "I thought about sending a telegram that I was coming but decided just to come." He could have sent a telegram ordering immediate cessation of work, but he owed the men some face-to-face explanation.

"I'm glad you did." Loren beckoned him toward the mine's entrance. "Come on down."

Clifford pulled his watch from his vest pocket to glance at it. "Won't the men be coming up soon?" All unmarried—Clifford couldn't afford to pay men who had to support a family, and men couldn't feed children on speculation—the small crew of four bunked in a nearby boardinghouse. "I don't want them to miss their supper."

"We have time. Mrs. Mitchell knows not to set her table by our quitting hour." Loren's expression turned quizzical. "Aren't you here to inspect? Advise? I think you'll like what you see."

Clifford hesitated. What was the point of giving them false hope with an inspection of the vein they'd been working since his last visit? On the other hand, if the silver market didn't recover, he might never have reason to descend a mine he owned again.

In an oversuit to protect his good traveling clothes and armed with a hat and candle, Clifford followed the younger man down the ladder, remembering for a moment the way he used to scramble down in the manner Loren did now, mindless of how the rungs trembled beneath them, growing colder and damper with each yard deeper into the darkness. His spine tingled with crawling doubt as the shaft narrowed. Descending a hundred feet or more into pitch blackness was not natural, yet the thrill tantalized. The riches of Mother Earth were here, waiting to glitter in sunlight like newborns blinking in the first light of day. A drift ninety feet west had not yielded as much as they'd hoped two years ago, but another, shorter, in the other direction had done far better before it backstopped. Then they'd dropped down to create a second level. Many of the larger mines had four, five, or even six levels. Men descended in cages, not ladders, to work in teams around the clock, and mules that went down turned blind because they never again saw the sun as they labored moving cars through the tunnels. Horace Tabor could offer those more efficient conditions in large mines that churned out tons of ore daily, while Clifford still relied on his crew to push and leverage even the heaviest of work. Once the crew filled cars with ore, a hired team of mules dragged the cars to tracks to put them on a path to Denver. For all this Clifford needed strong, hardworking men.

Or he had.

All that was gone.

Clifford barely heard what Loren said about the new tunnel where three men were clearing up, making sure they left the work area safe overnight. He nodded thoughtfully and squinted his eyes where Loren pointed, aiming his candle as if to be able to see what made Loren so optimistic and enthusiastic.

Then they climbed the ladder to the surface, feeling the air warm and dry out. The other men emptied buckets into cars that could be moved to the rail tracks when the time came.

Clifford doubted he would go to the expense of moving them anytime soon.

In the waning sunlight outside the mine's entrance, the men splashed water on their faces and propped themselves up on the largest boulders. Clifford pulled a handkerchief from a pocket and wiped perspiration from his brow.

A pall of shock fell over them with his news.

No more shifts. Not even tomorrow.

What pained him most was that he couldn't pay their salaries for the last thirty days. The loss of his own salary and the precipitous drop in silver prices meant he probably should have closed his mines before this. He spared the men the details of how much silver sat idle in Denver, not worth the expense of preparing it for collapsing markets.

"What are we supposed to do?" one of the men asked.

Clifford exhaled. "I wish I could tell you. If you come to Denver, and you want to ride this out until we know if anyone can ever mine again, I'll do what I can to find you work. I would hire all of you again in a heartbeat. But I must ask you not to take that as a promise. This is not a time for promises. I can't guarantee I have any influence. Things are grim. I'm being honest. My own liquidity is limited, and I have two other teams who will be in the same position. Every man has to make his own decision. You might decide it's best to leave Colorado."

He spread his fingers across his face to pinch his eyes closed and inward for a moment before opening them again to meet each man's gaze. Loren, whose thoughts would be of Missouri. Wesley, who had promised to send for his sweetheart in Kansas as soon as he had enough saved. Clyde, who was sending money home to his parents in Ohio. Jasper, who dreamed of prospecting his own mine someday— sooner rather than later. "I'm so sorry. I wish there was something more I could do, but under the present circumstances, I just can't think what it would be."

Sullen, wordless faces bore back at him.

"I've done a poor job of thanking you for your faithful service," Clifford said. "I wish I'd said that first. Please forgive me. Please forgive me."

CHAPTER FOUR

O melets and hash browns?" Jillian took her favorite mug from the cupboard, the large taupe one with the maroon swirl around the bottom, and in the movement saw her mother reaching for the same mug for so many years. Jillian had only started using it a few months ago, but she made sure it was clean every night and available every morning. "And you turned on my fancy coffee machine that you make such a hobby of mocking?"

"I thought you might require fortification this morning."

Nolan chopped a row of green pepper slices with speed and precision Jillian would never aspire to. She pressed ground hazelnut coffee into the machine and selected her buttons before going to the refrigerator for half-and-half to steam.

"Fortification for Tisha, you mean." Jillian spoke over the noise of her morning beverage preparation.

"She's a child, Silly Jilly. We have to remember that."

"I'm not sure she does."

"That's not her job." Nolan whisked eggs and poured the mixture into the heated pan.

From its corner of the kitchen, the barista-quality coffee machine whirred and spun and dispensed Jillian's coffee. She stirred in her desired quota of sugar and topped it with the steamed milk.

Nolan dropped cheese into the omelet before flipping it without compromising its shape and turned the potatoes at the instant of perfect browning.

"What am I supposed to do with her, Dad?" Jillian carried her coffee to the breakfast bar and slouched into her favorite stool.

"I know you're self-employed and a solo practitioner used to doing everything yourself, but think of this as an opportunity to grow your supervisory skills. You can enhance your résumé."

"Ha ha."

"There must be some simple tasks that a bright teenager can handle to lighten your load."

"I already know how I want everything organized."

"Then let her help you organize faster." Nolan slid a loaded plate in front of Jillian and filled one for himself.

"Honestly, Dad, she doesn't seem that interested."

"That's because she doesn't understand what you do yet. She'll get there."

"I'm not so sure."

"Last night was weird for you." Nolan took his seat beside Jillian. "Think about how weird it was for Tisha."

"I suppose." Jillian moved some potatoes around on her plate. "Should we hide the valuables or something?"

"Jillian!"

"Sorry. I guess I just feel nervous about this whole thing."

"I know. It wasn't your idea. But it's only a few weeks, and it could really make a difference for Tisha."

Jillian set down her fork and turned up both palms. "Okay. I'll try. I really will."

"Be open to surprises."

"That's certainly your modus operandi."

"Life's too short to be bored."

"Says the man who drinks boring black coffee." Jillian picked up her much more imaginative concoction.

"Touché." Nolan sipped his plain green mug of plain black coffee.

"You're working at home today, right?"

"Correct. I have a meeting here in town later this morning with a potential client. Otherwise I'll have my nose to the grindstone upstairs."

"Good. I might need you."

"No, you won't. But if you do, I'll be around until you're well underway with Tisha."

Jillian cleaned up the kitchen, answered some emails, and stared at the piles of folders in the dining room, trying to imagine Tisha

Crowder bringing order to them.

Movement outside the front windows caught her eye, a flash of pink above spinning green. The neon-haired girl had arrived on her neon bike.

Jillian paced to the foot of the stairs. "Dad! She's here."

"Be right down."

Tisha rode her bike up the sidewalk, not hopping off until she was at the base of the steps of the porch that wrapped around the side of the house. She leaned it against the railing. Not especially tall, at fifteen she likely wouldn't gain much more height, yet the bicycle looked like it was a couple of inches smaller than ideal. With several gears, it would get the job done, but it was hardly a fancy flyer of a bike and certainly not a mountain bike to take off paved roads. The flashy color was consistent with Tisha's propensities. Instead of coming straight up to the doorbell, however, she paused to pull out her phone.

"Of course," Jillian murmured.

"What did you say?" Nolan stood beside her.

"She's on her phone."

"Is she late?"

Jillian glanced at her own phone. "Technically she has two minutes."

"Then leave it be."

Tisha walked slowly up the steps, still on her phone, and rang the bell.

"I'll get it!" Nolan called out.

"I'm right here," Jillian grumbled, raising a hand to cover her ear.

"That was for external effect."

Jillian glanced out the window. "She doesn't seem to notice."

Tisha pushed her oversized phone into a pocket. At least today her shorts had hems and covered a reasonable portion of her thighs. Her T-shirt even covered her belly button. Barely.

Was it possible she'd made an effort to dress appropriately for the first day on the job?

Clearly the pink hair was there to stay. Youthful experimentation with bold color had never seemed like an option for Jillian with her thick, wavy dark hair, inherited from her Italian mother—not that she'd been tempted. Tisha's blond base color made it much easier.

Nolan opened the door. "Good morning!"

Tisha squinted up at him. "Yeah. Hi."

"You ready to jump in?"

"I'm here."

A cagey response, it seemed to Jillian.

"Well, Jillian's ready for you," Nolan said. "Aren't you, Jillian?"

"We have lots of work to do." Jillian felt cagey herself.

"Jillian makes some amazing fancy coffee drinks," Nolan said. "Just tell her what you want, and she'll fix you right up."

"That's right," Jillian said. "Latte, espresso, cappuccino—whatever you like."

Tisha made a face. "I'm only fifteen. I haven't developed a taste for that disgusting poison yet. I hope I never will."

Wow. Three sentences. Rude and unnecessary but complete sentences. Plenty of teenagers drank coffee.

"If you don't mind, I'll make myself another cup," Jillian said. Without coffee, she didn't have any other icebreaker tricks up her sleeve. "Then let's get to work."

"I'm confident you'll make spectacular progress." Nolan winked.

"We'll do our best." Jillian rounded up what she hoped was a convincing smile. "Right, Tisha?"

"Yeah. Sure."

"Be sure to track your hours," Nolan said. "I'll be up in my office making some calls before I go out for a meeting."

"Come on in the kitchen with me." Jillian led the way. "We have some orange juice, or I can make you some cucumber water."

Tisha looked at Jillian with an expression that screamed, *Lame.*

Jillian tried again. "What do you like to drink?" *Please don't say Jack Daniels.*

"Italian cream soda."

"Really?

"Yeah."

"I like Italian cream soda too. My mom used to let me have it for a treat when I was little. It's sort of an American Italian drink, but she liked it." Jillian readied the coffee machine for her second cup of the morning.

"Does she still like it?" Tisha scanned the kitchen.

"I'm sure she would, but she passed away a long time ago."

"Oh."

"Do you want a glass of plain water?"

"No. I'll just bring my own drink from now on."

"Um, okay. I'm happy to buy something you like to keep it around."

"Nope."

Jillian pushed buttons and waited for the machine's sounds.

"What's that?" Tisha pointed at a small picture hanging on a short wall at one end of the counter.

"Something else my mother liked. She found it at a garage sale when I was little."

"No, I mean what is it? Like where?"

"Nothing in particular. Just a painting of the hills around Canyon Mines in the silver mining heyday, I think. She liked the colors. It's only a print. There are a few others floating around town. I have no idea where the original is."

"Huh."

"Are you interested in history?"

Tisha side-eyed Jillian. "You asked me that last night."

"Right. Not really your thing."

"I just feel like I've seen it before—that's all."

"Maybe you know someone else who has one of the other copies." Jillian grabbed her mug of coffee. "Let's get to work."

In the dining room, she set her coffee safely away from the files on the table and picked up a label maker.

"Here's what I'm thinking. The original folders are crumbling, literally, and the names on them are handwritten. Some of them are hard to read or might not be spelled the way you would expect. I'd like you to open the folders, check the spelling of the name on the outside of the folder against names you see on documents inside. If there are any discrepancies, carefully spell the name in the way that seems the most consistent. Print out a label on the label maker, put it on a new blue folder, and transfer the contents from the original folder to the new folder. Any questions so far?"

"Uh, no."

"Good. Then over here on the table you'll find some stacks of documents. These are records I believe may be related to the child or children listed in the documents in the blue folder. I've put large sticky notes with the same names and cross-stacked the piles. Not every name has papers on the table, but many do. Some of the names have only a sheet or two, and others have quite a few, so you have to be careful that you get them separated by the sticky notes. It's important not to confuse them because it could seriously derail the research efforts going forward. Do you understand?"

"I speak English."

"Sorry. It's just very important."

"Yeah. You've made your point."

This was going every bit as well as Jillian anticipated. "Anyway," she said, "what I need you to do is make a second label with the same name that you put on a blue folder and put it on a red folder. Then put the papers under the corresponding sticky note in the red folder. The last step is to stack the matching blue and red folders together. Can you do that?"

"Like in the fourth grade." Tisha took the label maker from Jillian's hand.

"Once we get everything in folders, it will cut down on the general sense of disorganization—which is not really disorganization, because I know where everything is—and then we can get down to more serious work."

"Okay. Sure. Read. Spell. Paste. Match. Paste again."

"Accuracy is paramount."

"So you said."

"We can work together. I brought my coffee in, after all." Jillian raised her mug.

"But we only have one label maker."

Jillian gulped coffee. "We'll figure out a system."

"Don't most people print labels with a computer these days?"

"Maybe. Personally I don't think that works all that well for this kind of project. You have to have an entire sheet of labels ready to put through the printer. This way we can smack the labels on the folders and be done with it."

"I guess."

"Let's get started, then."

"You don't have to hover." Tisha picked up a folder. "I know what I'm doing. See. This one says Reigland. R-e-i-g-l-a-n-d."

"I want to be sure you don't have any questions."

"It can't be that hard."

"Oh, I forgot to mention. Please use all caps."

"Got it."

"Okay. All caps. Blue folder."

"Remember to check the spelling inside, please. On a name like that, it could be R-i-e."

Tisha sighed. "You don't have to keep explaining."

Jillian gulped more coffee. "Thanks. I'll be back in a few minutes, and we'll see if we can get in a groove."

"Whatever."

Jillian backed out of the dining room with a smile pasted on her face. In the hall she pivoted and scurried to her office, closed the door, set down her mug, and pulled out her phone.

She punched in a speed dial contact. "Nia?"

"What's up?"

"You were a kid once," Jillian said.

"Um, yes."

"Even a teenager."

"Also correct."

"You babysat me when I was a kid while you were a teenager."

"Additional true information."

"Then you became a school guidance counselor."

"Yep, I did."

"For how many years?"

"I guess it was about eight years. You know that."

"Until you married Leo and you two decided to move back to Canyon Mines and open the Inn at Hidden Run."

"Jillian, you're being very strange."

"And you were a good enough counselor that the Canyon Mines School District would hire you in an instant if only you would accept one of their constant offers."

"Jillian," Nia said, "why are you telling me my life's story?"

"Because I can't take any chances that you're going to deny that you know a lot more about kids than I do. Teenagers in particular."

"Technically you weren't a teenager when I was your babysitter," Nia said, "but maybe you'd like to cut to the chase and tell me what has you so worked up."

"My dad got me into something, and I'm in over my head, and you're an expert, so you have to help me."

"I run a bed-and-breakfast now."

"You're not listening. You have to help me."

"Maybe you need to give me more context."

"Maybe you need to come over here and meet the context for yourself."

CHAPTER FIVE

Nolan hummed while he walked down Main Street, though neither the name of the aria nor any of the words took distinct form in his mind. Bellini? Donizetti? It would come to him the next time he was in the kitchen finessing fine cuisine. His meeting had gone well. Practicing law for more than thirty years primarily happened in Denver, with a couple of days each week working for his firm from his home office, but occasionally someone in Canyon Mines prevailed upon him for his services. Perhaps someday he'd hang out a shingle in town, when he was ready to startle Jillian with the concept of semiretirement.

He did love this mountain town with its quintessential main street only half an hour from the state capital. Nolan could stick his head into virtually any shop in town, and either the owner, customers, or both would greet him by name and ask how his daughter was doing as well. The town pulled together the way every town should. It was a fortunate day, all those years ago, when Bella told him she'd found the perfect old house for them to raise their daughter in—and the perfect town. As she was about so many things, Bella was right about the house and the town. Nolan never once thought about uprooting Jillian and moving back to the city when Bella passed away. This was home.

With his red leather-bound legal pad tucked under one arm, Nolan ducked into Digger's Delight to inspect the confectionaries on offer. Carolyn handed her customer a box of chocolates and a receipt before catching Nolan's eye.

"Have you come in search of chocolate-covered cherries?" Carolyn moved down the candy case.

"Please tell me you made some today."

"Dark."

"Perfect! I'll have six. And three dark chocolate marshmallow crèmes for you-know-who."

Carolyn reached into the case with tissue paper and began filling a small box. "Everything all set for the big day?"

"You're prepared for your part?"

"But of course. I'm not the part I'm worried about."

"O ye of little faith."

Carolyn handed Nolan the box and took the bill he offered. "Don't eat all of these on the way home."

"No promises." Nolan contemplated stepping to the other side of the building, which Carolyn shared with Kris Bryant's Ore the Mountain ice cream parlor, for a quick dish, but he had just come from a breakfast meeting and had a box of candy in his hands. Ice cream might be a bit much, and Kris looked too busy with a line of customers on a warm summer day for chitchat. He waved at Kris behind her counter and exited the shop to continue strolling Main Street toward home.

Next door, Luke O'Reilly was pulling down the Fourth of July sale banner from above the Victorium Emporium display window. Nolan paused to rap his knuckles on Luke's ladder.

"Don't play with me, dude." Luke scowled downward.

"I know Veronica doesn't like any out-of-date signs."

"She's not the boss of me." Luke gave the banner a final tug.

"Tell Not-the-Boss to be sure she's ready. You too."

Luke saluted.

Nolan moved on to Motherlode Books. Now that was a store he could get lost in if he didn't have three mediation files to read that afternoon. Maybe Saturday.

Kitty-corner from the bookstore, outside the Canary Cage coffee shop, Tisha Crowder boarded her green bike and leaned into one pedal to put it into motion, steering with a single hand while balancing a beverage on the handlebars with the other. Riding a bicycle in flip-flops and solidly managing the front end one-handed seemed precarious to Nolan, but Tisha's mastery kicked in within a few seconds, and she wheeled down Placer Street. In a few blocks, she would have to choose one direction or the other to either Westbridge or Eastbridge to get across Cutter Creek to her own neighborhood—assuming she was going home. It wasn't even noon, and what was waiting for her at home? Nolan didn't know where she might be headed.

Nolan crossed Main Street and entered the coffee shop, where clusters of patrons milled.

"Hey there," he said to the young woman behind the counter. "Where's your uncle?"

"In the kitchen," Joanna Maddon said, "making a batch of burritos for the lunch rush. Are you going to stay and have one?"

"Not today. A girl was just here. Tisha Crowder. Do you know her?"

"Large raspberry Italian cream soda. Extra syrup."

"Does she come in with friends?"

"Are you buying anything other than information?"

"Are you the mafia?" Nolan cocked his head. "Your uncle operates with more favorable terms."

Joanna raised baleful eyes. "He reminds me every day we're not just a free hangout joint."

"Blueberry muffin to go," Nolan said.

"No friends." Joanna reached into the case for a muffin. "A woman sometimes. Kind of young to be her mom, but sure sounds like she is."

"How so?"

"You know. In the naggy way that mothers can be."

"Not like hip uncles?"

"Ha ha."

Nolan added the boxed muffin to his collection of items to juggle on the way home. "So she's a loner?"

Joanna shrugged and rinsed out a milk pitcher. "She comes in by herself, but she's on her phone a lot. Who knows who she's texting?"

Indeed.

"Oh, there's Clark," Nolan said.

The Cage's owner came from the kitchen with a tray of lunch offerings and made room for it in the case.

"Uncle Clark, I need to scoot for just a few minutes." Joanna tossed her apron on the counter and left without making eye contact.

"Something is going on with her." Clark's gaze followed Joanna out the door.

"What do you mean?" The aroma of freshly made burritos

tantalized, and Nolan debated whether to take one to go after all.

"What you just saw," Clark said. "She's been doing that the last few days. Ever since she moved into one of the apartments above the bookstore."

"Her own place! That's progress. Wasn't that the goal when she moved out here from Chicago to work for you?"

"Of course. But she keeps shooting out of here on these long breaks. I see her running across the street toward her apartment. Why does she have to go home so many times during the day? What's she doing?"

"Valid question. But she's over eighteen. What were you doing when you were her age?"

"That's what worries me. If she's up to no good, how will I explain it to my sister, who thinks I'm looking out for her?"

"That is a conundrum," Nolan said. "I'd better get home and check in with Jillian before I succumb to the smell of what you've made for lunch."

"Jillian is at Nia's," Clark said.

"How do you know that?"

"I just do. Trust me." Clark opened a paper sack with sturdy handles. "Here, give me the evidence of your morning on Main Street. I'll throw in a burrito on the house and make it easy for you to transport since you have a detour."

"How do you know I'm going to detour?" Nolan surrendered his load.

"You are not nearly as whimsical as you imagine." Clark handed the filled bag to Nolan. "Questions about Tisha. Checking with Jillian. Not even staying to eat. You're up to something."

"Thank you, my good man."

Nolan carried his goodies bag in one hand and his legal pad in the other as he walked the short blocks along Main to Double Jack and turned north toward the Inn at Hidden Run. The rambling Victorian dominating the second block up was one of the most noteworthy structures in Canyon Mines. Nia and Leo Dunston had done a spectacular job of renovating it into a bed-and-breakfast that was busy even in the middle of the week at this time of year. Canyon Mines was a popular getaway spot for a few days of summer mountain recreation.

Nia and Jillian sat on the roomy front stretch of the porch that cloaked nearly the entire house. Jillian was on the swing and Nia in a rocker beside her.

Nolan approached.

"She doesn't want to do this, Dad," Jillian said.

"Was it that bad?" He leaned against the railing and set down the sack. "It was the first day."

"She has an attitude, and we didn't get much done. She didn't stay three hours, either."

He'd noticed Tisha had cut short her time. "Well, she has to do it. I'll talk to her."

Jillian pushed the swing a little harder. "I'm not the one who shoplifted. Why am I sentenced to community service?"

Nia laughed. "Grumpy a bit?"

Jillian glared.

"You called me over there because you wanted help," Nia said, "not because you wanted out."

"Maybe I changed my mind."

"Jilly called you?" Nolan said. "You met Tisha?"

"Very briefly. It's possible my presence may have contributed to her early departure."

"Based on how often her phone was buzzing," Jillian said, "I doubt that."

"Valid point."

"I'd love to hear your professional opinion," Nolan said, "if you don't mind putting on your guidance counselor hat."

Nia shrugged. "I saw a lot of kids like her when I worked in Denver. Jillian's right. She doesn't want to do this. And you're right too. She has to. So she knows she's cornered and has to put in the time, but nobody can force her to do things to standard. The question is, why did she shoplift to begin with?"

"And your answer?"

"It wasn't her first time," Nia said.

"Doubtful," Nolan said. "She just found out what happens when you get caught."

"Most kids steal because they don't know what to do with their feelings." Nia spread the fingers of one hand and ticked them off with the index finger of the other. "Anger. Loss. Disempowerment. Entitlement. Depression. Pick one."

"More than one," Nolan murmured.

"Well, there you have it," Nia said. "She wouldn't admit it, but she's asking for help."

"Exactly."

"So you two have this all figured out," Jillian said, "but you want me to spend the time answering her cry for help."

"She needs the work," Nolan said. "The purpose. And you do need the help."

"I have to agree with your dad there," Nia said. "I've seen your dining room. Your papers are multiplying like rabbits. What happened to living in the digital age?"

Jillian stopped her swaying swing. "The lost children in those files never knew anything about the internet. Maybe I'm just trying to understand them better by remembering what life was like. How confusing it must have been for them."

"Good," Nolan said. "We're on the same page. I'm just asking for help to understand one lost girl in front of us."

"When you put it like that."

Jillian looked at him with green eyes that matched his own. She reached up now with both hands and corralled the mass of dark curls she'd gotten from her mother, pressing it back away from her face.

"I'm really not trying to make things hard for you," Nolan said.

Jillian pointed at his paper sack. "What's in there? Didn't you meet someone at the café inside the art gallery? Why do you have a bag from the Cage?"

"Do you accept bribes?"

"Possibly."

"Let's go home, and you can have a freshly made steak-and-cheese burrito followed by a dark chocolate marshmallow crème."

"And you'll call Tisha?"

"And I'll call Tisha."

"Fine. But I'm eating the marshmallow crème first."

CHAPTER SIX

Denver, Colorado
Friday, July 7, 1893

Clifford wandered through downtown Denver. In the weeks since the price of silver collapsed below what it cost to produce silver from any mine in the state, with no hope that the price would rise soon, he wandered often. He couldn't simply sit at home. What could he do there?

Listen to Georgina give instructions to Graciela, who came in two days a week to help with the more consuming cleaning tasks? The truth was they couldn't afford Graciela much longer.

Listen to Decorah or Fidelity dreaming about when the new fall fabrics would arrive at McNamara Dry Goods and about the illustrations in the magazines and catalogs they would ask the dressmaker to imitate? His daughters would have no new dresses this year unless Georgina brought her old sewing machine down from the attic and they settled for making over last year's prints. That was hardly likely. Georgina had evolved past sewing her own clothes years ago, once Clifford was making a steady income in the employ of Horace Tabor, one of the wealthiest men in Colorado.

He no longer had an office to go to. Tabor wouldn't even come to the door of his mansion when Clifford tried to call on him and inquire whether he might be able to pay any portion of back wages—for the men if not for Clifford. From the looks of the place, the Tabors shuttered themselves in and avoided everyone. There was no telling how many people they owed money.

So Clifford wandered.

Today he'd been to a large meeting of men in the silver industry. A week ago President Cleveland called for repealing within a few weeks the Sherman Silver Purchase Act that obligated the nation's government to buy vast quantities of Colorado's silver every month. The president was determined to accomplish this goal with a special summer session of Congress. The nation had been watching for months. The silver men of Colorado were just as determined to mount an opposition, sending delegations to meetings in St. Louis, Chicago, and Washington, DC. The government owed the western states the economic support of buying their resources rather than throwing them deeper into turmoil.

Clifford believed the delegation would lose the confrontation and had abstained from voting in the tidal wave of support. Instead, he slipped out to wander before the meeting adjourned.

Past the cars of ore sitting ghostlike in Denver with no markets waiting for them.

Past the straggling, idle men with nowhere to go.

Past the People's Tabernacle at Blake and Nineteenth, where some men did go when they heard there might be aid. The Tabernacle, under the leadership of the Reverend Thomas Uzzell, had always been a church quick to offer relief when possible through various programs for the poor. Their work was in the newspapers frequently. Clifford ought to know more about them. He just hadn't needed to know. It wasn't where the Brandts worshipped regularly. The more traditional First Methodist was where he and Georgina were comfortable. The Congregational Church, with the Reverend Myron Reed, likewise organized alms for the needy. Clifford was certain, though, that both were houses of worship and not shelters for miners used to living rough in the mountains or in towns still fighting to be more than glorified camps. Canyon Mines was further along than many. With some resolve and ingenuity, it might survive the silence of surrounding mines that had thundered with the promise of prosperity, at least for a season.

Every day more men came. This might be as far as they could afford to travel without the back pay owed them. They might be hoping for work in the larger city for a few weeks or months until the mining industry righted itself. They might be hoping at least to earn train fare. They might have nothing waiting for them anywhere else, so

Denver would do as well as any city.

Every day as he wandered, sometimes having a discouraging conversation about his own prospects, Clifford looked at the faces of the men. *For* the faces of his own men. If he told himself the truth, that was what dragged his feet around the city—not knowing what had become of them. And knowing that some of them, or all of them, could be among the growing throng of thousands snaking out of the hills like dark, incriminating evidence of injustice.

Sending delegations to St. Louis or Chicago or Washington, DC, over the weeks of the summer would do little for the men out of work *now* because the mines shut down. It wouldn't help the shopkeepers whose businesses were imperiled because fewer and fewer people had cash to spend. Nor would it help the domestics, like Graciela, whose livelihoods would be the next wave when families like the Brandts were among those who could no longer keep up. Even Missouri had already been given notice from her work as a tutor for the children of one of the other more prosperous mine owners. It was difficult to see how anyone in Denver would remain untouched by the mine closings.

Clifford's feet, out of habit, turned toward the office, now abandoned, where he had happily gone to work for so many years. Overseeing the records of some of Tabor's mines, under Tabor's tutelage, had taught him well and inspired his confidence to make his own investments.

And for what?

Yes, he had—at the moment—more money than the men he'd had to let go last week. But he also had his own debts to bear.

Clifford had worked for Mr. Tabor long enough to have a reasonable grasp of the scope of silver mining in Colorado—both the number of men employed by heavy investors like Mr. Tabor and men who had staked out their own claims in hope of striking it rich and had perhaps finally begun to mill ore and send it to market before prices began creeping downward, chipping away at their meager success.

He knew what the People's Tabernacle and Congregational Church did not, perhaps even what officials of the city of Denver did not—the sheer potential numbers of men who would keep descending the mountains west of Denver but also come from other parts of the state, everywhere that silver mining had been active. The Sherman Silver Purchase Act contracted the government to buy four and a half million ounces of silver each month, and that required a great deal of men to produce. But the price had plummeted, and the government didn't care whether they got the silver no matter the price. Now the supply of men was greater than the demand for silver would ever support again. In only the last week, each day was worse than the day before.

And this was only the beginning. Denver couldn't possibly be prepared for what was coming. Whatever the city had been doing for the poor before this would be inconsequential compared to the need that lay ahead.

Haggard with dejection, Clifford opted to drag in through the back door at home.

In the kitchen Georgina looked up from the stove. Her gaze teased. "Why haven't you come in through the front door? You're not a delivery boy."

Clifford shrugged and kissed her cheek. "It's just a door. Dinner smells wonderful."

Georgina beamed and opened the ornate cast-iron oven. The stove had come from profits of the Decorah Runner, the mine named for their second daughter. Corah's name came from the city in Iowa where Clifford had discovered his lovely bride when he wandered out of Missouri after the War between the States had taken what little family he had. She was winsome and in love and would have followed him to the ends of the earth in those days. So with little Missouri and Decorah squirming in the wagon, they ended up in the Colorado Territory just in time to witness the transformation into statehood and welcome Lity to the family. Fidelity, their pledge to make a loyal life together in this wild new place. They'd come a long way. Life had been good.

And Georgina's dinners had expanded Clifford's waistline.

Carefully she lifted a beef roast from the oven now and inspected the assorted potatoes and vegetables arranged around it. Not every household task gave her equal pleasure—thus the presence of

Graciela—but Georgina was happy when she cooked.

"I've sent Lity out to the garden to see if there is anything we can put straight on the table," Georgina said. "How was the meeting?"

Clifford's hands dug into his trouser pockets. "They have made a plan to register their protests before the president can organize a vote to repeal." *They*. He hedged his own opinions.

"That sounds constructive." Georgina began transferring the meat to a platter. "Standing up for the western states."

"I walked past the People's Tabernacle." Cliff tested the waters with the simple statement. His wife stabbed the roast with a fork and her hand trembled slightly, the first sign of nerves. "The lines are lengthening."

"I know you are worried about your men, Clifford, but shouldn't your focus be our family? You cannot save the world."

He glanced at the steaming roast and the fresh rolls beside it. How was it they still lacked for nothing in a city of growing want? Georgina would be insulted if he did not eat, but he had no appetite.

"We could help some," he said softly. "So many people are losing so much."

Her fingers still gripped the fork. "We don't want our family to be among them, do we?"

"Georgie, we could help somebody, could we not?"

She picked up a serving spoon, and it clinked in a ragged rhythm against the china platter. "We have our girls to think about. Missy and Corah are old enough to wed. Once this business is over, we can arrange for them to meet men with prospects. And Lity is bright."

"Very bright."

"She must finish high school. We can't let this. . .distraction . . .interfere. It's important that a young woman be able to comport herself in cultured conversation."

"Of course." Cliff's fingers twiddled keys in his pocket. "We've always been of one mind when it comes to the girls. But the men, Georgie. Some of them worked for Mr. Tabor for years. Or my own men could be sleeping on the streets. A donation to People's Tabernacle could help."

He moved closer and with one hand stilled her twitching while he leaned his forehead into hers.

Her breathing slowed, and she let the weight of her face drop into his.

"Georgie," he said. "You know I'll take care of you."

With a small nod, she pulled back. "The table is set. Would you mind calling Missy and Corah down?"

"Of course." Clifford restrained his sigh. Georgina was not unkind. But somewhere over the years, she had become insecure, and their home was her cocoon. When she came home from the shops or visiting friends, she did not bring the world with her. In these last six months, she'd cushioned herself all the more.

He called Missouri and Decorah down from their second-story bedrooms, and Lity came in from the back garden with vegetables to rinse and take straight to the dining room table. Clifford managed to consume enough food to forestall questions about his health, and the girls chattered about not much of anything. Periodically Missy caught his eye, and he gave her a wan smile. While Corah and Lity cleared the dishes, Clifford took a book from the shelf and settled into an armchair in the parlor across from Missy and Georgina. Missy was mending, and Georgina had a needlework project that it seemed like she'd been working on for a decade. Many evenings she would make about two dozen stitches—it seemed to Clifford, who knew little about these things—and then declare she was ready to retire for the night.

Lity came out of the kitchen, a damp towel over one arm. "Missy! There's a man at the back door for you."

Missouri jumped up and glanced at Clifford.

"You tell him to go away." Georgina's tone clipped.

"Now Georgina," Cliff said, rising. "Let's see what this is about." Missy was already halfway to the kitchen.

Loren Wade was at the back door, as Clifford suspected. How the young man discovered the location of the Brandt home, Clifford did not know. Missouri might have slipped him the address at some point in the past, or perhaps he simply asked around until he found a shopkeeper who knew them. It wouldn't have been hard. Georgina had accounts all around town.

Corah and Lity's dark eyes were wide.

"Good evening, Mr. Brandt," Loren said.

"Evening, Loren," Cliff said.

"You know this man?" Georgina gripped Clifford's elbow.

"He works for me. Or he did until a week ago."

"Why has he asked for Missouri?"

Missouri took Loren's hand. "Because, Mama."

"Decorah, Fidelity," Georgina snapped, "please go to your rooms."

"What about the dishes?" Lity asked.

"Go."

They abandoned their towels and left the room, but Cliff doubted they would go as far as the stairs.

"So you've come down," Clifford said.

"Mrs. Mitchell won't keep boarders who can't pay. I. . .well." Loren glanced at Missy. "I wanted you to know I was here."

Missouri squeezed his hand and raised her eyes to her parents. "He can stay with us."

"That would not be appropriate." Georgina clenched her hands together.

"Mama!"

"Many men worked for your father, and many more knew him because he managed mines for Mr. Tabor. We can hardly take them in simply because of that association."

"This is not the same, Mama. Loren and I—you can see it's not the same. Papa, say something."

"It's all right." Loren untangled his fingers from Missouri's. "I didn't come to cause trouble for your family. I just wanted you to know I'm in Denver. I'll get by."

He slipped out before Missouri could protest again, pulling the door closed behind him.

Missy glowered at her mother. "How could you do that?"

"I've never even met this man before," Georgina said, "and you ask me to take him into my home?"

"I've met him before. Papa trusted him to look after the mine.

Isn't that enough? I could share a room with Lity to make space. She wouldn't mind. Loren would be no trouble."

"He's a miner, Missouri. You can do better."

Clifford winced. She might as well have slapped Missy.

"Papa was a miner when Mr. Tabor found him." Missy blanched.

"I believe I'll retire for the evening," Georgina said. "This has been quite enough distress."

Georgina headed toward the stairs. Clifford heard his younger daughters shuffle out of the way and scramble up the steps. Missy went out in the backyard, no doubt to her thinking bench, as she called the seat in the garden. Clifford went to his small study and took down his journal from the shelf. He wouldn't go to bed until he knew Missy was safe inside, her tears contained.

She came to him an hour later, and he looked up.

"So she knows now," he said.

"And she was awful, just as I thought she would be about a miner. She has no trouble living off the work of someone willing to go deep inside the earth every day to dig out silver, but she doesn't want to know the man who risks his life. What has happened to her, Papa?"

"She's afraid," Clifford said. "She didn't used to be, and I don't know why she has become afraid and anxious the older you girls have gotten, but she has."

"It's no excuse for being unkind or uncharitable."

Clifford shook his head. He could not disagree.

"She must know how I feel about Loren. Why else would he come here? Yet she sent him away. What will happen to him, Papa?"

CHAPTER SEVEN

Multiplying like rabbits—Nia's description—was an overstatement. Folders and papers didn't reproduce, but the piles were consuming. There could be no doubt about that, and it had been nearly three months since the boxes arrived from Maple Turn, the small town near St. Louis where Jillian's client was located.

Client.

Yes, Tucker Kintzler was her client—or the Matthew Ryder Foundation, named for his grandfather, was. The foundation would fund the search for as many people as she could find even the smallest leads for. This project was bigger than anything she'd ever undertaken before. Between the folders that held papers and the record books they'd found in the bottom drawer of the old file cabinet with names, dates, locations, and dollar amounts—she hadn't yet counted up the number of children.

Dollar signs next to names was a heart-wrenching telltale sight that Judd Ryder, Tucker's great-grandfather, no doubt never expected anyone else to see.

Tucker was now trying to redeem evidence of the wickedness.

A half dozen other genealogists were on board for handling some of the work. A semblance of organization came first, including admitting that some of the cases were so remote that it was unbearable to hope for resolution and nearly unreasonable to spend any time or money on them. Jillian hated the idea that their names should be shut away in files for another fifty years. Or forever.

But the dining room was the dining room, and her dad loved to cook and have people over for dinner.

Still, it seemed as if the more she pulled the files apart, the more questions she had about what they contained. The children's names—were they the names *before* they were taken from their families or names assigned to them by the people who took them? And of course the families who adopted them likely changed even the first names again.

She also had questions about where children were "found"—of course they weren't found in the true sense of the word. Tucker Kintzler's great-grandfather had sheltered and transported children he knew were stolen, some moments after their births and others when they were old enough to have reliable memories of the events if anyone had listened long enough to hear the stories.

Then there were questions about references to other people involved in the ring. These seemed to be carefully coded, but they did record who delivered the children to Judd Ryder's custody and to whom he passed them on.

Of course none of this was meant to benefit the children.

But the children and their families were out there. Matthew Ryder, Tucker's grandfather, himself a stolen baby, had passed last year, but many of the children were as much as twenty-five years younger than he was. Genealogically, there was every reason to expect most from that era were still alive, shopping Medicare supplemental plans, dreaming of retirement travel, debating whether to downsize from the family home.

Perhaps they were caring for the aging parents who had raised them in their failing health.

They had a right to reconnect with their first families if they wanted to. But Jillian was racing the clock. Finding the right leads—for so many—could take years, a phalanx of genealogists, and incredibly good luck in many instances.

Glancing at the antique clock that her own mother had loved, Jillian left the relative tidiness of her office. Only one side chair contained work folders at the moment, for Raúl, the insurance company client who gave her steady work ensuring they were paying out life insurance claims to rightful heirs when family lines ran thin. The pages of her latest contribution to a genealogy journal were printed and laid out on the desk ready for her own red pen to do one last round of editing before submitting the article. At the moment, though, she had to be ready for Tisha Crowder, due to ring the doorbell in approximately three and a half minutes.

Coffee. Definitely coffee.

Jillian gave herself an extra shot in this second cup of the morning. Something told her she was going to need it.

The doorbell didn't ring for thirteen minutes—ten minutes late. By then Jillian was halfway through her coffee, starting to move files around on the dining room table, and wondering why she hadn't asked Tisha for the phone number of that shiny new iPhone she was attached to.

Canyon Mines was a small town, so even though Jillian didn't know Tisha's family well, she knew the girl didn't come from the easiest of households. Brittany wasn't the first single mother in the family. When they were growing up, Brittany's mother was the only family member who turned up at school programs—some of the time, at least. But hers was one of many families with a vague long history in the area. In contrast, the Duffys, with a mere twenty-seven years in Canyon Mines, were virtually newcomers still on trial in the neighborhood.

When the doorbell finally rang, Jillian raced to answer it on principle. Tisha should have been on time. Whether she could do nearly as much for Tisha as her father believed remained to be seen, but she was not going to sign off on court-ordered hours trimmed around the edges.

"Sorry," Tisha muttered, not meeting Jillian's eye. "Line was long at the Cage." She held a large Italian cream soda.

"Come on through," Jillian said. Some people would come to work on time, even if it meant sacrificing the Italian soda. "We'll find a place to set your drink out of the way of the papers."

"I haven't spilled anything in, like, ten years."

Jillian produced a tight smile. "Let's keep it that way."

"I'm not a kid."

Jillian ignored the mumbling and indicated a spot at the end of the sideboard where Tisha could set her drink on a coaster and it would be within reach. For visual emphasis, it was right beside Jillian's own mug. She wasn't asking of Tisha any rule she didn't follow herself—no beverages in the immediate vicinity of ninety-year-old documents.

"I think for today," Jillian said, "we'll just work together. How does that sound?"

Tisha shrugged.

On the one hand, this felt like stepping back rather than forward, but if it helped Tisha grasp the details of the task, it would be worth investing the time.

"The label maker is there at the end of the table," Jillian said.

Tisha took a long slurp on her drink, set it down, and picked up the label maker.

Jillian pulled a chair up to the table. "Let's dive into this stack. It'll help us clear some space to work."

"Whatever."

Jillian picked up a brittle folder. "This one has already lost its original label. The ink got smudged somewhere along the way, so we can't rely on it."

"So you have to open it." Tisha was poised with the label maker. "I know all this."

"It looks like it's from September of 1942. A little boy. Age three."

"We don't need that for the label."

"It's the sort of thing we might need to remember later. A little boy with the last name of Renfeldt. Karl with a K."

"So you want the whole name or just the last name?"

"The whole thing is helpful," Jillian said, "when we have it. Last name first. R-e-n-f-e-l-d-t, K-a-r-l."

"You didn't say that yesterday." Tisha poked letters on the label maker.

Jillian let the comment slide and watched the lettering.

"Oops, looks like we missed the *d*," Jillian said. "There's a backspace button that makes it easy to correct spelling."

Tisha sighed but made the correction.

"That looks great," Jillian said. "Print two, remember?"

"Blue and red. Geez, this is like preschool or something." Tisha pressed PRINT, tore off the strip, and presented the result.

"Wait until we add in yellow folders. Then the fun really begins."

Jillian's attempt at levity collapsed. Tisha stuck the two labels on folders.

"Okay," Jillian said, "we don't have much to go on in this original folder, so we'll just move the sheets to the—"

"Original contents in the blue folder. I was here yesterday, remember? And two minutes ago." Tisha reached for her Italian soda and slurped.

"Of course." Jillian waited for Tisha to finish with her drink before handing her the contents of the original folder to slide into the new blue one. "I do remember I have a few pages on the table here somewhere with a sticky note that says *Renfeldt*. There was another name in that file that made me curious, and I dug up some things that might be related for the red folder. If you could help me look for the *Renfeldt* stack without disturbing any other piles, I'd appreciate it."

Tisha's effort appeared half-hearted to Jillian, but the girl found the papers before Jillian did. A large red paper clip bound them together, with the edge of a long orange sticky note tucked under the bottom of the clip to keep it from floating off.

"That's it!" Jillian took the find from Tisha and put it in the red folder. "Now we stack them together."

"Do I get a gold star?" Tisha matched up the edges of the folders perfectly and added them to the other paired folders at the far end of the table from the day before.

They did a few more folders like this, Jillian commenting on the contents, pointing out where she found confirmation of spelling for a name or a tidbit of information that could lead down a promising trail, before forcing herself to sit back and let Tisha look through the stacks on the table for what might belong in the red folders. Though Jillian handled the original documents and file folders around the edges, they were just old enough to leave a trail of dust on her fingers and clothing. Brushing off her khakis felt like brushing away the physicality of the past. These were not mere internet images of census entries or military records. Ghastly as the task was to identify where these children might have come from and where they might be now, with each crumbling folder Jillian opened, she caressed the past. The original folders were too fragile to stand up to use going forward. She had to relocate the documents and establish her own system. Nevertheless, the growing stack of discarded files from the 1930s to the 1950s was an aching sepulchre.

Discarded files. Discarded children.

Life was fragile.

Jillian's phone rang. The tune it sang told her it was Drew Lawson calling from the ranch where he lived with his great-aunt south of Pueblo.

Two months ago, Jillian didn't know Drew Lawson. Now she always took his calls. Hoped for them, even.

She snatched up the phone. "Keep going," she said to Tisha. "I'll be back in a few minutes to answer any questions."

In bare feet, Jillian skidded out of the room and around the corner to the privacy of her office.

"Hey you."

"Am I interrupting?" Drew's smooth voice lilted.

"I don't care if you are. Sounds like you're outside."

"The horse needed some exercise. Practically begged me to go for a ride."

Jillian laughed. The first time she met Drew, he was astride his white horse on his ranch, backlit by streaming spring sun.

"I can't wait to come down this weekend," she said.

"About that."

"Oh no."

"I have a chance for an engagement. It just came up."

"Oh. I see. If you have a chance to sing, you should definitely take it."

"I'll make it up to you in a big way," he said. "Promise."

"It's okay." Jillian swallowed back her deflation, reminding herself she and Drew were still getting to know each other. He worked on a ranch with his great-aunt, he took occasional catering jobs in Pueblo, he was the most amazing singer she knew—scheduling his life could be complicated.

"How's Aunt Min?" She shifted the conversation. As they chatted, she pictured the far-flung, enticing landscape of his family's land, with views of both the West Mountains and the San Isabels and thriving wildlife.

More time passed than she realized, and with a flash of anxiety about having left Tisha alone so long, she drew the call to a close.

In the dining room, Tisha was stuffing her own phone into the pocket of her shorts.

"It's time for me to go," she said.

"It's barely been ninety minutes today," Jillian said. "The goal is three hours."

"I can't stay. I'll make it up."

"You were already short yesterday."

"I'll figure it out, all right?"

"We have a lot of work to do, Tisha."

"I have to go."

And she did go.

Jillian picked up Tisha's abandoned Italian soda. The large cup was mostly empty, and Jillian disposed of it and rinsed out her coffee mug before returning to the dining room to inspect what Tisha had done on her own.

It only took a glance to see that on one pair of folders the spelling didn't match. Which was correct?

In another, Tisha had picked up a wrong spelling for a name, labeling with a version only used once while another spelling clearly prevailed with four uses on the documents.

One red folder was empty, even though Jillian was certain she had clipped together papers under a sticky note with that name on them.

And one of the crumbling original folders in the discard pile wasn't empty. The most important task of all was transferring the original—and irreplaceable—source documents to secure folders, and Tisha had left some to be thrown away.

Jillian discharged heavy breath. If she had to be physically present at every step or check and repair Tisha's work later, what good was it to have her?

CHAPTER EIGHT

J uvenile court?"

Nolan's assistant looked skeptical.

"Not court," he said, "not even adjudication in any sense. Merely a discussion about some arrangements."

"But you'll be back?"

"Absolutely. Run over to Colfax Street, iron out a few things, be back in plenty of time for the Mertenson meeting."

"Okay, but I'm going to have extra scones to offer them just in case."

"Perfect plan." Nolan slipped on his suit jacket and cruised down the hall to the elevator before anyone could stop him.

The excursion shouldn't take long. In the middle of the afternoon, everyone would be back from lunch and ready for a burst of productivity. Tisha's lawyer was on board with what Nolan proposed for the rest of the summer. After that she'd have to keep her grades up. It would be up to Nolan whether he wanted to check in with Tisha occasionally to see if she was staying on track and offer support, but the high school principal would provide the official communications of record and make a point to keep an eye on her so she didn't fall through the cracks. The prosecution was agreeable. They just needed to get the plan on paper. Nolan, Tisha, and her mother would present themselves to the case manager moving the paperwork along, describe the arrangement, get the necessary signatures, and he'd get back to the Mertensons. The day would still offer enough free time for some phone calls about the weekend, though he might have to make them from his truck during the drive home.

Tisha was there, outside the building at the designated spot. Nolan's instinct had kept him from suggesting she rinse the pink color out of her hair—or however kids got rid of what they put in their hair—but he was pleased to see that otherwise she wore pants, rather than shorts or jeans, and a shirt with sleeves and a collar. Very unTisha, but it would give a good impression.

"Where's your mom?" Nolan asked.

"She dropped me off." Tisha's neck sank into the oversized collar of her shirt, making Nolan wonder who she borrowed it from. "She had stuff to do, as long as she was in Denver, so she'll be back for me in an hour."

"Back for you?" Nolan shifted his briefcase to his other hand. "She's supposed to be here. She already missed the last meeting. Can you call her and ask her to come back?"

Tisha waved her phone in resignation. "She won't do it."

"I'm afraid she doesn't understand what's happening. This is not a court appearance, but it still is a legal matter. You're a minor. You need a parent or legal guardian with you."

"I'm all right on my own. I'll sign anything they want me to sign and do whatever."

"It's not that simple, Tisha. An adult has to be responsible. You need a parent here."

"Well, I only have one of those, if you can call Brittany that, since as you can see she made other plans."

"Let's go inside. I'll talk to the case manager. If you don't mind, please keep trying to reach your mother." Nolan held the door open for Tisha and scanned the block for Brittany. She was nowhere in sight.

They got in the elevator.

"I don't know how many times I have to say you people don't understand," Tisha muttered toward the wall as she stared at her phone.

"I'm sorry it's been this way for you." Nolan jabbed a button. "But I'm not 'you people.' And I will figure this out in a way that doesn't drop you off a cliff."

Tisha jammed a piece of gum through her teeth. Nolan winced at her timing, but allowing her to chew it might be the only thing that would keep her in the building at this point. If she would just not pop a bubble in the middle of a conversation, that might be the best he could hope for.

Tapping one finger against the side of his briefcase, Nolan offered a reassuring smile to Tisha as they took seats to wait for their appointment. Briefly he considered leaving her outside the case manager's office while he privately explained the situation, but the risk of opening the door again and finding daughter absent as well as mother—it was enough to decide that mediating the situation with Tisha present was the better approach.

Maddie Vasquez opened her office door. "Come on in." She looked from Nolan to Tisha. "Are we still waiting for Mom?"

Nolan cocked his head. "I'm afraid not. We'll have to go ahead."

"Nolan, you know—"

"I do know," he said, cutting Maddie off, "that there's almost always something we can work out in these situations."

Maddie pulled her blue-framed reading glasses down from the top of her head and settled them on her nose. "All right, then. Come in, and let's see what you have."

Nolan gestured for Tisha to enter ahead of him and take a seat at a small round table. Her jaw worked her gum with a steady rhythm.

"Denver's a great city." Nolan nodded toward a framed historic map hanging behind Maddie's desk.

"I've always thought so," Maddie said.

"It was your grandmother who first came to Denver, right?"

"Great-grandmother."

"Graciela."

"That's right."

"In the silver rush days. I remember you telling me that map had been hers."

Maddie opened her laptop on the table. "When she was very young, she did domestic work. One of the families she worked for gave it to her."

"I've always admired it," Nolan said. "I've offered you a good price more than once."

"Not for sale."

"Even back in those days Denver had a strong heritage for social services. Opportunity for young people to make something of themselves if they were willing to work hard. Kindness toward families in need. Generosity toward one's neighbor."

Maddie smiled, shook her head, and exhaled. "Yes, all of that is true."

"I'm pretty sure if we looked closely at that map, we'd see some well-known churches that had extensive social services programs serving the women and children of Denver."

Maddie typed a few keys. "I take your point, Nolan, but these days social services are official and require paperwork. This is not the days of the old miners. Besides, I may be a social worker by training and even intuition, but we're here because of a court order, and by my count we are still short one required parent in order to proceed."

Nolan held up a finger. "Not precisely. We will need a parent's signature on the final paperwork for the court to give its stamp of approval, but nothing stops us from doing everything except that step today."

Maddie looked over her laptop at Tisha. "Perhaps you'd like an opportunity to explain why your mother is not with you today. It's my understanding she arranged your legal representation and was present at your court appearance."

Tisha nodded.

"How did you get to Denver today, Tisha?" Maddie asked.

Tisha's shoulders sank. "She brought me."

Maddie's eyebrows arched. "Your mother brought you to Denver but didn't stay with you?"

"The family dynamics are a bit complicated," Nolan said.

"Are we certain this arrangement will be successful?" Maddie squinted at her screen and tapped a few keys.

"We have no reason to believe one isolated glitch will sink the whole effort," Nolan said. "As you said, Tisha's mother arranged legal representation and was present in court."

Maddie made a circle with one finger. "It's this part she doesn't take seriously."

"I only became involved myself the day before yesterday. Her mother wasn't present for that meeting, either." Nolan pressed ahead. "Yet already Tisha has met the business owner she'll be working with on Monday evening and begun accruing hours on Tuesday morning and again this morning. I would argue those positive steps on her part go a long way to offset the confusion on her mother's part about what was expected of her today after providing transportation. Tisha is a minor. We cannot unfairly punish her for what the adults in her life choose to do."

"Well, I'm not the court," Maddie said. "Tisha, I am required to record that your mother failed to attend this meeting, and we will require her signature before the court can formally approve any of the arrangements we've been discussing for alternative sentencing."

"But we can go ahead and create the documents," Nolan said. "Spell everything out. Clarify expectations for all parties. Tisha. Her mother. Me. The small business owner she's working with. I will personally take responsibility to get her mother's informed consent to the arrangements and submit the documents to both you and her legal representation of record."

"Tisha," Maddie said, "do you want to go ahead, or would you rather reschedule for a time when your mother can be present."

"Now is better."

Tisha's voice was small, defeated, cornered as she met Maddie's eye for half a second. Nolan hoped it was long enough to be convincing.

Maddie paused before typing a few words. "Very well, then. Let's proceed. Tell me about what you've arranged in Canyon Mines."

Nolan described. Maddie typed.

Maddie questioned. Tisha answered—haltingly and in as few words as possible, but without smacking any bubbles or looking at her phone a single time. Maddie clicked boxes and typed notes.

Question: Who lives in your home with you?

Answer: My mother, my grandmother, and my great-grandmother.

Question: Do any adults provide supervision to you during daytime hours?

Answer: My great-grandma is home. She doesn't work anymore.

Question: Does she require special care?

Answer: Not really. She's just retired.

Question: Do you feel safe at home?

Answer: Yes.

Nolan's eyes flicked toward Tisha. The response seemed a little too smooth and practiced, but he was in no position to dispute it, and Maddie didn't probe.

Question: Is there anything about the tasks you are being asked to do that makes you think you cannot fulfill them satisfactorily?

Answer: No.

Question: Are there any special supports you require in order to succeed in this work?

Answer: No.

Question: Is there anything about your family situation that would keep you from fulfilling the required number of hours per week?

Answer: No.

Question: Do you have transportation to get there on a daily basis?

Answer: My bike.

Maddie glanced at Nolan. "Is that safe?"

He nodded. "Yes. No dangerous streets."

Question: Let's talk about the fall. How would you describe what kind of student you are?

Answer: Average. Maybe above. Like B.

Question: Are you confident you can meet the court's requirement to keep your grades at least C or above?

Answer: Yes.

Question: Will you require any special supports in order to keep your grades at least C or above?

Answer: No.

Question: Do you have friends?

Answer: Yes.

Question: What do you like to do with your friends, Tisha?

Answer: Hang out. We live in Canyon Mines. What is there to do?

"It's a charming town," Nolan said.

Maddie half smiled. "I'm sure it is. When you're not fifteen."

Now Tisha half smiled.

Question: What do you do when you hang out?

Answer: Just hang out. Go to someone's house and hang out.

Question: Are your friends' parents usually home?

Answer: Depends.

Maddie tapped away at her questions, some predictable to Nolan and some less so. It was Maddie's job to make sure this arrangement had a strong possibility of success in meeting the purposes of alternative sentencing. Some questions likely gathered required information while others followed Maddie's nose as a social worker. Nolan listened carefully to the answers, both spoken and unspoken.

"Okay," Maddie finally said, "I will recommend proceeding. Since Ms. Crowder is not present to sign electronically, I will print the forms and trust you to get her signature ASAP so we can wrap this up."

"You have my word," Nolan said.

"Make sure she is aware of the next scheduled in-person check-in and that I expect her to attend."

The printer outside Maddie's office was already churning out paper, and she stepped outside to grab the sheets and slide them into a manila envelope to hand to Nolan.

"I really do like that map." Nolan stood.

"Yeah, yeah, yeah. You can stop smooth-talking me," Maddie said. "And I am never selling you my map, so don't even go there."

Nolan and Tisha descended in the elevator and stepped out into the afternoon sun.

"Now what?" She blew a bubble at last.

"Now we wait for your mother."

Tisha popped the bubble and sucked it back into her mouth. "You're going to wait with me?"

"You did say she'd be back in an hour. It's almost time."

"Brittany has her own sense of time and place."

"Then call her. We can meet her somewhere if we have to."

"Give me the papers. I'll get her to sign them."

Nolan shook his head. "Not this time. Your mother and I need to have a chat."

Tisha blew another bubble and popped it immediately. Her phone buzzed with a text message, and she looked at it and then down the street. "We got lucky. She's at that coffee place over there."

"Perfect," Nolan said. "Let's go."

He didn't have time to order anything. The Mertensons would be waiting soon.

Brittany Crowder, with the mixed blond hair the color her daughter's would be if she ever stopped experimenting with neon hues, was surprised to see him. Her brown eyes widened as Nolan and Tisha slid into the booth opposite her, and she pushed a shopping bag to one side.

"Why did you bring him?" she said to Tisha.

"I didn't bring him," Tisha said. "He came."

"Hello, Brittany." Nolan waved the envelope of papers. "When we spoke on the phone, I thought you understood it was important for you to come to that meeting. We need your signature."

Brittany shrugged. "Seems like things worked out. Do you have a pen?"

Nolan reached into his suit coat inner pocket and extracted a pen. "When you sign this, you'll be saying that you understand that the court is asking for your parental support of the alternative sentencing, including attending certain meetings in the future."

"I found her a lawyer, didn't I?" Brittany snatched the pen from Nolan. "Of course I don't want my kid to go to jail over a dumb scarf."

"I'm sitting right here," Tisha said.

"We all want this to work." Nolan laid the document in front of her and pointed to the signature section. "You have a good lawyer, so I'm sure he's aware that if this falls apart and if the store were to decide to bring a civil suit, as a parent, you, Brittany, would be liable for any penalties the court might award."

"But I didn't steal anything." Brittany's eyes threw a dart at her daughter, and her hand hovered above the document.

Nolan had Brittany's attention now.

"In this state in a civil suit, you could be liable for the damages caused by your minor child. The court could award other costs to the plaintiff as it sees fit," Nolan said. "It is to your benefit as well as Tisha's that you participate fully in this process."

Brittany scrawled her name on the paper and pushed it back across the table toward Nolan. "I don't know why everyone in Canyon Mines thinks you're such a nice guy."

CHAPTER NINE

Denver, Colorado
Monday, July 17, 1893

Nothing improved.

Clifford's waistline thinned from his lack of appetite, and Georgina chided him for thinning his shoe soles as well with all his walking, when he had a horse he could ride anywhere he needed to go and even a carriage to hitch to the mare—and of course the streetcars ran everywhere in Denver.

He didn't *need* to go anywhere—at least not for the economic welfare of his household. The daily wanderings were for the spiritual welfare of his own soul. Each day the miles he traversed took him more often to the People's Tabernacle, and he paused longer to observe the activities at the church and the other locations where volunteers tried to keep up with the streaming needs of men, women, and children who had nowhere else to turn.

Now he stood across the street from a free dispensary. They recruited doctors and nurses from among the congregation, Clifford supposed, or perhaps the hospital. People with professional training could be prevailed upon to be charitable to the poor under ordinary circumstances, with the support of volunteers who could follow instructions for providing basic care. These were not ordinary circumstances, though. How did the Reverend Uzzell find enough people to keep the dispensary running for all the hours it must take to diminish the line that now wound, serpentlike, out the door and along the walkway?

A slender young woman, aproned in an unfamiliar way, exited the building and began speaking with people in line one at a time.

Missouri?

Clifford crossed the street.

"Papa! What are you doing here?" His eldest daughter smoothed the white apron meant to be a sign she was part of the dispensary staff.

"My question for you as well," he said.

"I wanted to help. I've lost my tutoring position, and I'm no better at sitting at home at a time like this than you are."

"Apparently you are more successful at putting your shoulder to the task than I am."

"You have a lot on your mind, I'm sure. Thinking. I'm just thinking with my hands."

Clifford glanced at a pair of little girls hanging on to their mother's skirt. "Children will always need schools. You could apply for proper credentials to teach if you want them."

"Mama would never agree. Being a tutor until I'm wed is one thing. Aspiring to a career is another."

"Don't underestimate your mother. She was a hard worker when we were first married. I could not have achieved what I did without her."

"That was before you worked for the famous Horace Tabor and became a mine owner yourself. Mama has rather a different picture of life these days."

"Life is changing. You'll need something."

"If I'm to marry Loren, you mean. The Missouri Rise might not be much of a dowry after all."

Cliff shook his head. Missouri's dowry was sunk in the front room renovation. "It's not quite the reliable revenue I'd intended for you."

Missy gasped and bustled down the sagging line. Clifford followed in her wake. What a difference ten days had made. Loren Wade was fifteen pounds lighter and his beard fuller than Cliff had ever seen it.

"Where have you been?" Missouri cried.

"I told you I'd get by," Loren said.

"Are you ill?" She sank her fingers into his beard, feeling for his face. "Is that why you're here?"

"I'm fine." Loren grasped both her hands with his. "Someone I met was headed this way this morning. I wondered how he made out."

"What's his name? I'll help you find him."

Cliff was used to the odor of sweating men setting dynamite, blasting rock, and swinging double jackhammers, but at Mrs. Mitchell's boardinghouse the men had access to hot water in the evenings and weekly baths. The fact that Loren smelled like he'd had neither for at least two weeks seemed not to bother Missouri.

"I only know him as Mickey," Loren said. "An Irish redhead."

"That could be a lot of men." Missy sucked in a breath and let it out with a tilt of her head. "I've only been here a little while today, but I can see if one of the nurses recognizes that description." She took Loren's hand and led him toward the building's entrance.

She'd always been the most self-sufficient of the three girls. Whether Georgina ever accepted her choice of a miner for a husband, Missouri would marry Loren. Clifford certainly would not stand in her way.

"Are you Mr. Brandt?"

Clifford turned toward the unassuming man approaching him. His wide, high forehead accentuated the unusual line of his hair, which at the moment could have used a good brushing.

"Yes, I am Clifford Brandt."

"I thought you might be when I saw Missouri speaking with you. Your daughter is very capable. We're grateful to have her."

Cliff placed the face. The man's photo had been in the newspaper on many occasions. No doubt the disarray of his hair was a sign of his unending busyness. "Reverend Uzzell. It's a pleasure to meet you."

"My flock calls me Parson Tom. Are you interested in volunteering as well?"

"I want to help in some manner," Clifford said. "I seem to find myself drawn to your work."

"Walk with me for a few minutes, and I will tell you more."

Cliff fell into step with Thomas Uzzell along Blake Street. "They just keep coming. How are you managing?"

"By the grace of God," the pastor said. "We've always been doing what we could to care for the sick here at the dispensary. In the winter we provide warm clothing to those who need it. We have a bath house where the indigent can clean up at no charge. We teach women to sew so they have a skill to earn some income as well as make clothes for their families. And we have our own department of justice, you might say, to help men who have been cheated out of wages they deserve."

Clifford winced. "I imagine you are hearing quite a few of those complaints right now."

"We have had to put some constraints around the cases we can actually help," Parson Tom said. "We must have some hope of recovery of the funds, and we only deal with the businesses in Denver. We don't consider the mines to be our jurisdiction."

This information made Cliff feel no less remorse at having been unable to pay his men their last month's wages, though he had not shorted them with any intention to cheat. Yet if he had paid them out of the diminishing balance in his bank account, would Georgina's concerns prove true? Missy might find herself in the line rather than serving those seeking aid.

"To be honest, Mr. Brandt," Parson Tom said, "I'm uncertain how much longer we can continue our efforts. Caring for the poor who have lived among us in Denver has been a challenge, of course, and one which the congregation has answered with the love of Christ. And while we have no shortage of love for the thousands of miners who have come down from the mountains with nothing but a pack of personal belongings, our resources are stretched. We must depend on the generosity of the faithful in ways in which we have not experienced before this—even as many of them have suffered a reduction in their own circumstances."

Clifford slid his hands into his pockets. What else could he do? "Please accept this donation for now. When I can manage more, I will come prepared."

"Jesus said, 'What you have done for the least of these, you have done for me.' " Parson Tom shook Cliff's hand.

At home Clifford satisfied Georgina's preference and entered through the front door. She was in the dining room with Graciela, replacing the knickknacks and display pieces they systematically removed once a month for a thorough dusting.

"Hello, Graciela," Cliff said.

"Good afternoon, Mr. Brandt." The glass shelves in the corner piece sparkled, as did the crystal vase Graciela was setting in its spot. She'd been with the household long enough to know the precise angle Georgina would accept.

"Clifford," Georgina said, "might I have a word?"

"Of course, dear."

"In your office, then."

They left Graciela to her tasks. Georgina closed the door behind them once they were in the small room.

"You'd think after all these years," Georgina said, "I would get used to how much dustier Colorado is than Iowa. I would be lost without Graciela to keep the dirt at bay."

"It's the dry air," Cliff said. The dirt never settled. "Couldn't the girls help more?"

Georgina looked at him as if to inspect whether the screws in his neck required tightening.

"Decorah is quite helpful with the daily chores," she said. "Missouri can put a lovely meal on the table on her own. Fidelity is barely more than a schoolgirl, but she does quite well also."

"I realize they all pitch in," Cliff said, "but our budget is growing tighter right now. We might need to cut back on how much Graciela works for the time being."

"We hardly live like the Tabors," Georgina said. "Goodness knows every spare penny has gone into investing in the mines for the girls, but our daughters are not scullery maids."

"Of course not." Even the Tabors did not live like the Tabors anymore.

"I hope better for them than that once they are settled. One day the mines will be working again."

One day? Perhaps, but they could not plan based on vague speculation. How were they to manage in the meantime?

"I need to pay Graciela, of course," Georgina said, "but that is not the only matter I wanted to discuss with you privately."

Clifford fingered the money still in his pocket, hoping he hadn't given away Graciela's wages at the People's Tabernacle. That was more explaining than he felt up to offering his wife just then. He would manage the coins to pay Graciela today—after all, she had already done the work—but he would have to find the right moment to have a realistic conversation with Georgina about Graciela's ongoing employment.

"What else is on your mind, dear?"

"The banks."

Clifford lifted his eyebrows. It was unlike Georgina to talk about the financial institutions so candidly. She had no privileges on his bank accounts.

"I was out this morning to see what the butcher had—precious little—and I heard the rumors. Surely you have too. Why didn't you tell me?"

He sighed. "You don't often wish to speak of these matters anymore."

"You must get our money out."

"If I do, I'll be contributing to the downfall of a bank that has been good to our family for many years."

"I don't know where you spent your time today," Georgina said, "but I was downtown. The news is everywhere. People's Savings Bank. Rocky Mountain Dime and Dollar. Colorado Savings. They've all failed this very day."

Clifford raked his hand over his head. "I thought they might." The reports in the financial section in the newspapers suggested there could be runs on some of the more vulnerable institutions.

"You must go down to Union National before it's too late." Georgina rapped the desk with her knuckles. "You can't ask me to scrimp on what I'm paying Graciela while you risk everything we have by leaving it in the bank. This is no time to be weak."

Cliff nudged closer to Georgina, cradling one of her elbows in each of his palms as he leaned in toward her forehead. "Georgie."

She nuzzled his forehead but remained adamant. "Clifford, this is urgent."

Cliff pulled his watch from his vest pocket. In the hall, the grandfather clock chimed a warning that he would not likely make it to the bank before closing time.

CHAPTER TEN

J illian tried a new approach with Tisha, a completely new task.

Her dad's account of the previous afternoon was a mixed review, with enough drama that Jillian withheld chastisement for his failing to mention to her that Tisha would be running off to Denver and likely have a short morning. He didn't often draw a hard line as he had with Brittany, motivating her to do the best for Tisha by planting threats of the worst in her mind. Time would tell if Brittany would truly come through. But Tisha arrived on Thursday at nine o'clock sharp with her raspberry Italian cream soda. She politely set it on the space Jillian had cleared on the sidebar.

"I decided we need to get stuff off the floor," Jillian said. "The folders can wait. It might even be easier to do them if we get these loose piles grouped better first."

Tisha nodded mutely and reached for a slurp of her cream soda.

"I found this stack of bright blue construction paper," Jillian said. "That's what gave me the idea. The sheets are a little bigger than most of the papers, certainly easy to see. We can use them to separate piles. If we offset the piles with the construction paper separators, things will get much more organized on the table, and we'll have space to get papers off the chairs and floor."

Tisha looked confused.

"Do you know how to play solitaire?" Jillian asked.

Tisha shrugged.

"Like that. You stack the cards so you can see the top of each one. Ace, King, Queen, Jack, and on down the line. We'll paper clip each pile and stack them that way, with the blue sheets like the cards."

"What about your sticky notes?"

"Great question! You can leave them, but also use a marker to make a larger label at the top of a blue sheet. Then if we discover things that go together logically, we can put those piles together. Like suits in a deck of cards."

"What do you mean, go together logically?"

"Another great question. I'm still figuring that out. You might even come up with some connections yourself. Feel free to ask if you do. Be on the lookout for things like sibling groups, or infants as opposed to older children, or even simply boys or girls." Jillian picked up a stack from a chair. "For instance, I already know this stack contains all boys under the age of two."

"Some of them are the old folders," Tisha said, "and some are just sheets of paper."

"Exactly." Jillian set the stack down. "Some of the file folders I received had groups of single sheets, rather than being about one child, and I've been trying to figure out if there were patterns to them."

"Like if the file mentions a city anywhere?"

Jillian perked up. "Yes. That's a great example. We may not know for sure if the city has to do with where children came from or ended up, but it could be useful information in tracking someone down, so we'll want to figure out a way to track it. And if there's a group of kids associated with the same place, that could be significant."

"Isn't this kind of sorting going to be different than the names on the folders?"

Tisha's questions encouraged Jillian. She was starting to think about what they were doing.

"We'll still put everything in folders," Jillian said, "but eventually I'll also need more than names to add to a computer software that will cross-reference details of the leads we find. This is all preliminary organization. I've cleared up some other work, though, and I should be able to give this more time. Soon we'll get to the point where you can help with scanning."

Tucker Kintzler's retainer fee was considerable. Jillian didn't want to cut off all her other steady clients, but she would prioritize the St. Louis files enough to bring order, create a plan, and subcontract some of the searches to other genealogists.

Jillian wrote a label for her stack of boys under the age of two and nudged some cross-stacked piles aside to make a small space on the table for it. Tisha slurped her soda again before picking up a marker, a blue sheet, and a sticky note from one of Jillian's piles. Jillian side-eyed the girl while she marked up another large blue page herself and set it atop seven files that clearly contained information on groups of siblings. Most likely few of them had ended up together, but finding one might begin a trail to finding another. Tisha wrote in large, clear letters, to Jillian's relief, and carved out a clear space on the table for a stack of papers related to a particular last name.

Jillian labeled another stack and offset it from the boys-under-two and sibling piles. At her end of the table she had three stacks now, like three cards turned up in a game of solitaire.

"There's only one page with this sticky note," Tisha said. "Do you still want a blue sheet?"

"Yep. Just clip it together. We might find something later that goes with it, and now we'll have a place to put it."

Tisha wrote the words on the blue sheet and set it on top of her first pile.

"Don't forget," Jillian said, "offset, like solitaire."

Tisha huffed, but she rearranged the piles.

Jillian marked several more divider sheets at her end of the table and added the corresponding stacks to her own solitaire-style arrangement. Eventually she had fifteen blue cards along the edge. Looking at them, she pulled out three stacks to begin a separate line of files.

"What happened?" Tisha asked.

"I saw something," Jillian said. "I have three stacks that have to do with places, so I thought I'd start a separate line for those. Have you got any places?"

"I think so."

Jillian winced as she watched Tisha look through her blue labels. At least half of them were not offset, leaving the labels out of sight.

"Remember, like solitaire." Jillian pointed to her offset stacks.

Tisha handed her a half dozen pages clipped together under a city label. "I knew this was here without playing some dumb game."

"But I wouldn't have seen it if you weren't here," Jillian said.

"Okay, fine. Whatever." Tisha rearranged her clipped groups of papers so the blue labels were all visible.

"What's this?" Jillian carefully removed one of Tisha's stacks and flipped up a few pages to find one of her handwritten sticky notes in the middle of the pile. "This should be a separate group."

"Whatever." Tisha snatched the papers back. "I'll make another label."

"Are you sure the rest are appropriately separated?"

"Well, I guess since you found one little mistake, I'd look pretty stupid if I claimed I was sure there weren't any more." Tisha pushed back from the table and reached for her Italian soda.

"It's easy for small things to slip by." Jillian swallowed back a stream of thoughts before they left her mouth. "But the work is full of details, and we do have to be accurate."

"Fine. I will check every single pile I've done so far." Muttering, Tisha took her entire line of blue labels into her lap. "But it's just a bunch of old papers. Who really cares?"

Jillian's hackles raised. "I care. This is my work. And right now it's your work." *If you didn't want it to be your work, you shouldn't have shoplifted.*

"It's too little too late. You can't find any of these families. Even if you did, the parents who lost their kids are long dead. Most of the kids are too."

"We don't know that." Jillian evened out her tone. "We don't know what kinds of holes have been left in families for generations because they don't know what happened to the children who were taken from them. We might still bring peace to someone."

"What difference does it make?" Tisha began laying her blue cards on the table again, properly this time. "My family was rich once, and look at us now."

"What do you mean, your family was rich?"

"Rich. Had money."

"What kind of business was your family in?"

"I don't really know. It was a long time ago."

"Maybe I could help you find out. Clearly I'm a history nerd."

"No thanks."

"I'm actually pretty good at digging around in the past."

"It doesn't matter. Just like none of this matters."

Jillian stood, stepped over the trail of piles leading into the living room, and found the small stack of yellow folders sitting on the purple ottoman.

"Do you see these?" she said.

"Yeah. So now we're switching back to folders again? You never said anything about yellow."

"These are the ones I found already," Jillian said. "And the families *do* care. It *does* matter."

Tisha reached for her soda.

"Sophie Ballard's little sister, Talia, didn't remember the first family they had, but Sophie did." Jillian thumped the folder. "And she held on to those early memories, how her mother loved the color green and didn't like apples and sang lullabies like an angel. She knew her mother was doing the best she could on her own with two little girls and would never, ever have given them up. Something happened when their mother wasn't there. She whispered those stories to her sister when they went to their new family. At least they got to stay together. And she told them to her children and grandchildren over and over. Do you know how I know all that?"

Tisha shrugged.

"Because I found Sophie. Her mother is gone now, but she married again and had other children who knew they had two older sisters out there somewhere, and they're thrilled to know Sophie and her little sister. After a lifetime of feeling lost, it means the world to Sophie to be found." Jillian pointed to the dining room table. "Sophie was in those piles. Being careful matters, or we'll lose people like Sophie all over again."

"Well. That was a speech."

Jillian exhaled. "I'm just trying to explain the work so you know you're doing something that matters."

"Sorry." Tisha slurped her soda in a distinctly unrepentant manner before replacing it on the sideboard and going back to the piles, head down. "You know what? I never once in my life played solitaire. No one ever taught me."

Jillian swallowed hard. "Maybe I can teach you."

"Don't."

"Don't what?"

"Just don't." Tisha snatched up another blue sheet and attacked it with a marker. "I hate it when people placate me."

"I need to make a phone call," Jillian said. "Excuse me."

"Whatever." Tisha clipped a new stack and placed it with exaggerated deliberation perfectly offset from the last one.

Jillian managed to keep her stride at a normal pace until she rounded the corner into her office and closed the door. She paced as she waited for Nia to pick up.

"I cannot do this. Why do I have to go through this?"

"What happened? Did Drew call? He's not backing out, is he?"

"Backing out of what?" Jillian stilled her steps.

"This thing that the two of you never quite define," Nia said.

"No, he did not call." Jillian resumed pacing. "And we've only known each other a few weeks. You don't define anything that fast. Why would you ask if he called?"

"Because you sound so upset. What else would it be?"

"Tisha Crowder, that's what. You have to talk to her."

Nia laughed so hard that Jillian pulled the phone away from her ear.

"I don't think she wants to talk to me," Nia said.

"I didn't ask her to talk to you," Jillian countered. "I asked *you* to talk to *her*."

"All the difference in the world."

"You know how to talk to sulking teenagers!"

"Even you are observant enough to see that I gave up guidance counseling for innkeeping."

"You can moonlight."

"Jillian, my friend, you underestimate yourself."

"She pushes my buttons."

"Count to ten. Snap a rubber band on your wrist. Rock up on your tippy toes. There are strategies."

"I know. And mine is calling you."

"I'll think about it," Nia said. "Have you called Drew?"

"Why would I call Drew about Tisha?"

"Not about Tisha specifically. Just about how you are."

Jillian dropped into a chair and fiddled with an uneven pile of folders on her desk. "I'm trying not to. He did call the other day to cancel my visit to the ranch this weekend. He has a chance to do some sort of gig."

"I see. And that means you can't talk about anything else?"

"Nia, stop it! You call me for help and I help. I call you for help and you help. That's how we roll."

"I think I've known you long enough to have an interest in your love life. Stop trying not to call him. I'm sure he'd like to hear from you."

"You think?"

"I know."

"What about Tisha? Are you extorting me?"

CHAPTER ELEVEN

A re you sure this is going to work?" Nia repaired the end of her long dark braid, twisting it into subservience with a tight red band and letting it hang forward over one shoulder.

"Not in the least," Jillian said, "but that's why you're here."

"Against my better judgment."

"You're having coffee at the Canary Cage." Jillian tapped Nia's latte mug. "It's an ordinary thing for us to do together. Just be cool."

"You're the one losing your cool."

Jillian scowled and sipped her own latte. By temperament she was not much of a gambler. The worst that could happen is she would dash home at the last minute and risk not getting there before Tisha, but it was Friday and her father was working at the house. He could let Tisha in, pick some random conversation topic, and keep her there until Jillian hightailed it up the street. For just such a scenario, she'd brought her small SUV rather than walk the mile down Main Street.

"Well, there you go." Nia picked up her latte as her eyes drifted to the coffee shop door.

Tisha left her green bike leaning against the front window and entered, walking directly to the counter.

"The usual?" Joanna Maddon asked.

Tisha nodded, and Joanna moved to begin assembling the soda.

"Here's your opening," Nia murmured.

"Yep." Jillian breathed through her words. "Here goes."

She got up from the table and brightened her face. "Tisha! Hi!"

The girl turned her head. "What are you doing here?"

Jillian chuckled. "Having coffee, of course. You remember my friend Nia."

Tisha gave a small nod.

"Nice to see you again," Nia said.

"Aren't we working today?" Tisha looked back at Jillian. "Your father will kill me if I lose any more hours this week."

"My father is not the murdering type, I assure you. Why don't you sit with us?"

"So we're not working?"

"Yes, we're working. But we can sit for a few minutes and go back to the house at the same time."

"I was just going to get my soda and go like I've been doing."

"I was thinking about ordering breakfast. I'm happy to treat you."

Tisha rolled her eyes. "I already ate. My great-grandma—she has a thing about it."

"That's nice of her."

"She burns the toast."

"They don't burn the toast here. You could even have a bagel. We could just relax for a few minutes. The piles aren't going anywhere."

Tisha glanced at Nia. "I'm not hungry."

"Raspberry Italian cream soda." Joanna set the drink on the counter, and Tisha snatched it up.

"Although you didn't give me any notice that we were changing the schedule," Tisha said, "I will rearrange my day for your convenience. If I come an hour later than usual, will that be enough time for you to have breakfast?"

"I don't have to order breakfast," Jillian said. "We'll just go back to the house now and get to work."

"No, by all means, eat." Tisha gestured expansively toward the table where Nia still sat. "Do what you came here to do, except the part where you and your friend think a plate of eggs will bribe me to listen to some pseudo-lecture about living up to my potential."

"It's just breakfast."

"Obviously it's not."

"It can be." Nia's voice came from the table.

Tisha shook her head, her pink hair swinging. "I'll be there in an hour."

Her nose was back in her phone before she reached her bicycle.

Jillian and Nia watched her set the soda on the brick ledge that ran across the front of Canary Cage so she could text with both thumbs.

"I suppose she's arranging to go hang out with some friend and kill an hour complaining about the wacko boss who offered to buy her breakfast." Jillian slumped back into her chair.

"Don't worry," Nia said. "Her friends are not your friends. Your reputation is safe."

"Very funny."

"Besides, you hardly ever leave your house, so you can just lie low until the whole scandal blows over."

"Ha ha. You're so helpful." Jillian watched through the window as Tisha picked up her drink, mounted her bike, and pedaled off. "She ought to wear a helmet. Isn't there a law or something?"

"The great state of Colorado does not deem this issue worthy of legislating."

"You're just full of jokes. Did you see her? She's barely holding the handlebars because she has that stupid drink in one hand and her phone in the other."

"Jillian, are you listening to yourself?" Nia sipped her latte, her lips turning up at the corners.

"You can sit there and grin at me with that foamy mustache you don't even realize you have," Jillian said, "but in an hour, I have to be ready to spend three or four hours with her again."

"Isn't there anything she can do where you don't have to be in the room the whole time?"

"Only if I want to take it all apart later and do it all again myself anyway."

"She might get better. She's plenty smart."

Jillian threw up her hands. "That's the thing. We can all see she's smart."

Joanna paced out from behind the counter and planted her feet at their table. "Seems to me you're the one who needs to smarten up."

"What do you mean?"

Joanna rolled her eyes just the way Tisha sometimes did. Something told Jillian she'd had plenty of practice. Joanna was only four years older than Tisha.

"You put up with that sass?" Joanna said. "Obviously you two thought you could casually run into her here. Lame move. She called that one. But you said you didn't have to order breakfast and could just go home and work, and what happened?"

Jillian puffed out her breath. "She dressed me down, and I'm still sitting here in a breakfast place."

"That's right," Joanna said. "She walked out of here with the upper hand. Now I know a workaholic like you has plenty to do at home, but I recommend you let me bring you eggs and toast so you can eat while you figure out your next move. That girl is trouble."

"We'll have two orders," Nia said.

Joanna stuck her head into the kitchen and called to her uncle to cook and returned to the counter to get the coffee machines hissing and steaming again for a pair of customers.

"I'm twenty-eight," Jillian said. "When did I become old and lame?"

"Well, there you have it. It sneaks up on you."

At the table next to them, an older man scraped back his chair. "Don't ever label a child as trouble."

Jillian and Nia turned their heads toward him.

"Dave Rossi." He extended a hand, which they shook. "Retired high school history teacher, recently relocated to your lovely mountain town."

"Welcome to Canyon Mines," Jillian said.

"I agree with your sentiment," Nia said. "I'm a former guidance counselor. I avoid labels like that too."

"I have a feeling Jo recognizes something of herself in that girl," Dave said.

"Do you know Joanna?"

"A little. I moved here to be near my daughter and granddaughter, but I took a part-time job in Motherlode Books. I see Jo coming and going since she moved into her apartment upstairs. We chat in passing sometimes."

"Your teacher instincts tell you something?" Nia said.

Dave chuckled softly beneath his gray mustache. "Enough to

believe Joanna's parents might have had some sense of relief when she moved from Chicago to work for her uncle here. Now she's talking about California someday."

"But she just moved into an apartment," Jillian said.

"A girl can dream," Dave said. "LA. The city of angels."

Joanna came out of the kitchen with two plates. "Did you decide what you're going to do about Raspberry Italian Cream Soda?"

"We thought we'd start by calling her by her name," Dave said.

"You're in on this now?" Jo set the plates down in front of Jillian and Nia.

"Probably not much I can do," Dave said, "but I couldn't help overhearing earlier."

"I'm sure it was hard not to," Jillian said. "I didn't mean to get loud."

"Raspberry Italian Cream Soda was the loud one." Jo pulled cutlery wrapped in napkins from her apron pocket to add to the table.

"Tisha," Nia said. "Maybe Mr. Rossi here didn't know her name, but the rest of us do."

"Call me Dave. I'm glad to have her name. Tisha. Unusual."

Nia picked up her fork. "Something in my brain tells me formally it's Letitia."

Dave gave a small grunt. "Well, the traditional names are coming back, but that one doesn't quite fit this girl."

Jillian surveyed the perfectly scrambled eggs—not too runny, nowhere near rubbery, and still steaming—and the golden toast placed artfully beside a small fruit cup. She hadn't had much appetite to begin with, and the conversation-turned-confrontation with Tisha had chased the remnants away.

"You might as well eat," Nia said. "You're here, the food's hot, and you won't have a chance to eat when you get home."

"I'll refill your coffee," Jo said, "and then I have to take a break."

Jillian glanced around. No line formed at the counter. Satisfied customers curled their hands around mugs and breakfast pastries. Joanna left a pot of coffee on their table, tossed her apron over a chair, and dashed out the door just as a part-time barista came through.

Clark emerged from the kitchen. "Where's Joanna?"

Jillian shrugged. "Said she was taking a break."

"Again? It's barely nine thirty, and this is her second break since we opened at six."

Clark pinched his eyes together beneath his gold-rimmed glasses. With his gray hair pulled in a ponytail, he looked more like an annoyed librarian than the relaxed former hippie he espoused to be.

"But she comes back, right?" Jillian tore off a piece of toast and dipped it in the eggs.

"Not fast enough. She won't let me see her new place, even though it's right across the street. But she needs to do her decorating on her own time. Maybe I'll dock her pay and see how she likes that."

Jillian tucked her chin against her neck to hide her smile. Clark would never dock Jo's pay. But he was more frustrated than she'd ever seen him. She squelched the temptation to offer him Tisha in exchange for Joanna.

"I'd better help Patsy move things along." Clark strode away to work the counter.

"He thinks Patsy is on the sluggish side," Nia said.

"He just likes all evidence of the morning rush cleared up before the lunch breaks start," Jillian said.

"It's nine thirty."

Jillian shrugged. She had more to think about than when people on Main Street would start dropping into the Cage for sandwiches.

Dave Rossi stood and gathered dishes to self-bus his table on the way out. "Bookstore opens at ten. Stephanos asked me to set up a new sales rack. Nice to meet you both."

"Likewise," Nia said.

"I'm sure I'll see you," Jillian said. "Motherlode Books is a favorite place."

Dave nodded and paced away.

"Jo's attitude about Tisha is what's trouble," Nia said. "Joanna doesn't even know her—not well anyway. You and I know the Crowders just enough to recognize they can all be a little rough around the edges at times, and that still doesn't entitle us to be judgmental about what we don't know."

Jillian swallowed the eggs in her mouth. "Are you talking about me right now or Joanna?"

Nia fiddled with her braid. "All of us."

"So what do I do?"

"Go one step at a time."

"But what's the next step?"

"I really believe you'll know it."

Jillian stabbed her fork into a melon ball. "Nia, come on."

"Joanna's not wrong about how Tisha manipulated the whole situation when you asked her to sit with us. But why did she learn to do that so well? That's an important question."

"Answering it will not get the papers cleared off my dining room table in an orderly manner."

"Maybe not today, but the answer is a piece of the puzzle that is Tisha Crowder."

"I suppose you're going to say that's more important."

"I doubt I have to."

Jillian had parked her car on the side of the street pointed toward home. With no traffic lights and only one stop sign, the short drive home allowed little time to devise any more profound strategy than to try to recognize the next step when it came—which Jillian found thoroughly unsatisfying.

She turned into the driveway, and there was Tisha, sitting on the top porch step. Fifteen.

Jillian had lost her mother when she was fourteen. She barely remembered the daily details of being fifteen, which were adrift in the morass of grief. They'd had a lot of burned suppers while her father learned how to put a meal on the table. Jillian remembered that much, because she missed the comforting smell of the food her mother used to make. She still did. Her father had turned into a remarkable cook and enjoyed it far more than he ever imagined. But the dishes he chose to prepare never carried the same aromas of her mother's meals. Those were gone for good, reduced to wisps wafting through Jillian's olfactory memory at unexpected moments.

Fifteen. Defiant. Stubborn. Arrogant. Self-protective.

Fifteen. Angry. And lost.

Jillian had been fifteen and angry at what she lost when tragedy kicked her moorings out from under her.

This teenager on the steps with the pink hair and the incessant bubble gum—underneath it all, she was a lost child.

As she parked her car, Jillian waved a couple of fingers and tried out an anemic smile in recognition of what she might have become half a lifetime ago.

CHAPTER TWELVE

Denver, Colorado
Tuesday, July 18, 1893

They gaped at the orderly banded piles snug up against each other in irregular heights in a single row, Clifford from behind his desk and Georgina on the other side. Finally, he raised his eyes to hers.

"I thought it might be more," Georgina said.

"Some of it is large bills." Cliff picked up a stack. "It's a mishmash. I couldn't specify what bills I preferred. I had to take what the bank had left after all the withdrawals."

He hadn't made it in time before closing the day before. Even though he left the house very early this morning, he still found a line at the bank by the time he arrived well before it opened. The Union National was facing a run. They would be shuttered before the day was over, probably by midday, their cash reserves exhausted. And he would have contributed to the demise.

Yet if he had not, he would not only be unemployed and a deed-holder of three worthless silver mines, but also penniless in his own home.

"How much is it?" Georgina asked.

"It's everything. They didn't short me." Clifford avoided specifying the amount. While Georgina had no reference point for what it might have been had silver prices not begun dropping as long ago as January, it also was not as robust a sum as she likely imagined. In the old days, when they counted their dimes, they both knew the precise value of their joint net worth. But in the years after he began working for Horace Tabor, and they moved into this house and invested in their own mines, that changed. Clifford earned money and Georgina assumed it would be there when she asked for some or charged accounts around town.

"What now?" It was Georgina's turn to pick up a stack of bills and feel the heft of them.

Cliff inclined his head toward the safe in the corner. On the day Mr. Tabor announced operations at the office would cease, he'd brought it home to safeguard a few essential documents against the day they could open again. Now he did not believe that day would come for Horace Tabor. His audacious business ventures had made him famously rich—and too overextended to recover from the bankruptcy that collapsed like an iron anvil on his web of investments. With the banks failing and the repeal of the Sherman Purchase Act looming, there was no one to shore up Tabor.

"It's a good thing you brought the safe home, then," Georgina said, "but filling it with cash and leaving it in plain view hardly makes sense."

"I'll find someone to help me carry it upstairs." Although its cast-iron construction made it heavy, the safe wasn't large. In the grid of family bedrooms and wardrobes, Clifford could find a place for it that would not readily announce its presence.

"You did the right thing," Georgina said.

"Did I?"

"Yes, Clifford. You had no choice. You said yourself that people were clamoring to withdraw their savings like a mob. Our money was not going to keep the Union National Bank open. We would only have lost everything. You must remember that when your conscience gets the best of you."

He nodded.

The front door banged open, and Corah and Lity tumbled in.

"Papa." Decorah's eyes widened. "How rich are we?"

"Hush," Georgina said. "Don't be so impolite. Clifford, you'd better take care of this immediately."

"They're old enough to understand," Cliff said. "After all, the whole city is suffering."

"It's the banks, isn't it?" Fidelity said. "We just came from Kittie and Cecilia's house after the shops. Their father had to go back to the newspaper office to write the story."

"And what story is that?" Georgina asked.

"All the closings, of course," Corah said. "He's writing an editorial about the panic for the evening edition."

"Surely he is overstating things," Georgina said.

Clifford fastened his gaze on hers. What point was there in trying to water down what their daughters could see and hear for themselves? They weren't children. They were nineteen and sixteen, and if pressed by circumstances, they could run a household. Whether together or independently, they navigated Denver with ease, and for all her aspirations for their future marriage matches, Georgina wanted them to be capable in all these ways. She was the one who made them capable, despite her nervous spells. There was no reason to protect them.

"I'm sure he will write wisely and truthfully," Clifford said.

"The miners are everywhere, Papa," Corah said. "We could hardly get into any of the shops without them looking at us."

"What do you mean, looking at you?" Georgina barked.

"Not like that, Mama," Lity said. "I really would like some new canvasses and a few tubes of paint, but I didn't want to buy anything with all those men around. It didn't feel right to put anything so frivolous on our accounts when they looked so. . .I don't know. . .hungry."

"You've got your father's conscience," Georgina muttered.

"What did you say, Mama?" Lity asked. "I didn't hear."

Clifford heard.

Georgina waved a hand. "Go. Clean up. Please don't track street dust all through the house."

Clifford came out from behind his desk and spun the dial on the safe. "I'll put this away for now until I can arrange help to move the safe. I'm going to take a walk."

"Where in the world are you going this time?"

"Please, Georgina."

"You don't need to be out there. Who knows what might happen?"

"I need to make a plan to take care of us, where there might still be an opportunity for business. I've never been much good at thinking while I sit still."

"Be home on time for dinner." She eyed him with suspicion. "Don't leave me worrying that you fell into a ditch or something." She huffed and pivoted out of the room.

Clifford missed the old Georgie.

He transferred most of the bills to the safe, folded a few dollars into his money clip, and dropped some coins into his pocket. At the last minute, he shirked off his suit coat before quietly leaving the house. Georgina would disapprove, but this was no time to draw attention to finery.

Besides, it was the middle of July and the day was warm.

The tenor in the streets was not much different than when he came home a couple of hours earlier with two bags bulging with his financial liquidity. He'd taken two of the largest saddlebags. Delivering payroll to the mountain mines he oversaw for Mr. Tabor gave him some idea of what amount of cash might take up what amount of space, depending on the bills the bank disbursed. But he also hoped that it looked like he was carrying nothing particularly important when he strapped them to his horse and trotted home. He hadn't dared walk far with that much money. Even the streetcar made him nervous.

Now Clifford crossed a grassy area, nodding and tapping his hat at each man who had not been there yesterday or the day before. They clustered in the shade of trees or in the open sunshine, or they sprawled, solitary, on their backs in the grass.

Sweat found the groove down the center of his back. Whether it was from the heat of the day or the heat in his soul, he did not know. What did it matter?

By the time he got downtown again, passive desperation had given way to panic. Shop doors were slamming closed even though business hours were far from finished. Shades came down in the faces of customers knocking on the windows to be allowed in.

Customers without cash, no doubt.

Shopkeepers who could no longer sustain lines of credit.

Because they no longer had a bank to do business with.

It didn't take more than thirty minutes for Clifford to verify that Union National, National Bank of Commerce, Commercial National, North Denver, the Mercantile, and Capital had all suspended transactions—in addition to yesterday's closures. Mentally he ticked off the banks that might still be open. They were very few, and only the largest ones with national backing. At this point money would have to be coming from New York. Boston, perhaps. But why would anyone take a risk on Colorado's collapsing economy?

Clifford rubbed the tight spot in his chest. It seemed nothing he did eased it these days.

"Mr. Brandt."

He turned toward his name. "Wesley! I thought you might have gone home to Kansas."

"I don't have the train fare, Mr. Brandt. My Betsy doesn't even know about any of this, except if she reads the papers. I can't even send her a telegram."

"Surely I can help you with that." Clifford took some coins from his pocket. "Are you managing something to eat?"

Wesley shrugged. "If I get to the soup kitchen early enough."

Clifford hesitated and asked, "How much is train fare home?"

"They say the railroads might accept six dollars."

Cliff hadn't tucked that many bills in his money clip. "Would you like to go home?"

"I want to work, Mr. Brandt, and earn my way. It's been weeks now. I know it's hard times all around, but we need to be men. To work. To make our own way."

"I'm sorry again about what happened with the last payroll." The image of the stacks of bills in the safe at home stung Clifford's mind. If he had paid fifteen men a month's wages while he himself had no wages for months and all three mines were running at a loss during that time—Georgie would have his head. Yet did not Wesley at least deserve train fare home to his sweetheart? The spot in his chest tightened even more.

"Minin' is speculatin'," Wesley said. "We all know that."

"Have you been to the People's Tabernacle?" Clifford asked. "Loren Wade has been there. I saw him just yesterday."

"Loren?"

Cliff nodded. "I'm sure he would be glad to see you. And I had the sense he is finding his way around the city as well as any man, considering the circumstances."

"I'll ask around for him. Thank you, sir."

Don't thank me. Please don't thank me. I have done this to you, and now I offer no true balm.

Clifford patted the young man's arm. Perhaps if he saw him again he would have train fare. In the meantime, he suspected now that Loren and Missouri had found each other at the People's Tabernacle, they would not lose one another again. Wesley would have a good chance of finding Loren there.

He was home in time for dinner, and Missouri arrived on his heels and scooted into the kitchen to help her mother complete preparations with sufficient competency and resolution to avoid chastisement or interrogation as to her whereabouts during the afternoon. At the table Georgina shut down any conversation about the dismal state of things outside the family home, which left little to talk about since miners, bank closures, and social charities were the main topics of the city these days. After dessert—where had Georgina come up with ingredients for a chocolate cake, and at what price?—Missouri offered to do all the dishes, and her sisters disappeared upstairs before she could change her mind. Georgina predictably declared her intention to retire early within twenty minutes, and Clifford reached for his journal and pen.

July 18, 1893. A word here and there will solve nothing. Or perhaps I need only find the right words and the right place to speak them. Yet is there hope I can soothe anything with the resources I have left? They can stretch one direction or another, but not two and not three.

And not far enough for long enough.

I cannot even soothe my own wife, my own household. My men, when they stumble upon me, no doubt think me rich, and I suppose I am, for I still have my home—for now. I doubt it is worth as much as the mortgage is in these times. When I rearranged finances the last time to improve cash flow for the mines, I should have been more specific with Georgina about what I was doing, for now she has no inkling that the new bank, which is still open, will expect a rather large payment by the end of next month. If I don't satisfy them, they will take the house and every dollar in that safe across the room.

And then what? I may as well give it all to the People's Tabernacle, because it is not enough to save us.

CHAPTER THIRTEEN

Jillian closed the door behind Tisha's departure. The three and a half hours had been the longest she'd endured since last fall, when an insurance client required her to sit through a mind-numbing workshop to keep up to date on regulations related to rightful heirs for life insurance and estate settlement. The good news was that her breakfast and caffeine infusion at the Cage that morning tided her over well into the early afternoon despite starting work with Tisha at ten o'clock rather than nine. Further good news was that Tisha hadn't brought a soda into the house to slurp, only looked at her phone twice during the entire time, and though silent and sullen in expression, had remained better focused than any day earlier in the week. The dining room table was well organized under offset blue divider sheets, including space for the piles previously on chairs and the floor, and they'd even made a bit of progress with labeling folders again. After all the false starts, the end of organizing was in sight.

The bad news was—well, there wasn't much to complain about. Jillian had stayed in the room with Tisha the whole time, flicking her eyelids up often enough to monitor what the girl was doing. Whether Tisha was making an honest effort or proving some unarticulated point left over from the morning's encounter, Jillian was unsure. Jillian had reached over a few times to gently rearrange Tisha's efforts or point out that she'd separated piles with blue sheets without labeling them. Tisha's eyes rolled, but she repaired the errors and didn't throw her marker down in a huff a single time.

Before Tisha left, Jillian insisted they double-check everything together.

"You want me to stay extra?" Tisha was flabbergasted.

"It happens sometimes when you have a job," Jillian said. "It will save me time if we check everything together. Don't worry, it counts toward your hours."

The proof check, as Jillian thought of it, had taken thirty minutes, but it yielded another three errors in Tisha's work—and none in Jillian's.

"It pays to be careful," Jillian said.

"Nothing satisfies you."

"I didn't say that."

"No, I said it."

"You did a lot better today, Tisha. Let's go with that."

"Whatever."

At least the work was getting done. This was the first day all week that felt like substantial progress.

And it was Friday. Jillian would have a welcome breather for the weekend, during which she could pick her father's brain about what to do with Tisha next week.

Nolan had worked upstairs all morning, only briefly greeting Tisha when he came downstairs to borrow printer paper from Jillian's office. Then he'd left the house before Tisha did, with a vague, unpersuasive explanation of a commitment that would take him away from his usual Friday routine in his home office. For now Jillian was alone in the house.

She padded in bare feet through the front rooms, down the hall, and into the kitchen in search of lunch. A plate of thinly sliced pot roast and a bag of washed spinach leaves suggested a sandwich, and Jillian assembled it and took it into her office to sit at her desk and sort through unread emails.

> *To: Jillian*
> *From: Nia*
> *Subject: Have you called Drew yet?*

The body of the email was empty. Jillian hit Reply.

> *Very funny. No.*

Jillian kept scrolling. Raúl, her regular insurance client, wondered about her availability for a quick-turnaround project. She hesitated. Was she available? Being in the room with Tisha all the time might not prove to speed up the work. For now she didn't answer Raúl.

A couple of genealogist friends had questions about what they might be getting into if they signed on as subcontractors to the St. Louis project once it got into full swing. Tucker Kintzler, who was funding the project, had sent an update on setting up the foundation according to Missouri law, under which most of the work would happen. He'd copied Nolan on the message because it involved legal issues, even though he was working with a Missouri firm Nolan had recommended.

The rest of the emails were blog posts Jillian could read later—or not at all—and junk mail she could delete immediately. She munched the last of her sandwich, brushed the crumbs off her desk into the trash can, and looked at her to-do list for the day, which seemed more aspirational than doable at two o'clock on a Friday afternoon.

One hand moved to her phone, just to be sure she hadn't missed a text or voice message from Drew.

Nope. Nothing there.

If plans hadn't changed, she would have been loading her suitcase in the car by now and heading for I-25, hoping to beat the rush-hour traffic through Denver and Colorado Springs and get down to the ranch for a weekend visit. Instead, she'd heard crickets ever since he phoned to cancel.

If he'd known how much it meant to her to receive an invitation to spend her birthday weekend at a place that had been so prominent in his childhood, and where he now lived by choice as an adult, would he have changed his mind about accepting the opportunity that kept them apart now? His great-aunt Min would have been around. Jillian was set to stay up in the big house with Min. It's not as if she and Drew had planned a secluded romantic getaway. But was he not ready even for her to visit his home the way he'd visited hers a couple of times since they met?

Don't ask questions you don't want to know the answers to. That's what everyone always said. And that's probably why Jillian didn't just pick up the phone and ask.

The side door outside her office, a vestige from the days when the house had been two mirroring cottages joined by one shared wall, rattled against pounding from the outside. Only one person ever bothered to come around to the small porch on this side of the house, where Jillian sometimes worked outdoors in nice weather.

"Hold your horses, Kristina!" she called.

Jillian brushed her hands against each other to relieve her fingers of the last evidence of her lunch and went to the door to unlatch the locks.

Kris Bryant and Veronica O'Reilly both pushed past her.

"Where does she keep her shoes?" Veronica asked.

"Check the landing at the top of the stairs," Kris said.

"She'll need to do something about her hair."

"I'm on it."

"Did she drop her lunch on her shirt? Do I need to grab a clean one while I'm upstairs?"

"I beg your pardon." Jillian resisted Kris's efforts to steer her toward the mirror in the half bath between her office and the kitchen. "I'm perfectly capable of dressing and grooming myself."

"You just weren't expecting to leave the house." Kris handed Jillian a hairbrush. "So we wanted to be sure."

"What are you talking about?" Jillian glanced at the mirror. She had to admit her mass of black curly hair could use tending.

"What's the verdict on the shirt?" Veronica was back with Jillian's sandals.

"Clean," Kris said.

"Will somebody please tell me what's going on?" Jillian tugged the brush through her hair and grabbed a large clip from the edge of the sink to fasten her stubborn tresses away from her face.

"Girls afternoon out," Veronica said. "Nia's waiting."

"But I had breakfast with Nia at the Cage," Jillian said.

"You didn't invite us?"

"It was sort of special circumstances."

"So is this. Let's go."

"Resistance is futile, I suppose." Jillian eyed her to-do list, which she had lost interest in anyway.

"You got it."

"You know I can only lock this door from the inside."

"Then do it, and we'll go out the front," Veronica said. "Kris is driving."

Kris's ice cream parlor, Ore the Mountain, was more or less across the street from the Cage. She parked her car behind the store, and the trio entered through the rear door to walk through the kitchen into the main space. As Jillian expected for an afternoon in July, the parlor, and Carolyn's adjacent Digger's Delight candy store, was busy. It took only a few minutes, though, to realize the faces crowding the parlor weren't tourists or random citizens of Canyon Mines but people who would be there for her.

"Happy birthday!" they shouted in chorus.

"Girls afternoon out, eh?" she said to Kris, grinning. Veronica's husband, Luke. Nia's husband, Leo. Leif from Catch Air, the ski shop that was far busier in the winter than it was right now. Marilyn from the Heritage Society. Ben from the bakery. Both Clark and Joanna from the Cage. Lizy, a favorite clerk from Motherlode Books. Rachel from Candles & Cards. People from church who had known her since before she could talk. The head librarian who had suffered Jillian's incessant questions since she was a child—and still did—and taught her the basics of research. And Nolan, standing to one side with a loopy glow on his face.

"Well, look at you all," Jillian said, "looking so proud of yourselves. There are so many of you here, I have to wonder who is running most of Canyon Mines."

Chuckles curled around the room.

"We have the occasional employee," Luke O'Reilly said.

"Seriously, though," Jillian said. "You got me. Thank you. You know my birthday is not until Sunday, right?"

"That's the point of doing it today," Nia said. "Surprise!"

Joanna motioned people away from a center table to reveal an elaborate cake—it had to have come from Ben's Bakery—with a stout candle in it, and the gathering began singing "Happy Birthday."

Kris said anyone who wanted ice cream on their cake could simply go to the counter and ask for a scoop. Clark Addison produced plates from the Cage and handed Jillian a cake knife. She loaded plates for one friend after another, not focused on the other customers in the parlor at the tables on the fringes of the party.

The voices rose to a stinging inflection, until no one could ignore them.

Jillian dragged in breath in dread.

Tisha sat in one corner with her mother, Brittany, and grandmother, Peggy. Given the half-eaten state of their ice cream treats, they must have been there the whole time Jillian was absorbed in the celebration her friends had thrown her.

"It's a reasonable question!" Tisha slammed the table. "Why won't you ever answer it?"

Conversations around the parlor hushed.

"I never knew who my father was," Brittany said, "and I turned out all right."

"Brittany! Who your father was is not anybody's business," Peggy shrieked.

"You two are nuts!" Tisha yelled. "I had a father. It's who I am and who I came from. It is so my business. As for you, Brittany, if you ask me, you didn't turn out all that great." She stood up and tossed her ice cream into a trash can.

"You ungrateful punk," Brittany hissed.

"Yeah, right. Whatever."

"You've never deserved a single thing you've had in your entire life."

Tisha swiped at the Styrofoam coffee cup beside Brittany's ice cream, knocking it over, and stomped out of the parlor.

Peggy snatched a handful of napkins and began sopping up brown liquid. She glared at the speechless onlookers. "What are you all gawking at? You never saw a girl learning the truth about men before? Mind your own business. You look like a pack of village idiots."

Brittany and Peggy whirled out the front door, leaving a parlor of stunned bystanders. Gradually the comments began.

"Whoa."

"That was wild."

"I'm not sure who was more out of control."

"Can you imagine?"

"What in the world?"

"I pity going home to that child."

Jillian was frozen, cake knife in midair.

"Perhaps we should pity that child," she said. *Perhaps I should pity that child.*

"She's out of control," Joanna said. "Behaving that way is not going to solve the issues."

"Jillian, did you get any cake?" Nia asked. "It's pretty good."

"Maybe I'll have some at home," Jillian mumbled.

Nia nodded. "Looks like there's plenty. Take the rest of it. Kris will probably give you a quart of ice cream." The party was over.

"Absolutely," Kris said. "Chocolate chip cookie dough?"

Clark started cleaning up. "We'd better get back to the Cage, Jo. Patsy has been on her own long enough, and it's time for her to clock out."

"I'll be right there." Jo held up one finger.

"No, Joanna, not another break. I need you back at the shop."

"I'll be right there. Promise." Jo dashed out the door.

Clark notched a fist into one hip. "This is getting out of hand."

"I'll help you, Clark." Nia started to load leftover supplies into canvas bags.

Nolan rubbed the back of Jillian's left shoulder. "This isn't quite how we all had in mind for this to end."

"I don't guess it was." Jillian buzzed her lips. "This thing with Tisha, it's—"

"Complicated?"

"Yep. And I don't think it's just about Tisha and her mom. Or her grandmother. I think it goes back farther than that."

"Your genealogist's nose is sniffing something?"

"I'm not sure what, but it's not exactly perfume."

"I admit there are layers I was not fully aware of when I signed you up for this. But now that we've both witnessed some of what Tisha is up against, as well as what she can dish out, I hope you'll hang in."

One of the things Jillian liked most about looking in her father's face was seeing the green eyes that bound them. She fastened on them now and nodded.

CHAPTER FOURTEEN

Nolan's favorite long-handled spoon clanged against the edge of the iron skillet, and he made no effort to diminish the sound. In fact, he knocked it three times with enough force to start a person's ears ringing if they weren't already. These days he was having a bit of tinnitus, but it was Jillian's ears he was trying to annoy with clamorous cooking. The hash browns were approaching golden perfection, and the bacon in the oven would soon be at maximum crispiness without slipping toward burned.

Humming, Nolan sauntered from the stove and into the hall at the base of the rear stairs before he let loose with full voice.

"Che gelida manina, se la lasci riscaldar."

There. Puccini. That should do it.

Nolan returned to the oven to remove the bacon and began laying it out on paper towels to drain. He reached over and turned off the burner under the just-right potatoes speckled with chopped onions and green peppers. A smaller skillet was warming for eggs. Two place mats framed plates, flatware, and juice glasses.

A hearty Saturday breakfast. One of his favorite habits since the earliest days of his marriage to Jillian's mother. Even before that, his parents had done the same thing, with a traditional Irish breakfast with their three sons—and usually a cousin or two—most weekends.

He sang again. *"Cercar che giova? Al buio non si trova."* Who didn't love waking to the drama of a good Italian opera?

Finally, Jillian stumbled into the kitchen in a green T-shirt and yellow-and-blue-checked lounge pants she liked to sleep in.

"LaBoheme, Dad? Are you trying to depress me?"

"Eggs?" Nolan held one, ready to crack on the side of the pan.

"I had eggs yesterday. Just potatoes and bacon for me." Jillian pushed unkempt hair out of her face. "Some people are entirely too cheerful in the morning, especially while singing about tragic stories."

"It's not exactly sunrise, my darling daughter."

"But it is exactly Saturday."

"Do you think you can find your way on your own to that contraption you claim makes coffee?" The eggs Nolan dropped in the skillet sizzled.

Jillian offered a doleful look and poured beans into a grinder at the top of the machine before pushing a power button.

"I stayed up really late," she said, "after getting next to nothing done yesterday."

"Between recovering from entrapping Tisha in the morning and being kidnapped in the afternoon?"

"Something like that. Though *entrap* is a strong word. I would not have chosen it. Pass me the half-and-half, please."

"I wouldn't say you got nothing done, Silly Jilly." Nolan set the half-and-half where Jillian could reach it and then put a plate of bacon and potatoes at her spot at the breakfast bar. "The piles on the dining room table are quite attractive now. And did you know we had hardwood floors in there under all those papers?"

"Aren't you the comic today." Jillian filled a small stainless pitcher and positioned it under a steamer arm.

"Every day, actually."

"Hmm." Jillian took her favorite mug out of the cupboard, placed it under the dispenser, and pushed another button on that do-everything-but-mop-the-kitchen-floor coffee machine. Nolan was quite content with the small machine next to it that gave him one cup at a time of real coffee. Jillian slumped into her stool.

"Breakfast looks good, Dad. Thanks."

"I'm going to build you shelves for your boxes." Nolan slid his eggs onto his plate and came around the island to sit next to her.

"Shelves?"

"In the big guest room. That's where you're going to store your boxes when you get them organized, right?"

"That's the plan."

"They should be on shelves. Besides, we've been talking about shelves for that room for years."

"All true. When are you going to build shelves?"

"I promised Leo I'd help him set a new window at the Inn today, so not today."

"The window Nia has been asking him to work on for five months?"

"That might or might not be the one." Nolan bit into a slice of bacon. "Tuesday. The shelves will be a Tuesday project."

"You're supposed to work on Tuesday."

"I will take the day off. I'll be at home anyway, and believe it or not, I have zero phone meetings on the schedule."

"But you're so busy lately. Can you really take a day off?"

"Jillian Siobhan Parisi-Duffy! Are you trying to discourage my carpentry efforts?"

She laughed. "Not at all. Shelves on Tuesday. Got it."

"Tisha can help."

Jillian grabbed her napkin, put it to her mouth, and coughed.

"Don't choke on the idea," Nolan said. "Maybe she'd like to stay all day and get hours in."

"Go for it." Jillian sipped coffee. "I have to go to Motherlode Books this morning. A book I ordered came in."

"I'll go with you. It's a nice morning. We can walk."

"I was thinking about getting in a run and just ending up there."

"Even better."

"You really think you can keep up with me, old man?"

"We'll see who gets there first."

Jillian snorted. "You're already planning to cheat with some short-cut while I get in an extra five miles."

"Do you think so little of me?"

"Whatever." She popped the last of her breakfast in her mouth. "I'm going to get some running clothes on and be back in twenty minutes tops. Be ready."

They left the house, both in shorts and running shoes, heading away from downtown and toward the mountain vista their house faced at the end of Main Street where the neighborhood petered out as the street curved. In his midfifties, Nolan power walked in Denver when he could get away from the office at lunchtime, and he and Jillian both walked the mile from their home to the downtown Canyon Mines shops frequently, if time allowed and they were not carrying home large loads of purchases. He was in good shape. Nevertheless, he had no delusions of keeping up for long with a daughter who would turn twenty-nine tomorrow, had run track and cross-country in high school, and could still outrun everyone she knew no matter the age. So the point came when he waved, let her pull ahead with the speed he knew she was ready to unleash, and turned on a loop that would take him back toward town at a more manageable rate.

At the water fountain at the back of Motherlode Books, Nolan refilled his water bottle and guzzled the contents straight down as he paced the aisles and caught his breath. The air-conditioning cooled him off enough that, after a few minutes of browsing, he would be able to face the final mile home—at a stroll, not a sprint.

Behind the counter, Dave Rossi looked over his glasses at Nolan. "You're not going to faint, are you?"

"What gave you that idea?" Nolan straightened his shoulders.

Dave smirked. "I used to be a runner. I had one knee replaced, and the other is just bad enough to take the fun out of even pretending to run. Plus I'm pretty sure I have a dozen years on you."

The shop door opened, and Jillian blew in. "You made it."

"Not only have I made it, but I have read six books while waiting for you."

Jillian dragged an arm through the perspiration on her forehead. "You can give me the SparkNotes on the walk home."

"Nolan, is this your daughter?" Dave asked.

Jillian pivoted toward the counter. "You know my dad?"

"He's my lawyer."

"Your lawyer? I thought you were new to Canyon Mines."

"I am. Just updating some documents. Stephanos not only employed me but recommended a good attorney."

"Full-service bookstore," Nolan said.

"Jillian," Dave said, "I hear our girl Tisha was the subject of some commotion at Ore the Mountain yesterday."

Nolan winced. "I guess it would have been too much to hope that incident would have been contained."

"Last I looked, this isn't Vegas," Dave said.

"What do you mean, 'our girl'?" Nolan asked.

"I met Dave at the Cage," Jillian said. "You know. When I was entrapping Tisha."

Dave bellowed. "Is that what we're calling it?"

"Grandpa Rossi?"

A tiny voice made Nolan spin around. "I'm sorry. I'm in your way."

"That's my grandpa." The little girl looked fourish, perhaps a young five, with dark bangs colliding with long eyelashes when she blinked. "He said I can have a new book."

"Put it right here on the counter, sweetie," Dave said. "Your mom will be here soon."

"Grandpa Rossi, can I have two books?"

"Well, I'd like to read a book about baseball with you. What do you think?"

"I like baseball." The girl scampered back to the children's section.

"Nadia," Dave said. "Spitting image of her grandmother. She doesn't remember her, but she'll see the pictures someday. I'll ring up your book, Jillian."

Joanna careened through the store, sneezing three times on her way and too busy to stop and say hello.

"Does she always come through the store?" Nolan asked.

"There's an outside entrance at the rear," Dave said, "but I suspect she thinks this is faster when she's in a hurry to get back to work."

"I guess it would be more direct to go straight out to the street than walk halfway around the block." Jillian slid her debit card into the machine at the counter.

"She has a puppy, you know." Dave bagged the book.

"A puppy?" Nolan said.

"Strict schedules. Comes back down with a silly grin on her face and hair on her jeans. And sneezing. Every time."

"She's allergic."

"Yep. She takes that puppy out in the alley and then back upstairs."

"A workable theory."

"A confirmed theory. In the evening, after dark when she thinks it's safe, she has it out for a good long walk away from any streetlights. I've seen her."

"It makes sense! But how does she keep it quiet?"

"That I don't know. But I'm fairly certain Stephanos knows nothing about it, and it's against the lease." Dave handed Jillian a receipt. "I'm not going to snitch, but it's not going to last much longer. I've seen the size of the dog."

Nolan laughed. "I can't decide if I'd like to be around when Stephanos and Clark find out, or if it would be better to be on the other side of the county."

"Let's go, Dad," Jillian said. "Leo will be waiting for you, and we both need showers."

Nolan sniffed. "You think? But we have time for the hardware store."

"Hardware store?"

"Let's go look at shelving supplies. I don't want to be caught short on Tuesday. We want something nice in that room."

They went down Tram Street to the hardware store in the next block, where Nolan made sure an order of finished wood, brackets, and assorted other hardware would be waiting for him when he returned to town on Monday evening with his truck.

Then they headed home, going up Ore Street to get back to Main.

One last shop window drew Nolan's gaze. Ordinarily he didn't pay much attention to Candles & Cards. He probably hadn't been in there a half dozen times in the last five years. But he knew Brittany Crowder's latest job was inside.

"Is she working?" Beside him, Jillian's voice was soft. At least her presence gave him a credible cover story for pausing to look through the shop's window and pretend to be interested in the display.

"It looks like she's keeping her head down and minding her own business."

"I guess being mean to your daughter in public is not grounds for dismissal from your job."

Nolan shook his head. "No, but the gossip must be terrible after yesterday."

"She's been living with gossip her whole life. It's true that after Mom died I stopped caring about the gossip at school, but it was always there. There weren't that many pregnant girls at Canyon Mines High."

"And now Tisha lives with it."

"Dad, Tisha said the other day that her family used to be rich. What did she mean?"

Nolan lifted one shoulder. "A lot of families around here did well in mining for a blip in time."

"It takes more than a blip to get rich."

"In your line of work, you know better than most that family lore tends to enrich the facts." Nolan chuckled. "I made a joke!"

"A bad one." Jillian rolled her eyes. "Dad, look!"

Across the street, at the Canary Cage, Joanna rushed out the door. Clark followed, calling her name. Nolan hustled enough energy for one more sprint and headed Joanna off, forcing her to stop running on her path up the sidewalk. Clark still had one hand on the shop door, as if he couldn't leave the place unattended.

"Let me get past," Jo said.

"Give me two minutes," Nolan countered.

Jo squeezed her eyes closed. "This is not going to go well."

"But you know it has to happen."

"Two minutes!"

Nolan had no proof of Dave's puppy theory, and the Cage was too busy on a Saturday morning to pull Clark away for a true calm mediation with his niece, but Nolan could get them to look each other in the eye. He walked behind Jo as she shuffled back toward her uncle.

"Explain yourself once and for all," Clark said.

"I have a proposal," Nolan said. "Carry on today without changing anything."

"What sort of proposal is that?" Clark said. "She'll just run off again."

"A temporary truce. Finish the workday. I'll be back at seven o'clock tonight when the Cage closes, and I will help you talk to each other."

CHAPTER FIFTEEN

Denver, Colorado
Sunday, July 23, 1893

Μy favorite store!" Georgina's lament was pure and palpable. "McNamara Dry Goods. What will I do without them? 'Forced into reorganization.' What does that even mean?"

"It's better than point-blank bankruptcy." Clifford held his wife's hand to stop it from flapping against the arm of the dark green upholstered chair in the front room, which she had appointed with fine detail. "It may open again under new ownership or with new financial backing."

"It won't be the same." Georgina resisted his comforts. "And assets seized by Union National of all things."

"The bank is trying to recover as well," Clifford said. "McNamara's owes them a great deal of money—seventy thousand dollars, the papers say. If they can recover the store's debts, it might be their best chance to open again."

"What will a bank do with a dry goods store?"

"Georgie, we need to talk about a few things." She was already upset. Clifford had little to lose.

She focused her eyes on him at last.

"Even if McNamara's hadn't closed—for now—we would have to close our account there," Clifford said.

Georgina pushed her eyebrows together.

"We must economize more than we have, dear. I have to ask you not to make any new purchases for the house or clothing, and we could eat simpler meals."

She huffed. "We may have to anyway. So many of the shops have shut. Who knows what's happening in the cattle yards, but you can hardly get a decent cut of beef at the butcher."

Cliff nodded. "And I'm afraid it's time to let Graciela go."

"Graciela!"

"Yes. We can help her out with food and a little money here and there, but I don't see how we can keep paying her the wage she is used to when we have nothing coming in."

"I saw the money from the bank just a week ago," Georgina countered. "I did think it might be more, but it was hardly nothing."

"Yes, we have something. But we have to manage it well. I have no hope of recovering what I'm due from Mr. Tabor. The inquiries I've made about other employment have led to nothing."

"You'll find a position. You are well thought of. This can't last forever."

"In the meantime, we have obligations." Cliff's throat had gone dry. "You know we've always had a mortgage on the house, Georgie."

"But you've been paying it down. We agreed. I can see now that you were right not to carry the mortgage at the same bank where we did our usual banking, or they might have taken our house last week instead of giving you what we had on deposit."

"I made some. . .adjustments. . .in the mortgage a few months ago."

"Adjustments?" Georgina sat up straight.

"Silver has been falling since January. I needed to ease the cash flow for our mines, so I rearranged our personal debt with another bank. A New York bank."

Her eyes turned to gray slits. "What have you done, Clifford?"

"I have done my best to take care of you and the girls," he said. "That's what I have done. And I have tried to spare you unnecessary worry, as much as I could. But our circumstances have changed in a downward manner nearly monthly since the beginning of the year, and now we face a significant payment on the mortgage at the end of August. We must economize. There is no question that you—we— must accept that our lives are affected by all that is happening beyond our control."

"Clifford." Georgina's hand began flapping against the chair arm again.

"We will weather this, Georgie, just as we weathered everything we faced in our early days. Together."

"We are not those people, Clifford." Her voice was a growl. "We built something. A life. And *you* have put it all at risk."

"Georgina, you don't mean that."

"Don't tell me what I mean."

"We all feel the distress. And you're upset about McNamara's. It may open under another name, but chances are once it's reorganized it will be back with all the departments you expect."

"I always thought I could count on you, Clifford."

"Of course you can. You're my Georgie, and I will always look after you."

She stood up. "It's a sad state that women need men at all."

Her words cut through him. Theirs had never been a marriage of necessity. At least he hadn't thought so. Clifford had always felt incredibly lucky that a woman of Georgina's loveliness and determination had chosen to settle her affections on him, and he thought she knew how much he treasured her. But she left the room and climbed the stairs without remorse for slicing into him and laying bare his efforts to care for her to hemorrhage on her imported rug.

Clifford forced air out of his lungs, deciding he needed a glass of water for his suddenly parched throat.

"What's going on here?" Perspiration broke out at Clifford's hairline as soon as he went through the kitchen door. How Missy tolerated the heat standing right beside the oven, he did not know. He took a glass from the cupboard and a pitcher of cold water from the icebox.

"Reverend Reed from the Congregational Church gave an appeal for bread money." Missy flipped a mound of bread dough on the floured counter and dug the heels of her hands into it in a vigorous kneading motion. "Have you forgotten? Just this morning after church you gave me money for ingredients to help feed the unemployed so I can replace Mama's supplies first thing tomorrow."

"Oh yes." Clifford swallowed a long draught of water, letting it flush through and cool him before swallowing another. "I see you are quite ambitious in your goals."

"I calculated carefully. We had plenty of yeast and sugar. Mama will never miss what I used. Mrs. Benedict gave me the eggs. Her hens are laying very well right now, and she's been quite eager to find someone who can take eggs. When I told her what it was for, she wouldn't even accept any money. And a little goes a long way for flour. Obviously I can't buy anything on a Sunday, but tomorrow I will go right out and purchase enough flour to fill the bin again. Surely one of the grocers will be open. Someone will find a way to manage for those who can still pay."

"It certainly smells delicious in here."

"I've already set aside three loaves for us, and I promised Mama I would make a nice family dinner before I go out tonight to help distribute the other loaves."

"Out? Where will you be?"

"Just at the People's Tabernacle. Parson Tom is overseeing the distribution. We're hoping and praying that between the two congregations we'll have hundreds of loaves to give out."

"I'll go with you."

"That's not necessary, Papa."

"The streets are getting rougher, Missouri." Clifford filled his glass a third time. "Your mother has given you a wide berth and holds her tongue during the daytime because you are not a child, but it is unrealistic to expect her to approve of your going out to give food to homeless men on your own in the evening."

"I'll be with other people."

"Loren?"

Missy's face blanched. "I hope so. I'm never sure."

"Well, I like Loren. He was a fine foreman at the Missouri Rise. But right now he's one of the homeless men who make your mother nervous. So if it's all the same to you, in the name of Christian charity and to keep the peace at home, I will accompany you to feed the hungry tonight."

Missouri flipped the bread dough again and leaned into it extra hard but nodded.

For an early dinner, Missy made a hearty dish from leftover pot roast and vegetables Lity harvested from the garden that, thankfully, was yielding steadily through the summer. Lity's interest this year had prompted planting a larger vegetable garden than most summers, long before the family knew they would come to rely on it as much as they had. At least Clifford had been relieved to see the bills from the greengrocer go down once the growing season was fully underway. Now he wondered if it was too late to plant squash or something else that would take them further into fall. The stew paired well with a loaf of Missy's bread and seemed a soothing offering. Georgina ate without giving anyone at the table the benefit of full connection with her eyes.

Perhaps it was better that way.

Lity and Corah cleaned up, and Missy and Clifford filled empty flour sacks with the ten loaves she'd managed to bake. The evening was cooling nicely as it did most nights. They could have taken horses or the carriage—the animals weren't getting enough exercise these days, and Clifford wasn't sure how much longer he could afford to keep feeding both of them—but they opted to ride a streetcar and have the freedom to move as needed among the throngs of hungry men. Clifford hated to think the worst of anyone, but right now a horse out of eyesight was a horse ripe for stealing. If circumstances got much worse, he might be able to sell a horse to someone who could put it on a train and auction it off in a city that still had currency circulating among its citizens. Georgina wouldn't like it, but the carriage was disposable as well. He had to keep every consideration in mind.

Clifford and Missy walked a few blocks, carrying the bread sacks.

"I would think a streetcar would have been along by now," he said.

"They aren't running as many," Missy said. "People can't afford to ride them."

He sighed. How had he not noticed in all his voluntary pedestrian wanderings? It did feel like a splurge for the two of them.

"I supposed some of the drivers have lost their positions, then," Clifford said.

Missouri nodded. "We can walk. We're both used to it."

"I'm proud of you, Missouri. You're doing a kind and generous thing."

" 'Verily I say unto you, Inasmuch as ye have done it unto one of the least of these my brethren, ye have done it unto me,' " Missy said. "I have so little to offer. But I can at least offer some balm to those who have even less than I. If I don't at least do that, I have heard nothing Jesus ever said."

Clifford drew in a slow, deep breath and only nodded as he shifted his bread sack to his other shoulder.

When they reached the People's Tabernacle, even though it was past time for the evening meal for most residents in their homes, lines of those who had no homes still slithered in several directions, waiting for food.

"Do you know where to take your bread?" Clifford assumed there was a process.

"I think so." Missouri led, and Cliff followed.

"It's nice to see you." Parson Tom greeted them both. "And with alms for the poor in your arms. Thank you."

"Where shall we go?" Missouri asked.

"Mr. Wade has pitched in over there." Parson Tom pointed. "I'm sure he would appreciate your assistance."

Missouri blushed and glanced at her father.

"Go." Cliff handed Missy his sack. "I'll find you."

"It seems to be going well," Cliff said.

"It's hard to keep track, but my guess is that since Reverend Reed asked for a bread offering this morning, we've had a thousand loaves—and fifty pounds of meat we didn't expect. Jesus would have been pleased with the multiplication of our simple gifts, don't you think?"

"Certainly." Cliff swallowed. "And your less edible donations?"

"Those are a bit harder to come by, but we continue to ask in faith."

Clifford nodded. He no longer carried bills in his money clip. And after impressing on Georgina the necessity of economizing that very afternoon, it hardly seemed like the time to come prepared to make a cash donation to the Tabernacle.

"This is not sustainable," Parson Tom said softly. "We need to be able to care for the women and children who were our focus before this crisis. The men need jobs that we do not have. Many of them would gladly leave for other cities if only they could afford it."

Like Wesley, who was only still in Denver for simple lack of train fare.

"Perhaps a special fund for transportation," Clifford said.

"I'm not sure how much longer the railroad companies will agree to reduced rates, but it would be something. If we cannot find a way to help the miners go to where there may be jobs in other industries, the city must be better organized about providing services. We can't just leave them on the streets and in the parks. I'm going to press for a relief camp along the river."

"Thank you for the information," Clifford said. "Something to think about. I'll go find Loren and Missouri and see if I can be some immediate help. Loren is one of mine, you know."

"I do know."

When all the bread had been distributed, Clifford let Loren walk Missouri home, keeping them within view but lagging a considerate distance behind the pair and closing the gap only when they were within a few blocks of home. If they were sneaking kisses—and he was sure they were—they would have to do it when they managed to find each other during daytime hours apart from his observation.

"I'll speak to your mother," he said to Missouri after Loren left them and they continued alone toward the house. "Not tonight, but perhaps later this week. I don't think she will ever allow Loren in the house, but if he is willing to stay out in the stable—"

"Papa!" Missy threw her arms around his neck. "Anything to get him off the streets and know he's safe!"

In the morning, news scorched the city that People's National, German National, and State National were all on the brink of failure.

That brought the total to twelve shuttered banks.

Still, the one that held Cliff's mortgage survived—which meant both that they would not be coming for his house today and that he must make his payment in another five weeks or they would. In this climate, no bank would offer extensions to a man whose income and assets were fully bound up in the failed silver industry.

The other news was the city's decision to open a relief camp at Riverfront Park to house eight hundred men. Efforts of groups like the People's Tabernacle were still needed to feed and clothe the men, but at least some of them had a place to go.

Very few, considering the numbers that had come down from the mountain mines, but if a few hundred at a time stayed while they could find their way out of town, it would be progress.

But they *must* get out of town. The city approved funding for some construction projects that could employ a couple of thousand men temporarily, but for most of them—and the best way to relieve pressure on the city—the greatest hope was to find ways to help higher numbers of men leave for other parts of the country.

It was after lunch when Clifford decided.

He went upstairs to the closet where he had hidden the safe and dialed the combination.

It opened. He pulled out some bills.

"Clifford?"

He turned.

"What are you doing?" Georgina stood with fists clenched at her sides.

"I had nothing at all in my money clip."

"And what do you need money for? I thought we were economizing."

"My men are suffering, Georgina. Wesley can get home for only six dollars. Maybe I can help one or two others."

She closed the distance between them and snatched the cash out of his hands. "You most certainly will not. You told me I must let Graciela go, but you have money to give strangers? No. I won't do it. Not on those terms."

"Mama! Papa!"

Lity broke into the room. "Kittie's father is writing another story for the paper. The men are taking over the train!"

"What men?" Clifford asked.

"What train?" Georgina asked.

"Miners," Lity said. "They want to ride the train, but they don't have money for tickets. They're demanding the railroad let them ride anyway. They've taken over entire passenger cars, and they say they're not getting off until the railroad takes them away from here. I need my sketch pad. I didn't see it with my own eyes, but I can imagine, can't I? I'm going to draw what that must have looked like."

Lity left the study. Georgina tossed the loose bills back in the safe, closed the door, spun the dial, and glared at Clifford.

CHAPTER SIXTEEN

Jillian's new book was a historical volume about the families and counties surrounding St. Louis in the midtwentieth century that would be of no interest to anyone else she knew, but it might aid the project in the dining room. She dropped it on the ottoman in the living room as she passed through and went up the stairs to the shower. She'd been neglecting her morning runs lately, but today's seemed to be giving her perspective. Drew was preparing for this weekend, and she was happy for his sake that the opportunity had come along. Being focused on singing in a concert didn't mean he wouldn't call her the minute it was over.

Jo couldn't run from reality forever, whether it was the reason she came from Chicago to Colorado, why she was dreaming of Los Angeles in the future, or why she was so intent on a puppy—if Dave Rossi was right—that she was allergic to and her lease didn't allow. Nolan might help both uncle and niece find a starting point of understanding instead of chasing each other around the table.

And Tisha. What a tangled string of knotted attitude. The explosion at Ore the Mountain the day before had opened Jillian's eyes.

"You ungrateful urchin." Brittany's words might have leaped straight out of a Dickens novel.

Yet the point of the work assignment for the rest of the summer was not merely to get signatures on a time sheet and send Tisha out to shoplift again—to get somebody to notice her pain. And Jillian couldn't afford to spend the next six weeks being physically present in a room to perform constant quality control on someone working at subpar speed with subpar accuracy without making forward progress.

They had to come to an understanding.

They had to talk.

No more entrapping Tisha to talk to Nia with her invisible

guidance counselor hat on or relying on Nolan to fix what he'd gotten her into. Jillian had to do this herself, but away from the stacks of work making every phrase feel urgent might still be the best way.

Jillian dressed in fresh khaki shorts and a loose red T-shirt before constraining as much of her mass of dark curls into a ponytail as she could. The weight of it wouldn't take long to droop, but for now she'd enjoy having it off her neck on a day when the temperature was pushing eighty degrees. A couple of minutes of internet sleuthing produced a specific address to support Jillian's vague idea of where the Crowders lived, and she stared at it on her phone. Three digits and a street name dared her to go while at the same time reminding her she wouldn't know what to say when she got there.

Tisha might not even be home. Who would blame her if she was off somewhere licking her wounds after yesterday's outburst at Ore the Mountain?

Jillian scooped up her keys and headed downstairs, calling to Nolan on the way. "Going out for a while."

Jillian turned west on Main Street, away from downtown, opting to use Westbridge to get across Cutter Creek. Getting to Eastbridge would have taken her past too many distractions, too many people waving, too many friendly onlookers wondering where she was going. This way she could get across the water and into the neighborhood at the foot of Eastbridge with a minimal number of curious spectators. As she drove, Jillian tried on some opening lines by speaking them aloud.

"I was hoping we could talk."

"We seem to have gotten off on a bad foot. Let's clarify things between us."

"I'd like for us to have a fresh start when you come to work on Monday."

"Can I have a small piece of your Saturday so we can both feel better about things going forward?"

"I haven't listened enough to your feedback about how I can help you be successful."

None of them sounded right, and some of them sounded

downright dumb, but here she was, pulling up in front of the Crowder home. Jillian put the car in PARK and shut off the engine. A few streets over, she knew, was a more modern subdivision with homes that didn't date back to the Victorian days of Canyon Mines's roots. The "new" houses, as everyone called them, only dated to the 1980s, a solid century more recent than most structures in town. This cluster of homes off the bridges, where the Crowders lived, was thrown up quickly for efficiency by people who lived south of Cutter Creek and ferried goods across to the main town in the days before permanent bridges. The oldest buildings, shored up and remodeled through the decades, had housed miners who came to clean up in the nearby water and sleep between long shifts in underground darkness.

The Crowder house was Victorian in era but small. Its original style was hardly recognizable under poorly executed efforts to modernize. Jillian guessed it had not more than three bedrooms, counting the attic, where an old-style air-conditioning unit sagged beneath a yellow curtain in one window. The exterior, screaming for attention, probably hadn't been painted in Tisha's lifetime. An old miner's pickax hung on the front of the house in a peculiar attempt at decor but doubled as a threat to someone who felt as out of her depth as Jillian did at the moment. A pickax wasn't a strange artifact for the old mining region, but hanging on the front of a house? That was a first.

Jillian was out of her car and only halfway up the overgrown, irregularly spaced pink pavement tiles that led to the front door when the rising voices erupted. Her steps froze.

"I'm not going to give up. Not ever!" That was Tisha.

"We can keep having the same fights we had when you were four," her mother screamed back, "but you didn't win then, either. I don't know what's worse, your stubbornness or your stupidity. You don't learn."

"I learn plenty."

"You don't learn when to shut up."

Something crashed. Jillian winced.

Over a chain-link fence, a neighbor pulling weeds in a flower bed caught her eye. "Every day is like this. The landlord failed to mention it before I signed my lease. I guess I looked at the place when everybody was at work and school. I'm moving as soon as I can break the lease."

Jillian nodded. Who could blame him?

"If I'm so stupid, maybe it's because I have a stupid father. But how would I know?" Tisha shouted. The front door was open. Nothing but the screen door was between the family's argument and the ears outside who didn't want to hear it. "Maybe I'll shut up if you tell me what I want to know."

"Letitia, could you just give us some peace and quiet for once?" That sounded like Peggy, Tisha's grandmother.

"I'm not the one who started the yelling!"

"Well, you're yelling now, and you're hurting my ears."

"Didn't I tell you to put your laundry away?" Brittany again. "Why are you always so lazy?"

"Maybe because you always think I am. I might as well be."

"Don't get smart with me."

"I thought I was stupid. Now I'm smart?"

Jillian took a couple of steps back. She didn't want to hear this. Or she'd heard enough.

"Just get out. I'm tired of looking at you."

Jillian backed up again, faster.

"You don't have to tell me twice."

The screen door flapped open, and Tisha stumbled out, phone in hand. With no closer arm to slow its speed, the screen door slammed as soon as she let it go. Or she might have given the door a shove for emphasis. Jillian wasn't sure.

Practically at her car now, Jillian glanced over her shoulder. Tisha caught her eyes.

"What are you doing here?"

"It doesn't matter." Jillian jangled her keys. "It's a bad time. I'm leaving."

"You think I don't know I'm in trouble." Tisha charged at her. "You think I don't know you're not happy that I don't make perfect labels and perfect solitaire piles in your high and mighty important work? Or do you think I'm stupid too?"

"I didn't say that, Tisha."

"Well, I have bigger things on my mind right now."

"I can see that."

Tisha exhaled a hard breath. "How much did you hear?"

"Enough."

"I'm not so stupid that I don't know it's terrible that anyone should hear that."

"No, you're absolutely not stupid at all."

"It's just. . ." Tisha dug a side of one flip-flop in the crack between pavement tiles and stared at the ground. "Well, none of it matters."

"Yes, it does, Tisha. How you feel matters." Jillian gestured toward the house. "Living with that. It matters."

Tisha raised her eyes for a second. "Do you really believe that?"

"I wouldn't say it if I didn't."

"Whatever. Forget it. Not that this matters, either, but I figured out where I've seen that painting your mother liked. The original is up in our attic."

"That's incredible. Was it in the house when you moved in?"

The screen door squealed open, and Tisha flinched.

"Hey!" Brittany stepped out on the stoop. "Why are you out here talking to my kid?"

"Mom, stop it," Tisha shouted.

Brittany flashed her daughter a scowl before rapidly shifting her attention back to Jillian. "Mind your own business, Jillian."

Jillian's heart rate throbbed like Cutter Creek rising in a storm. "As you know, Tisha is working for me. I wanted to check in with her about how things are going."

"You think because you live in that fancy house, you're better than we are."

"I never said that."

"You didn't have to. None of you has to say it. Nobody asked for your help."

"My dad asked for my help," Jillian said, "because your lawyer asked for his help."

"That's right. Rub it in. This one has to get in so much trouble that it takes *two* lawyers to dig her out. But you can get out of my yard."

"Mom, leave it alone," Tisha said.

"I told you to shut up," Brittany snapped. She followed Jillian's gaze. "Ah, you see the pick. It's some old thing my grandma Ora is attached to, but I can always yank it off the wall and use it if I need to."

"Brittany!" Tisha cried.

"I've told you a hundred times not to call me that. I'm your mother."

"Then act like one!"

"No need to take anything off the wall, I assure you." Jillian gestured to her car only a few feet away. "As you can see, I was just about to leave."

"Not fast enough." Brittany retreated into the house, and the screen door slammed once again.

Jillian turned to speak to Tisha one last time before she left and discovered the girl was halfway up the block, gone without even her bike. She sprinted after her.

"Come home with me," Jillian said, finding Tisha's pace.

"You want me to work today?"

"No. Not that. You need to be away from here, so come cool off with me."

"Thanks, but I have my own friends."

"My dad would be glad to see you."

"Everybody always thinks they can fix me. Fix that!" Tisha jabbed a finger back toward her house. "No stupid alternative sentencing is going to fix that. It won't change anything, so what's the point?"

"It might not change them, but it might change you."

"What? Change stupid, lazy, stubborn, piece of trash Tisha?"

"I don't think you're any of those things."

Tisha stopped now and met Jillian's eyes. "Yes, you do."

"No, I don't."

"You use different words, and you don't scream, but it's the same thing. Nothing ever changes." Tisha resumed stomping down the sidewalk.

"Tisha, please."

"Give it up, Jillian! And stop following me."

CHAPTER SEVENTEEN

"July 12 has been one of my favorite days ever since I started babysitting a little girl with that birthday." Nia flashed a grin at Jillian.

Jillian returned the smile. "Thanks for suggesting a hike today."

"I'm no substitute for a weekend on the ranch with Drew, but since that didn't happen, I thought this would be nice."

"It is." Jillian placed her hiking boot solidly on the incline and pushed off. "But promise me we won't dissect my relationship with Drew on my birthday."

"You got it." Nia huffed slightly, coming up the hill behind Jillian. "Lots of nice birthday greetings at church this morning."

Jillian nodded. "I was prepared, after going to that church since I was two."

"And the whole business of putting everyone's birthdays in the newsletter."

"Right."

"It's nice to have a place where you belong. You have a lot of big fans in this town."

Jillian pushed out her breath. "None of them has the last name Crowder, however."

"What you tried to do yesterday took guts. I'm sorry it was so rough."

"You wouldn't believe what it was like."

"Pretty sure I would. Every former guidance counselor has some bad war stories."

"Good point. I just don't feel cut out for it. I didn't take the right college classes, or get a master's in social work, or any of that stuff."

"Maybe not, but your instincts to want to help are right, as usual."

"Even if I go about it in my typical cloddish way."

"You always say that, and it's never true."

"I never squared off with Brittany Crowder before. I barely knew her in school and haven't done more than hand her cash or a debit card at an occasional checkout counter since. Suddenly she's everywhere."

They crested a small rise and paused to catch their breath and marinate in the vista. They were west of town, out past the old mine Tony Rizzo operated as a tourist attraction, in a network of trails. In midsummer, the mountains were their most blazing verdant cacophony above the browns and blues of Cutter Creek as it rushed through the canyon below.

"This view is worth every drop of sweat it takes to get here," Nia said. "Every time."

"Agreed." Jillian pointed at a massive pile of boulders and stones. "Although that can't have been part of the original view, and it seems like we're too far above the old mine for these stones to have come from there."

"The name of the town is plural for a reason," Nia quipped. "There are dozens of abandoned mines up here. That was long before the Environmental Protection Agency or state regulations. They dug out the mountains, mined in a frenzy, and when they got what they wanted or went bust, they just left it all."

"How do we know there's not a mine entrance behind that pile of stones?"

Nia shrugged. "I guess we don't know for sure, but most people left because the assay office told them what they were digging out was worthless after all or because the markets fell apart. Spending money to pay men to move rock *back* wasn't high on anyone's priority list. You can't put a mountain back together. Much later there was some effort by authorities to at least put some grates over known entrances for the sake of safety, but I'm not sure anyone claims to have found them all."

"How do you know all this?" Jillian took a long gulp of water.

"Have you met my husband?"

Jillian laughed, spitting liquid. "Leo and his books."

"And the way he likes to wax on, sounding erudite, over breakfast with our B&B guests." Nia shook her head. "I try to get him to tone it down at least until people have had their morning coffee, but enough of them find it fascinating that he keeps going. I've heard the same lecture umpteen zillion times."

"Good grief, he's going to scare them off from hiking for fear of falling in a mine."

"Well, there you have it." Nia flipped her fingers into Jillian's shoulder. "That's exactly what I tell him."

Jillian capped her water bottle and turned back to the trail. "Thanks for making me laugh. I haven't been able to shake thinking about Tisha since yesterday afternoon. To be honest, I'm dreading tomorrow when she comes to work. *If* she comes to work."

"Do you really think she might not?"

"She hasn't wanted to be there in the first place. Then half the town saw what happened on Friday, and I probably only made things worse by turning up at her house on Saturday. Why would she show her face again?"

"Because she has to."

Jillian shook her head. "It's hard for me to understand not caring about being in trouble when there could be legal consequences for blowing off the deal my dad has arranged, but I really don't think that's a factor for Tisha Crowder. Every step we try to take with her results in backward progress—which I guess is not actually progress. Regression."

"If what you saw of her home life is true all the time, coming to work tomorrow morning is the least of her mental worries at the moment. But she also knows she has to, and if she doesn't show up tomorrow, Nolan is not going to let it go, and she's smart enough to know that too. So I think she'll be back."

"In the long game, this option could make all the difference for a kid like Tisha."

"We all have reasons for the ways we express how we feel, even if we don't understand them. Teenagers with troubles are not always the best at thinking about the long game."

"I guess I can't argue with you there." Jillian pushed her sunglasses to the top of her head to absorb the nuances of the palette before her unfiltered. "How could this view not make anyone feel better?"

"It certainly does my spirit good," Nia said. "This spot always reminds me of that little painting in your kitchen."

Jillian turned to look at Nia and then back at the view. "Do you really think this could be it?"

Nia lifted one shoulder and let it drop without commitment. "It's a wide view. The exact vantage point could be anywhere along here. But don't you think the hills look right?"

Jillian considered the question. "I do. You know, on Tisha's first day, she said my picture reminded her of something. Yesterday she said she figured out it was because the original is in their attic."

"No way!"

It was Jillian's turn to shrug.

"You're not the only person in town who has a reproduction of that picture," Nia said. "There has to be a story."

"Given Brittany's mood, I'm not counting on hearing it. I didn't get much of a chance to ask." Jillian flipped her glasses back onto her face. "We're heading downhill again. You know what that means."

"No, no, no!" Nia crisscrossed her arms in front of her face. "That's not even a real trail you have your eye on."

"Looks pretty good to me. Think of it as a shortcut."

"You're killing me with these downhill sprints on mountain paths. I won't be able to move all week."

Jillian wiggled a hand over her shoulder, already ten steps ahead of her friend. The stretch she'd chosen was wide and relatively free of obstructions like wayward tree roots. It would dump them on a level length of trail that wound much more gradually toward the lot where they'd left the car.

"I'm older than you are!" Nia's plaintive cry came from behind.

Jillian grinned but didn't slow down until she got to the flat path. She bent over, hands on knees, for a moment, easing her breath before reaching for her water bottle and pacing while she waited. Nia wasn't walking, but neither was she sprinting. Jillian had plenty of time to recover.

"I suppose you're very proud of yourself." Nia finally reached the security of level ground.

"Quite."

"My calves will never be the same."

"You should do more running."

"Go to your room, young lady."

"You're not the boss of me."

A sheepadoodle lumbered across their path, chased by two giggling little boys who couldn't be more delighted to own a dog twice as big as the two of them combined. It took both of them, under supervision of their mother, to manage the dog's long leash.

"Grandpa Rossi, I want a dog like that!"

Jillian and Nia turned their heads toward the determined little voice. Dave Rossi gripped his granddaughter's hand. Clearly she wanted to race after the sheepadoodle.

"Hello," Jillian said.

"Hello there," Dave said. "Nadia, these are my new friends, Jillian and Nia. Can you say hello?"

She leaned into his leg as she greeted them.

"A dog, eh?" Jillian couldn't help smirking.

"I want a puppy, Grandpa!"

"Nadia, we've talked about this," Dave said. "I can't just give you a puppy."

"But you love dogs. You said you do. You're always happy to see doggies."

"If the puppy was yours, it would live at your house, and your mother would have to say yes. Remember?"

Nadia's lower lip pushed out. "My mommy doesn't want a puppy. She says a puppy is a lot of work."

"She's right. A puppy is a lot of work."

"But puppies are so cute, Grandpa Rossi! And so fun! You used to have a dog."

Jillian laughed. "She's got you cornered."

"My dog was an old dog. I'm too old myself to chase after a puppy."

"No you're not, Grandpa! No you're not! You're not too old. Don't say that."

Jillian tried to stifle her laugh, but Nadia's earnest appeal was too much not to evoke any reaction.

"I admit I miss my dog." Dave glanced at Jillian. "My yellow lab died about a year ago. Maybe someday I might be ready for another one, when I feel more settled in. But a puppy? They definitely are a lot of work."

"Are you getting an especially close opportunity to observe that truth right now while at work?" Jillian winked.

Dave chuckled. "Might be."

"What am I missing?" Nia asked.

"Tell you later," Jillian said.

"We gotta go, Jillian," Nia said. "Leo is hanging out with your dad, but we have stuff to do to be ready for tomorrow."

"Then don't complain to me about how your calves or your quads or any other body parts are screaming." Jillian waved at Dave and Nadia. "Nice to see you both."

"This was supposed to be a hike, not a race," Nia said.

"Whatever."

"Suit yourself, but remember I have the car keys."

"Well, when you put it like that." Jillian dumped the last of her water down her throat. That would have to last her until they got back to the car, where a cooler held backup bottles on ice.

Under other circumstances, Jillian would have had a couple more hours to enjoy being at the ranch with Drew before getting in her own car for the drive back from south of Pueblo to Canyon Mines. Maybe he would still call to wish her a happy birthday. In the meantime, she'd just about hiked off the excess nervous energy his silence fueled and Tisha stoked.

"Shall I send Leo out?" Jillian asked when Nia pulled into the Duffy driveway.

"I'll come in and get him." Nia unstrapped her seat belt. "Otherwise I could be sitting out here till the cows come home."

"I hear your cows have a late curfew."

"Cut it out, smarty-pants."

They climbed the front steps together. Jillian wouldn't admit it, but her own calves and quads were starting to talk back. Nia hung back a few steps to let Jillian go through the door first.

The shouts of "Surprise!" rattled Jillian's eardrums. She spun around to look at Nia.

"You!"

"Strictly diversion duty."

Kris. Leo. Luke and Veronica. Connie. Marilyn. Clark and Joanna. And Nolan, grinning at the dining room table, laden with food. He must have been cooking the entire time they were hiking.

"But the cake and ice cream party on Friday," Jillian said.

"Also strictly diversion," Nia said.

"Well, it worked. I didn't expect this. I'm a sweaty mess."

"You are glowing with age." Nolan came and kissed her cheek. "Officially twenty-nine."

"My piles of papers," Jillian said.

"Carefully and temporarily moved to the kitchen table," Nolan said. "I promise now that you had a recognizable system, I did not disturb it."

"Well, this does look much more enticing," she admitted.

Connie's chocolates. Kris's ice creams. Nia's scones. Her favorite meatballs in a sauce. Olive cheese bread. Two kinds of quiche. Little pastry cream puffs that looked just like the ones Drew, a master dessert chef, made and which Nolan had been feverishly determined to learn to make himself. Apparently he'd finally done it. Jillian couldn't tell the difference.

Even with her large, wild, noisy Irish family based near Denver, and as much as she enjoyed them, the moment before her swamped Jillian with gratitude for *this* family—people who chose her and loved her and stood by her every day.

Tisha Crowder had never known such a moment. Her family was wild and noisy, but not in the joyous way of the Duffys or these friends.

Where did Tisha disappear to when her own mother told her she didn't want to look at her?

Jillian pulled herself back to the moment. "Nice job on the pastries, Dad. You've finally done it."

Nolan laughed. "In my dreams. Those aren't mine."

Drew burst out of the kitchen and opened his arms. "You didn't really think I'd miss your birthday, did you?"

CHAPTER EIGHTEEN

Denver, Colorado
Wednesday, July 26, 1893

It's much too late to walk home," Clifford announced. "We'll take the streetcar."

Missouri glanced at Loren.

"He can ride with us for a while," Cliff said, "and then. . ." His words trailed off because he didn't know where Loren spent his nights. Loren didn't always know.

"You said you were going to talk to Mama." Missouri's tone threw a dart of accusation.

"The moment hasn't been right."

"Please don't argue about me," Loren said. "As you can see, I'm well enough."

Well enough. Hardly. Loren ran himself ragged making sure other miners knew where they might find help, and he would gladly hand his meager charity meal to another man in the bread line. If he got any thinner, he would have to make another trip through the charity clothing the People's Tabernacle offered, looking for smaller garments, rather than only directing others there. If Loren weren't so much taller, Cliff would have given him some of his own clothes. Clifford suspected the thought of seeing Missy kept Loren going. Most of the men had no such hope.

"Soon, Missy, I promise," Clifford said. "In the meantime, Loren, please ride with us part of the way, and then take the streetcar back to find someplace for the night."

Already it was well after nine. Over the protest of Georgina's silent scowl, Cliff had accompanied Missouri after dinner back downtown for a special shift on a food wagon to distribute food among the men who did not make it to organized food lines. Parson Tom was right.

They couldn't keep up. The church couldn't take care of everyone. But a couple of evening food wagons operated by volunteers could fill a few more bellies before night clasped the city. Georgina didn't want Missy to go at all, and even Clifford felt better if he went with her, no longer only to mollify Georgina.

Fewer streetcars ran every day, and even fewer in the late evenings, but the food wagon had finished its work circling around Union Station, leaving the trio at Fifteenth Street. Walking all the way across town to Champa and up to Twenty-Fourth to get home was too ambitious at this hour even for Clifford's wandering spirit. Though they might have to wait for a streetcar, they would be home much sooner than on foot. Before long Georgina would be ready to set aside the reading material she habitually took to bed when she retired early, and her irritation at his absence would breed anxiety. She never slept well without him beside her where she could reach for his hand, although she had been reaching for it less of late, her fomenting distrust of his decisions seeping into private spaces.

A car arrived a few minutes later, and they boarded.

"This seems unnecessary," Loren said. "We can say good night here."

"You're coming." Missouri shut down his protest with a tug on his hand.

Running along the rails that made it so easy to navigate Denver, even with frequent stops, at this hour, the streetcar should have had them to Curtis Street swiftly enough, and their route would have turned toward home. Instead, in a matter of blocks, traffic congealed in a throng of pedestrians.

Missouri gripped the seat in front of her. "What's going on?"

Their streetcar wasn't the only one clutched in unseen events. Several were backed up along both Fifteenth Street and Larimer where the two streets crossed.

"How could that many men be getting out of those streetcars?" Clifford mused—just as a stream of men pushed past him out of their own car. By the moment, the streets filled both with disembarking passengers and, more voluminously, pedestrians who mobbed their way down Larimer.

"The jail!" Missouri shouted. "It's in the next block. That's what is stopping up everything."

"What could possibly be happening to warrant this crowd?" Clifford couldn't count. Hundreds—no, thousands—of men swarmed, shoved, shouted.

"Some of them have picks." Loren swung out of his seat, his pack of personal belongings over one shoulder. "Miners."

Missy grabbed his arm. "You can't go out there."

"We're not going anywhere else. We might as well find out what's going on."

"It's dangerous!"

"I'll just get off and ask."

She couldn't stop him. When the streetcar began to rock, she screamed, and Loren turned around and reached with both hands for Missouri and Clifford.

"We have to get off. Now! All of us!"

Clifford instantly agreed. On the pavement outside, the men linked arms with Missouri in the middle and shuffled as a block to lean against a building on the corner. Even the driver sought escape from the streetcar's impending danger.

"We have to get out of here," Clifford said.

"But how?" Missy had to shout to be heard above the cries of the mob.

Loren reached out for a brawny miner's arm. "What's going on?"

"Dan Arata is in the jail," the man said, "and we intend to get him out."

"With sledgehammers and picks?"

"They won't give him up any other way?"

"What has he done?"

"Murdered a war hero, that's what. Over a nickel bar tab."

"Isn't that a matter for the police? They've already arrested him, haven't they?"

"We'll make sure there's justice in our own way." The man stomped off.

"What madness!" Missouri clung to the wall and her father. "This is not Denver."

"Arata may have killed a man," Clifford said, "but his greater crime in their eyes is being Italian."

"Stick together and stay to the walls of the buildings," Loren said. "Head away from the jail."

Missouri's breath convulsed as a gang of men ripped the lights from the streetcar the three of them had just occupied. Others thundered down the block with lamps from other cars.

"They mean business," Clifford said. "They want to see what they're doing." He gripped his daughter's arm so tightly he might well leave a bruise. If that's what it took to keep her safe, he would risk it.

No matter how far they walked or in which direction, the riot hampered any normal movement. More than once they were pressed so tightly together or against a building, their lungs scarcely found space to expand. Blocks that seemed familiar and open in daylight—or a normal evening under streetlamps—were horrific, bloated distortions of anything Clifford ever imagined might happen in the only city Missouri remembered calling her home. He could not begin to estimate the assemblage—and that was too kind a word for the intentions of this evening.

Pressing against the tide, they gained a few yards at a time until they reached Seventeenth Street, barely advancing two blocks from where they'd first boarded a streetcar. They had no hope of another as long as they remained on Larimer, but there might be one if they could thread their way eastward to Curtis. Just when Clifford thought it was safe to let out his breath and they would find safety on the avenue that would carry them home, the sound of the crushing horde shifted. It followed them now.

"Papa!" Missy's terror rose again.

The men had Arata, and they moved faster than Clifford could aspire to move in these circumstances, reaching Seventeenth and Curtis ahead of them and shutting off the possibility for a streetcar.

"It's only a few more blocks now," he said. "We'll keep trying to go northeast. We'll get ahead of them."

"We don't even know where they're going, Papa!"

"Yes we do," Loren said.

"Where?" Missy asked.

"Don't look. Just head for home." Loren turned her shoulders and nudged her away from the intersection.

"You're coming home with us," she insisted.

Loren met Clifford's eyes.

"I'm not going if Loren's not coming." Missouri set her feet solidly. "Papa, you cannot think I would leave him in the middle of this."

"No, of course not. Loren is coming." Clifford pushed his daughter forward again.

"Just don't look," Loren said.

"What is it you don't want me to see?" Missouri asked, though she did not crane her neck to look.

Clifford was not sure of the answer to her question. Whatever Loren was protecting her from would be in tomorrow's papers. Kittie's father would be sure of that.

When they heard the gunshots, Loren only tightened his grip on Missouri's hand and pulled her forward.

"What happened to your pack?" she asked.

"Someone snatched it three blocks back," Loren said.

"But that's everything you own."

Loren shook his head. "It was nothing of value. Keep going."

The grandfather clock in the front room gonged midnight when Clifford and Missouri, grimy and exhausted, crept in the back door and paused long enough in the kitchen to wipe the worst of the night's misadventure from their faces and arms before climbing the stairs. Surely, Clifford told himself, by now Georgina would have surrendered to her own exhaustion and gone to sleep. If she woke during the night at this point, she would find him there beside her. Loren was tucked into a corner of the stable on a bed of clean hay. Humble as it was, it might have been the best accommodations he'd seen since leaving Mrs. Mitchell's boardinghouse. Missouri had promised breakfast at dawn.

Over muffins, eggs, and coffee considerably after dawn, Clifford read the morning newspaper. The man Daniel Arata was believed to have killed, because he did not pay a five-cent bar tab in the early hours of the day before, was Benjamin Lightfoot, a Civil War veteran. The crowd that broke into the jail demanding Arata be handed over to them numbered ten thousand. Very few could possibly have known Mr. Lightfoot. That he was a veteran and that Arata was an Italian immigrant were the more salient facts. Though Arata had first denied killing Lightfoot and then said the mob had the wrong man, eventually he confessed. They'd strung him up, naked, on a cottonwood tree at Seventeenth and Curtis—that must have been what Loren did not want Missouri to see—before filling his body with bullets. Satisfied that they had accomplished justice, the rioters dispersed, and the police cut down the body and took it away, presumably to the morgue. Considering the nature of his crime, the newspaper estimated that the lynching saved the county between three and four thousand dollars, while the damage to the jail was only a thousand dollars.

Clifford folded the paper once and then again. No one else in his household needed to read the gruesome details. Certainly not Missouri. Certainly not Georgina. If Corah and Lity heard them from Kittie, he could not prevent it, but they need never know their father and sister had nearly been trampled in the riot.

And they must not know about the man who'd slept in the stable.

He caught Missy's eyes and offered a half smile to her blanched expression.

"I'm going downtown today," he announced to Georgina. "The city is considering some decisions for addressing the issue of all the unemployed men, and I'd like to hear what they have to say."

Georgina eyed him. "Where's your money clip?"

"On my nightstand. Empty."

"I'm sure you'll have some good ideas to contribute. I know you care about the men."

"Thank you. I'm just going to check on the horses first."

He kissed Georgina on the cheek, nodded at Missouri, went out the back door, and strode down the side of the vegetable garden to the stable. Loren peeked out from around one corner. Clifford waved him out with a tilt of his head, and they fell into a quick pairing of pace away from the house.

"The relief camp is opening not a day too soon," Clifford said.

"Though perhaps a day too late," Loren said. "I can't thank you enough for taking me in last night. I'll find someplace to go tonight."

"I think we're past that," Clifford said. "What would I say to my daughter?"

"What will you say to your wife?"

"I'll figure that out. She likes having a carriage, but the truth is, she rarely uses it anymore. And she sends Lity to the garden. She prefers using the front door. You don't have anything to worry about."

"Mr. Brandt, I don't want to make things complicated."

Clifford looked at Loren out the side of his eye. "You already did that when you stole my daughter's heart. But I know who you are, Loren. Everything is complicated right now. You wouldn't do anything to hurt Missouri. Georgina will see that eventually."

They strode a block in silence.

"So the relief camp," Clifford said. "Eight hundred men, they say. Hopefully it will help quell some of the violence starting to foment."

"Maybe last night wouldn't have happened if they'd opened the camp sooner," Loren said.

"They're promising employment for some of the men on city projects."

"It won't be enough. Not nearly. And once word gets out about a camp and jobs in Denver, miners from all over the state will head here."

"That won't solve anything."

Loren shrugged. "This is far from over."

CHAPTER NINETEEN

The *whop* of a door slamming before he even got in the house startled Nolan. Then he spied the green bicycle propped against the porch, beneath the open living room windows on the front of the house. It was nearly three in the afternoon. He hadn't expected to find Tisha anywhere in the neighborhood when he came home from Denver a few hours early. Drew was staying over a couple of nights, and they'd planned a few hours of cooking together. And there might be some singing.

Shenanigans, Jillian called it. But so far she'd never not smiled all the way through an episode of the *Drew and Nolan Show*.

Tisha stomped down the porch steps on the side of the house.

"Tisha, we need to talk about this." Jillian stood framed in the doorway.

"You decide what you need," Tisha said, "and I decide what I need. And it's not this."

Nolan met Tisha at the bicycle, and his fingers gripped one side of the handlebars. "What's going on?"

"Just make sure she signs off on my hours, okay? And let go of my bike." Tisha yanked her bike out of Nolan's grip. "I worked hard to win this bike in that stupid eighth-grade science quiz contest so that at times like this I could get away from the adults in my life who think they're so brilliant but actually aren't."

At least Nolan now understood why an otherwise savvy, modern teenager was so attached to a mode of transportation most kids abandoned by middle school. Nolan watched her pedal furiously for a couple of seconds before shifting his attention to his daughter and climbing the steps. "I guess there's a story here."

Jillian threw up both hands as they went into the house together. Drew met them in the living room wearing a white apron over his jeans and T-shirt. She went right to his arms, and after a brief hug she plopped into the sofa.

"It was horrible, Dad. *I* was horrible."

"That wasn't the way I heard it." Drew sat beside Jillian and took her hand.

"Smells good in here. You started without me."

"Just raspberry turnovers for dessert," Drew said.

Nolan glanced at the dining room table, once again coopted by the St. Louis files, but in a more disheveled state than he'd expected, considering the care Jillian had taken to sort and label everything—and how cautious he'd been not to disturb the system when he transferred everything to the kitchen for yesterday's party.

"What happened?" he asked.

"Let's start with she showed up three hours late," Jillian said, "and wouldn't answer my texts or take my calls. "Drew and I couldn't make any plans."

"It was all right," Drew said. "We had time we didn't expect to talk and catch up just hanging around here."

"Sure, I guess. But how did I know she was coming at all?"

"I guess you didn't," Nolan said.

"So, fine. She shows up at noon. I figured we'd have more space to work if we moved everything back in here. The nook in the kitchen can be cramped."

"I would agree. I should have helped you do that last night."

"The point is, I waited for her to help because I kept thinking she'd be here any minute. *For three hours.* And then she wasn't being careful about it at all. I tried to just let it go, Dad. I did. I know she had a horrible weekend. But everything I asked her to do just made things worse. I couldn't let *everything* go, could I?"

"You didn't say anything unreasonable," Drew said. "She was pretty sensitive."

Jillian shook her head. "I'm embarrassed you saw that. In my head, I knew I had to be delicate. But my frustration got the best of me, and the words that came out of my mouth—well, they weren't always what I meant to say, but I had to say something unless I was willing to just start the whole project over again by myself. In the middle of the night. Every night. And make up work for Tisha to do during the day."

"Do I dare ask who slammed the door I heard?" Nolan said. The doors between the kitchen and dining room and between the kitchen and the hall swung. No one could slam them. And he doubted Jillian would have let Tisha near her office.

"The powder room," Jillian said. "She asked to use it and stayed in there fifteen minutes. When I asked if everything was all right, she barked at me and stayed another ten. Then she came out, slammed the door, and went straight out the front door."

"You saw the rest," Drew said.

Nolan dropped his briefcase into a chair. "I'm going after her." The Mertenson mediation continued to be fruitless. Clark and Joanna hadn't opened up on Saturday night. If anything, those failures fueled Nolan's determination not to let Tisha's situation fall apart as well.

"Dad, she could be anywhere," Jillian said.

"She hasn't been gone that long." Nolan jiggled his keys. "She's on a bicycle—a bright green one. I'll spot it parked, or someone will have seen her."

"Do you want help?" Drew reached behind his waist to untie his chef's apron.

Nolan held up a hand. "You stay here. But Jillian, when I get back, I want to sit with the two of you."

"Drew and me?"

"Tisha and you."

"To make her understand, right?"

"To find common understanding."

Her green eyes widened. "You're talking about a mediation."

"Please promise me you'll be here."

She hesitated a few seconds and then nodded.

Nolan went out to his truck and backed it out of the driveway. Other than her family's home or the Canary Cage, he knew nothing of where Tisha might go. She might go home during standard business hours if both her mother and grandmother were working. Her great-grandmother was the one who provided most of her daily care, and as far as Nolan knew, Tisha's relationship with her wasn't as hostile as the others. But she was a fifteen-year-old girl glued to her phone, and it was the height of summer. She'd told Maddie Vasquez she liked to hang out with her friends, and she went somewhere when her mother threw her out or when she just wanted to leave. Chances were that home wouldn't be her preferred destination in the middle of the afternoon. Perhaps it was time he knew more about where she spent her hours away from home anyway.

Nolan fastidiously observed the speed limit as he cruised residential neighborhoods. In fact, he drove as if every block were a school zone with hordes of young children present, crawling down the street looking at porches, garages, sheds, fences, sides of houses—anywhere that might make a good parking spot for a bicycle. He alternated north of Main Street and south, moving west to east. If he didn't find her on this side of Cutter Creek, he'd cross at Eastbridge, close to Tisha's neighborhood, and work his way back toward the west on that side of the water.

On the east end of town, on the far side of the athletic fields the schools shared, in the middle of a knot of midsize Victorian homes painted in hues of blue and beige with white accents, sunlight glinted off the green bike leaning against a chain-link fence.

Right after this episode, Nolan would advise Tisha to invest in a lock.

He pulled up as close to the bike as he could, opened the rear of his truck, slid the bike in beneath the topper, and locked it in.

Then he approached the house and rang the bell. Inside, a dog went wild.

A teenage girl, dark hair and dark eyes, answered, listing to one side to curl fingers through the black lab's collar. "My parents aren't home, so whatever you're selling. . ."

Nolan smiled. "Not selling. Looking. For Tisha Crowder."

"Who is it?" A boy came around a corner. Unmistakably, he was related to the girl. Same hair. Same eyes. Same cheekbones.

"I'm looking for Tisha," Nolan said. "I know she's here."

"Um, stalking creep weirdo. Whoever you are, go away." The girl started to close the door.

"I'm her lawyer." That was close enough to the truth, and it got the attention of the sibling duo.

The boy stepped forward, nudging his sister aside, to square off with Nolan. The protective one. The one Tisha came to see. The boy-friend Brittany knew nothing about. The person she ran to when she had nowhere to go.

"What do you want with Tisha?" he asked.

"Attorney-client privilege," Nolan said. "She can tell you later if she wants to, but I'm not going to. Just ask her to come out here, please."

The boy nodded to his sister, and she went up some stairs. The dog offered one last round of territorial assertive barking before following.

Great. The boyfriend Brittany knew nothing about entertained Tisha in an upstairs room with no adults on the premises.

The girls thundered back down the stairs, and Tisha came out on the concrete stoop, closing the door behind her.

"What do you want?"

"I'm inviting you to come back with me to my house for refreshments and conversation." Nolan smiled.

"You're weird, you know that?"

"I've been told."

"Whatever you heard, there's another side to the story."

"Thus the conversation."

"Not interested."

"I can sweeten the deal with fresh raspberry turnovers coming out of the oven as we speak. I hear you like"—he waved one hand—"raspberry things."

"Still not interested."

"Would you like a ride home, then?"

"I have my bike."

"No, I have your bike."

Tisha's glance scudded to the fence. "You stole my bike?"

"Fortunately, I have the legal services of a very good lawyer, and I'm sure I can get off."

"You really have my bike?"

"I really do."

"And you won't give it back to me unless I go with you for this 'conversation'?"

"You could put it that way."

"Isn't that extortion or something?"

"It would be a shame to have your current legal circumstances still on your record and keeping you out of a good law school someday."

"Are you trying to intimidate me or just making a stupid joke?"

Nolan did not break from her glare.

"You don't seem like the intimidating type, so I'm going with stupid joke," Tisha said. "But then I didn't take you for the stealing type, either."

"I watch a lot of crime shows on TV."

"Somehow I think that's a lie."

"Let's just call it an exaggeration." Nolan pointed. "I'm parked right over there."

"What about my friends? Or are you adding kidnapping to the list of crimes this awesome lawyer is going to defend you from?"

"Good one. Text them."

"How do you know I didn't leave my phone inside?"

"You always have your phone. Back left pocket."

Her hand moved as if in a reflexive response, confirming the phone was there.

"All right," she muttered. "You win this round. But only because I want my bike back. It's the only thing that's truly mine."

"You should be proud of yourself for winning it."

"Whatever."

Tisha slammed the door of the truck as she got in and again when she exited in front of the house. "I'm here. What about my bike?"

"The conversation, remember? Jillian's waiting inside."

"Jillian! You didn't say anything about Jillian. This is, like, false pretenses or breach of implied contract or something."

Nolan laughed. "Seriously. Law school. Jillian doesn't bite."

Tisha dragged her feet. "I don't really want to go inside."

"Fair enough." Nolan took out his phone. "I'll call Jillian and ask her to meet us in the outdoor conference room."

Tisha rolled her eyes. "You have an answer to everything."

"I try to be prepared." He pushed Jillian's number. "Hey, we'll be on the porch. Can you join us?"

Nolan offered Tisha her choice of seats, and once she selected the rocker, he angled the double-wide wicker seat so he would be in a neutral position once Jillian took the remaining chair. If anything, he wanted to lean toward supporting Tisha. Jillian could stand solidly on her own two feet. Tisha was the one likely to try to bolt. With that thought, he also positioned his chair to make it a little harder for her to get around him.

Once Jillian was also settled, Nolan laid out the facts.

"Tisha, you're in a legal pickle. You have a lot riding on making this alternative sentencing work, and you have a responsibility to give it your best effort. Jillian, you're a professional with every right to expect someone working for you to meet expectations. So let's see if we can figure out how to make the two ends of this problem come together in a way that works for both of you."

Tisha slumped back in her chair, arms crossed over her chest, jaw clamped shut.

Jillian shifted in her seat, as if she might say something, and Nolan held up one finger.

"If you don't mind, Jillian, I think Tisha has something on her mind, and I'd like to hear it."

Tisha glared.

Nolan waited.

"Tisha, would you like to say something to Jillian?" Nolan asked.

Tisha huffed. "It's what you said to me."

"I've said a lot of things to you," Jillian said.

"Today. You said, 'You're never careful enough. You always make the same mistakes.' "

Nolan nodded. "Now we're getting somewhere."

CHAPTER TWENTY

S orry about breakfast." Jillian settled her hand in the open palm Drew offered on Tuesday morning as they walked the final stretch of Main Street between downtown and the Duffy home. "I never realized how limited morning fare is in Canyon Mines until I started going out to eat with a chef."

"The company is all I care about." He squeezed her hand. "Besides, Ben's Bakery puts out an impressive spread for a casual ambiance."

"Ben makes everything himself. He doesn't bring in frozen food from Denver like most of the other places."

"It shows. In a few more weeks, I imagine he'll go crazy with Palisade peaches from the western slopes."

"It's a peach-apalooza around here!"

Drew moved his arm to Jillian's shoulder, and she leaned into him. "I wish I could stay longer, but I've already had three text messages from Aunt Min verifying that I plan to be back at the ranch in time for the meeting with the zoning commission."

"Are you really going to sell off some acres?"

Drew shrugged. "Just talking about it. It's a generous offer, and the acres are in a corner of the ranch we rarely even ride out to anymore. It won't affect the seasonal route the deer take up into the mountains and back down, which is something Min cares most about these days."

They reached the house, and Drew gathered her into a full embrace beside his truck. "Sorry again about the radio silence last week. I didn't trust myself not to give away the surprise."

Jillian poked his chest playfully. "Well, don't do it again. I'm incredibly insecure."

She tilted her face up and waited. He'd better not even think about leaving without kissing her.

"Do you want to try again to visit the ranch in a couple of weeks?"

Drew's gray eyes danced above that dimple she loved, and she couldn't resist touching the dark curls that perpetually clung to the back of his neck.

"I thought you'd never ask."

"I'm coming back up to do a concert at an alumni event at the University of Denver in September. I hope you can be there."

"I wouldn't miss it."

"Don't you need to check your calendar?"

"I'll reschedule." *Are you going to kiss me or not?*

"Maybe you have to go to St. Louis that weekend."

"I don't."

Drew laughed softly, his warm breath spilling in gentle ripples across her cheeks. "Your father can come too, but you'll have to explain that he really shouldn't sing along."

"Done."

Finally, he lowered his lips to hers, lingering long enough for her to taste the rich, soft, sweetness of this man who had only entered her life two months ago. She'd very nearly chased him away by jumping to multiple erroneous and insulting conclusions about his genealogy before breaking through on the right path. What a shame it would have been if he hadn't returned to hear her out and find the truth together.

With a moan, Drew broke the kiss. "I really have to go."

"I know," Jillian murmured. "Tell Min I said hello."

She stayed on the sidewalk long enough to watch him pull away and turn the next corner out of sight. Already she missed him. A day and a half weren't enough.

Tisha's bicycle had appeared while Jillian was in town with Drew having breakfast. Nolan's intervention the previous afternoon between Tisha and Jillian had been bumpy. It hadn't lasted long enough to reach final resolution, but at least it had gotten a few things on the table. True to his word, Nolan was taking today off to construct shelving in the guest room, and he promised to occupy Tisha for at least three hours or as long as she would stay to help. A day of space between Tisha and Jillian—and perhaps reflection—might help reduce the temperature of their working relationship.

Jillian's phone rang, startling her, and she whipped it out of her pocket.

"Is he gone?" Nia asked.

"Just pulled away."

"Are you languishing dreadfully in despondence?"

"Are we speaking to each other from a Jane Austen novel now?"

"You know what I mean."

"I do wish he could have stayed longer." Jillian kicked a pebble. "Thanks for your part in getting him here and pulling off a second surprise party. That was crazy."

"My pleasure. The beauty was in the double whammy."

"You knew all along why he wasn't calling me, didn't you?"

"I might have. That doesn't mean I didn't think he should."

"So when it comes to Tisha, you don't want to meddle, but when it comes to Drew, you do?"

"I'm glad we understand each other."

"You are a curious friend, Nia Dunston."

"Let me know if you want to talk."

"About Tisha or Drew?"

"Boyfriend!" Nia's exuberance erupted.

"Okay, I'm going now."

"Not yet."

"Yes?"

"I do have one piece of advice about Tisha."

"I'm all ears."

"When it comes to the work, what is *she* good at?"

"What do you mean? There are certain things that have to be done."

"Because that's the way you would do them. But maybe the starting point is wrong. Just think about it."

"Okay. I'll try." Jillian ended the call. Inside the house, she paused at the base of the front stairs.

In one direction, she could see the papers still on the dining room table a week after Tisha's first arrival. Before this, Jillian hadn't imagined the room upstairs would have shelves before the papers even all had labeled file folders in boxes to go on the shelves. The St. Louis project was bigger than anything she'd ever done, and it had the potential to grow leaps and bounds larger than it already was. Though ideally most information would eventually be organized and stored electronically in ways that were backed up and secured from theft, corruption, house fire, flood—any number of things that could happen—Jillian knew her own brain. Undoubtedly there would be times when she recalled seeing an original paper document that came from a decades-old file or that she acquired by requesting future documents she didn't yet know existed related to the placement of a particular stolen child and the generations that followed. Even in the twenty-first century, there was a place for properly managed paper trails. If nothing else, they would serve as a quality-control cross-reference to an electronic scanned document that could so easily be misplaced and never found again.

In the other direction, Jillian could look up the stairs and listen to the sounds wafting through the hallway from the room above the living room and down the stairwell. The thud of boards being relocated and laid out around the bed in the larger of the two guest rooms. The occasional *thwack* of a hammer or the buzz of a power tool suggested the rearrangement of equipment. And laughter. Her father's laughter was a familiar sound in the house. He laughed every day, and he tried to make Jillian laugh every day. Most days he succeeded. Today, though, the second voice cavorting with his had the light treble ring of a girl.

Tisha was laughing. In an entire week, Jillian hadn't even seen her smile. Roll her eyes, smirk, pop bubbles, scowl, glare, sigh. But not smile, and certainly not laugh.

With placid steps, Jillian climbed to the landing and tilted her head to listen.

A tool whirred in a swift barrage. Jillian recognized the sound of her father's small cordless power drill.

"Whoa!" Tisha giggled.

"You've got it," Nolan said. "It just takes a light quick touch—when we're ready."

"I can put screws in with this?"

"I recommend it, unless you prefer to be twisting screws in until your high school graduation."

"This is my jam." Tisha pushed the button again for a few seconds. "At my house, we're lucky if we have a clean table knife to turn a screw."

"This is so much better, wouldn't you say?"

"Way! Are we really going to build a whole bookshelf?"

"Two! It would be a shame to burn all this perfectly good new wood in the fireplace."

Jillian moved through the hall and leaned against the wall outside the room.

"Why does this house have so many fireplaces anyway?" Tisha said. "Don't you have heat in these bedrooms?"

"Answering that question would require a history lesson."

"This whole town is a history lesson."

"Pretty much."

"Some sort of weird time capsule, if you ask me." Tisha ran the power drill again. "Bet they didn't have one of these when this house was built."

Nolan chuckled. "Doubtful. Maybe you'd like to holster that while we check to be sure the hardware store got all the measurements right on what they cut for me."

"Good idea. I saw a measuring tape in your toolbox."

"And we'll cover all the furniture with old sheets so we don't make a mess on anything we can't sweep up. There's a stack in the chair."

"Shouldn't we be building in the garage or on the porch?"

Nolan rapped his knuckles on something solid. "This is not pressboard. This is the real thing. Which means it's heavy. I decided I'd rather build in place than carry the finished product up the stairs."

"Makes sense, I guess."

"Because I'm of a certain age, you mean."

Tisha laughed. "Well. You said it, not me. How long are these boards supposed to be?"

"We're going to build two narrow, tall cabinets, one for either side of the fireplace." A paper rattled as Nolan consulted his notes. "Four at eighty and three-quarter inches for the sides."

A metal tape measure shot out of its case and flopped around a bit. Jillian looked around the corner to see Tisha wrangle it and stretch it across a long pile.

"Check. What's next?"

"Twelve at twenty-one inches for the interior shelves."

Tisha squared off in front of a stack of boards. "Check."

They worked their way through the cut list for shelves, backs, and trim. Then Nolan started explaining various types of screws.

Tisha's curiosity, questions, and attention to detail blew Jillian away.

Jillian knocked and revealed her presence.

Hands on his knees, Nolan greeted her. "Jilly. Hello. Want to help?"

She shook her head. "I just wanted to say something."

"Of course. They're your shelves."

"No, not about the shelves."

Nolan and Tisha, both squatting, looked at her. Jillian met Tisha's eyes.

"Tisha, I'm sorry. You were right yesterday. I haven't been careful with my words. I haven't given you the benefit of the doubt. I assumed the worst and had an attitude that I had to grin and bear it. We might still have a way to go in figuring out how to work together to get the job done, but right now I just want to say I'm sorry. I hope you'll give me another chance."

"Um. Okay." Tisha snapped the measuring tape back into its case. Her brown eyes were clouds of confusion, and she turned away.

"Well, that's all," Jillian said. "I'm sure the bookcases will be great. I'll be in my office if you need me."

She pivoted and started down the back stairs and was almost to her office before she realized her father was right behind her.

"Jilly, that was very brave. Thank you."

She shrugged one shoulder. "I'm not sure it did any good. You had to notice she didn't actually say she accepted my apology."

"I suspect that's because she has very little experience with receiving apologies."

Jillian's eyes flicked up the stairwell. "I hadn't thought about that."

"You just did something she didn't expect—and it probably shocked her. Give her some time."

Jillian nodded.

"So we'll build shelves, she'll have fun with my power drill, and when I have a chance I'm going to see if I can set up a meeting with Brittany for later today while Tisha is in a positive state of mind."

"Do you really think that will help?"

"I have to try to get somewhere with whatever is in the middle of the two of them. It's going to take more than a battery-operated drill to get Tisha to see she has power over her own future."

CHAPTER TWENTY-ONE

Nolan promised to buy every unsold burrito and dessert at the Canary Cage if Clark Addison would close to business as usual at seven on Tuesday evening but allow him to bring Tisha over to meet Brittany Crowder privately.

Clark harrumphed on the phone and said that if they wanted any food, they had to settle for paper plates and cups. He wasn't risking his crockery on the likes of the Crowders in a mediation gone bad.

"A fair compromise," Nolan had agreed.

He wanted a location that felt neutral—not the Crowder home—and close enough to Brittany's workplace that she couldn't claim inconvenience. She could come directly across the street from Candles & Cards when she got off. Once Tisha stayed through lunch, Nolan was sure he could keep her in a good mood the rest of the day building shelves, offer supper, and calmly explain what he had in mind for the evening.

Jillian slipped out to meet Nia for an early dinner, purposely absenting herself so as not to make Tisha's decision more complicated. Nolan's gentle request—an offer of help—hung in the kitchen, mingling with the aromas of a hearty garden vegetable soup he'd invited the girl to help cook and Irish soda bread she was curious about because she'd never had it. With the bread in the oven and the soup simmering, Nolan posed his question.

Tisha scrunched up her face. "Go to the Cage while it's closed?"

"Think of it as a private party."

"You asked my mom?"

"I did. I called and caught her on a break at work."

"I can't believe she said she would come."

"She said the same about you."

"But you hadn't asked me yet."

Nolan shrugged and ran water in the sink to rinse utensils.

"What if I don't agree to go?"

"I'll still meet your mother there and try to hear her perspective in a calm way."

Tisha rubbed both temples. "This has been such a great day. I actually learned stuff today, and it was interesting. I built something! Why do we have to wreck it by talking to Brittany?"

"I hope we're not going to wreck anything, Tisha. But Brittany is your mother. Wouldn't you like to build something with her?"

Tisha shuffled over to the nook at one end of the kitchen and sat with her head hanging between her elbows. "This is not going to end well."

"How about this? You put your phone on the table, you set a timer for the number of minutes you choose. When it goes off, you can decide if you want to reset it and keep going or whether you've reached your limit."

"How much time? Do I really get to choose?"

Nolan nodded. "I'd like to see fifteen minutes, and then evaluate, but if you're more comfortable starting with ten, or even five, then that's what we'll do."

"Does she get to do that?"

"Ultimately, I can't force anyone to stay, but I haven't made this offer to her. I'm hoping she'll want to stay because she's your mother and cares about what happens to you."

Tisha sighed, exasperated. "You're a glass half-full person, aren't you?"

"I like to believe there's always hope, Tisha. Will you let me hope for you?"

The oven timer went off, and Nolan reached for a mitt and pulled out the tray of bread. He set the steaming loaf on a board on the table in front of Tisha and returned to the stove to ladle soup into bowls.

"You said your great-grandma looks out for you. Jillian's great-grandma started a blessing our family likes to say." Nolan carried a bowl to the table and looked Tisha right in the eye as he spoke. "May you always find nourishment for your body at the table. May sustenance for your spirit rise and fill you with each dawn. And may life always feed you with the light of joy along the way."

She twiddled the handle of her spoon between thumb and

forefinger. "Pretty words but not real life."

"But they should be. You deserve for them to be *your* life."

He sat across from her with his own soup and cut into the bread. That was enough words for now. It was time for food, the labor of the day, and a trusting silence to do their work.

An hour later, Clark Addison latched the Cage's door closed, turned the sign to CLOSED, set a raspberry Italian cream soda in front of Tisha and two coffees on the table, and disappeared into the kitchen.

Nolan nodded at Tisha, sitting beside him, and she slid her iPhone on the table.

"Do you really have to play with your stupid phone right now?" Brittany said.

"The phone is a tool Tisha and I have agreed to," Nolan said. "Ten?"

Tisha nodded and hit START on the timer.

"I want to start by saying that Tisha and I had a delightful day," Nolan said. "She was a great help to me building some shelving that will be very useful for the project she's working on with Jillian. She has quite a handy touch with a power drill."

"Who on earth would let her use a power drill?"

"Me, of course." Nolan pulled out his own phone and showed Brittany the photo he'd snapped of the unit they'd finished. "We have a little more work to do on the second set of shelves, but this girl knows what she's doing."

"Well, I don't know what to say."

"I'm sure Tisha would like to hear you say she did a good job. Am I right, Tisha?"

"Yes." The answer was small but quick.

"Okay, then," Brittany said. "Good job."

Insincere at best, but it was a starting point.

"Thanks." Nolan eyed the timer. "She worked hard. I also was hoping we could begin talking about some of the conflict between the two of you. I help families with things like this all the time, and I would love to help you."

"You're talking about what happened at Ore the Mountain in front of all those people," Brittany said.

"That's certainly a place to start," Nolan said. Seven minutes left.

Brittany huffed. "Jillian didn't need to be snooping around our house on Saturday. That's the real reason why I'm here—to tell you to tell her to keep away."

"I'm quite sure she understands your feelings on that question," Nolan said. "Let's set Jillian aside for now and focus on the two of you. Tisha, what would you like to say to your mother about those episodes?"

Tisha glanced at her phone. "I just want to know who my father is. That's all. Doesn't everybody want to know that? Why can't we talk about that?"

Brittany snatched a paper napkin out of a holder on the table and began twisting two diagonal corners. "It's not important."

"It's important to me! That's what I'm trying to get you to understand. But all you do is yell. I have a right to know."

"I have a say in the matter too. It happened to me."

"What happened?" Tisha's voice rose. "Just tell me. I'm fifteen, almost as old as you were whenever whatever it was happened that I'm not allowed to know about. After all, *I* happened."

"No. You don't need to know. It's mine. You have me, you have your grandma Peggy and my grandma Ora. That's plenty of family. You don't need to know anything else. You're mine."

"I'm not *yours*. I'm *me*."

Nolan looked from Brittany to Tisha to the timer. Four minutes.

"Besides," Brittany said, "ultimately, in this town it's enough that you're a Brandt."

Tisha shoved her chair back a few inches. "No one is a Brandt. Not for generations. We're all called Crowder. Brandt is just a name on some building. It means nothing."

"The Brandt Building." Nolan pointed out the window and across the street. "The building where Motherlode Books is and the apartments."

"That's right," Brittany said. "Used to be ours."

"It was never *ours*," Tisha said.

"It belonged to our family, Letitia."

"Like a hundred years ago, if that's even a true story."

"That's something we can look into," Nolan said. "That's right up Jillian's alley. Genealogy."

"I don't need Jillian's help." Brittany tore off a piece of napkin and wadded it up in a tiny ball. "My grandmother has her own memories."

"Ora?" Nolan asked.

"That's right. She was a Brandt. Well, her grandmother was."

"Well, that's a great start." Two minutes. "No doubt there are some delightful stories to hear. Tisha also would like to understand more about who she is as a unique individual. Today, when we were building shelves, she described Canyon Mines as a history lesson. I think she's right, and she might enjoy learning more details about the Brandts in Canyon Mines. But as an individual she has a unique branch of the family that she doesn't share with any of the rest of you. That comes from her father, and she'd like to know more about that as well. Am I explaining that accurately, Tisha?"

Tisha nodded, her fingers creeping toward the phone.

"She doesn't need any of that nonsense," Brittany said. "I'm her mother. I tell her what she needs. She's a child, and we wouldn't be sitting here right now if I could count on her to make smart decisions. Instead, I have to clean up her messes. Find her a lawyer, take her to appearances, agree to arrangements or have you threaten me with liability."

"I'm sitting right here," Tisha said.

"Well, you might as well not be for the good you're contributing to this conversation."

"Let's all take a breath," Nolan said.

Mother and daughter glared at each other. Nolan considered his next tactic.

The timer went off, and Tisha pounced on it.

"Another ten?" Nolan said.

Tisha stood and picked up her phone. "You promised I got to decide."

"I will honor my promise."

"Why are you letting her decide anything?" The pitch of Brittany's voice, already sour, exploded with exasperation.

"Tisha has proven to me she can handle being in control of some things," Nolan said, "and we chose this."

"Well. Look what it got you. Not that I'm complaining. I told you why I really came."

"There's no point." Tisha pushed her phone into the pocket of her shorts. "She won't tell me who my father is because she doesn't know who my father is, the same way Grandma Peggy doesn't know who her father is."

Brittany nearly upended the table and beverages, reaching across to slap her daughter's face.

"Brittany!" Nolan jumped up and pulled Tisha back before her mother's open palm landed on its mark.

"She deserves more than a slap. You heard what she said."

Tisha's face reddened. Fury? Embarrassment? Frustration? Nolan wouldn't blame her for all three.

"I know who your father is," Brittany growled. "And I know exactly where he is. I've always known. I'm just not going to tell you."

"I'm going to do a DNA test," Tisha screamed. "I'll be related to someone out there. I'll find out who. Then I'll find him. I'll find another family that's better than these crazy so-called Brandt women."

Brittany scoffed. "You're a minor. You're stuck with the family you have unless I say otherwise."

Tisha charged the door.

"Tisha, wait." Nolan chased her.

"I'm out of here." She fumbled with the latch, arm upstretched and heels raised off the floor to give the extra height required.

"I'd like to see you calmer before you leave." Nolan couldn't imagine she would go home tonight—at least not anytime soon. Did she sneak into the boyfriend's house on nights like this without his parents knowing? The sister might provide cover. Or did she have another girlfriend?

Tisha finally wrestled the latch up, yanked the door open, and hopped on her bicycle outside. At least it was still light out—for now.

Nolan turned to Brittany.

She sneered. "Happy?"

CHAPTER TWENTY-TWO

Denver, Colorado
Wednesday, August 2, 1893

Clifford raised his coffee cup. "Why not sit with me a little longer? It's still early. Let your breakfast settle."

"Lity will be right back down to do the clearing up." Georgina's hat was already pinned in place, and her handbag dangled from one bent elbow.

Clifford knew better than to say he'd always thought that purse looked like it was made from remnants of a carpet bag, with its sturdy metal frame and heavy colorful weave. In one hand, she gripped leather driving gloves purchased from McNamara Dry Goods two years ago. Clifford couldn't recall that she'd ever used the new gloves. The carriage had its comforts, though it was too crowded for the family to occupy together comfortably now that the girls were grown, and its open design limited its use to fine weather. It could also be a nuisance to take downtown compared to the ease of the streetcars. Even Georgina agreed.

"There's still coffee in the pot," he said. "We may as well enjoy it."

"It's just coffee, Clifford. I don't know what's gotten into you. All I said was I was going to take the carriage to go see Mrs. Porter because she's feeling poorly, and suddenly you think we don't spend enough time together."

"We could do the clearing up," he said. "We always did when the girls were little."

"Is that how you remember it?" Georgina gave her hat a minute adjustment. "I don't know why the Porters moved so far south, but they have, and Mrs. Porter is unwell and I want to see her."

"You could take the streetcar." Clifford reached into his pocket for some coins.

"Clifford! It doesn't go all the way out there, and you know it. Besides, you told me yourself the horses are not getting enough exercise. If you won't hitch the carriage for me, I'll do it myself. I haven't forgotten how. I do remember a few things from the old days." She rotated away from him and headed out the back door.

Cliff scrambled to his feet just as Lity came back into the room. "Go fetch Missy," he said.

"But the dishes."

"They'll wait. Get Missy and send her out to the stable. Now!" Cliff thumped around the kitchen table and outside in Georgina's wake.

"Georgina, I'll get the carriage for you," he called from behind her.

She didn't break stride. "You made your point. I will manage."

"Please, Georgina. I was not trying to make a point. Wait here, and I will bring the carriage around."

She marched past the garden undeterred, not placated. If he'd simply offered to drive her to the Porters in the first place, he would have avoided this moment. Perhaps there was nothing to worry about. Most mornings Missy took food to the stable before the family breakfast and their guest was gone before anyone else was up. Clifford was likely borrowing trouble. Still, he didn't like the idea of Georgina poking around the stable. Even if Loren was gone, his makeshift bedroll might be in sight.

"Georgie." He wasn't sure what he would do when he caught up. He hastened his gait.

"Clifford, what has gotten into you?"

Georgina shoved open the stable door, a task she had not performed independently in at least five years, and paced in to yank on the carriage door and deposit her handbag.

The screech she emitted was everything Clifford had hoped to prevent. He winced.

"You get out of there right this instant!" She was beating the man with her miniature carpetbag, hardly giving him an opportunity to move.

Poor Loren.

"It's all right, Georgie," Clifford said, caught up at last. "It's Loren

Wade. You've met him. He worked for me."

Her thrashing ceased but not her indignation. She glared at Clifford. "You knew he was here."

Clifford caught Loren's sheepish glance. They'd said nothing of Loren curling up in the carriage, but Clifford didn't blame him for wanting to get off the ground. Why was he still there?

"I was going to speak to you, Georgina," he said.

"Papa! What happened?" Missouri burst into the stable. She saw her mother and Loren's disheveled form and understood. "He's staying, Mama."

"So you've all decided this behind my back," Georgina said. "The three of you. How long has this been going on?"

"A few days." Missy wound both arms around one of Loren's. "Since the night that Italian barkeep was killed by the mob. The streets aren't safe. Loren has nothing, Mama. Not even the pack he came down from the mine with. Either he's given away everything to help someone else or his things have been stolen."

"Keeping him here at night is the right thing, Georgie," Clifford said.

"Can't he go to that relief camp they opened along the river?" Georgina eyed her husband. "Isn't that what it's for? You're the one who told me about it."

"The camp has space for eight hundred men," Cliff said. "Do you have any idea how many homeless men are roaming around Denver right now? It's a place to start, but they never know if they'll have money to stay open tomorrow. We can ease the load in this very small way by giving shelter to one man we care about."

Georgina considered her husband's face for a few seconds. "You've eased their load another way, haven't you? A donation."

Clifford said nothing.

"Clifford!" Georgina shouted. "How could you?"

"I should go," Loren said.

Missy held him tight. "Not until we have this settled. You're coming back tonight, and that's final."

"Yes, it is," Clifford said.

Georgina huffed.

"Georgie, the railroads are no longer offering the six-dollar fare, and they won't tolerate being mobbed by men demanding to ride for free, either. Some of these men were my men. Others worked for Mr. Tabor, which makes them feel like my men. I can't stand by and do nothing."

"Mrs. Porter is waiting," Georgina said. "I'll need the carriage."

Loren and Missouri moved outside, and Clifford hitched up the carriage and sent Georgina on her way.

"What are we going to do?" Missouri asked. "She doesn't know a small fraction of the truth of that night."

"And we're going to leave it that way," Clifford said.

"I'll get by," Loren said. "I'm sorry I was in the carriage."

Missy shook her head. "Mama would have been just as upset to see you anywhere in the stable. You're going to stay. I only wish you could stay in the house. Papa, if he was in the basement, Mama would never know. She doesn't go down there."

Loren shook his head. "I won't go behind her back like that. Not again."

"The stable at least," Missy said. "Papa, you'll make it right with Mama for the stable?"

Clifford nodded.

"I promise to stay out of the carriage," Loren said. "I'll only come after dark and be gone before breakfast, like I've been doing. I slipped up just this once and fell back to sleep."

"You're exhausted. I'm going to find you a proper cot," Missouri said. "Somehow. And I want you to promise to go to the clothing bank to look for a few things to replace what you've lost. And something that fits."

Loren sniffed. "My clothes surely could use a wash."

Clifford slipped out of the stable. He'd let go the boy he'd been paying to muck the two stalls, so he'd have to put on work clothes and return later for the chore. Or perhaps if he promised Loren would do it in exchange for his shelter, Georgina would be more accepting. For now Missy and Loren could sort out their day on their own. An interesting inquiry awaited him in his desk drawer. He'd read it twice already. With Georgina out of the house for a few hours, he could take it out in plain sight and put to paper the response already formed in his mind.

The day's wanderings included posting the letter, visiting the camp along the South Platte River, and gathering news of the city's efforts to fund work projects to temporarily hire some of the unemployed men who still had no means of leaving Denver.

Georgina said nothing more about the guest in the stable—or the food that went missing from the kitchen in increasing amounts to sustain him. In solitary moments, Clifford used his journal to try to make sense of events that made no sense. A week passed.

> *Thursday, August 10, 1893. More than two months and the crisis seems unabating. I like to think that if I'd had the grand fortunes of Horace Tabor, I would have set more aside for circumstances such as this. If ever there was a time the city needs his philanthropy, this is it, yet he has nothing to give. I hear even the utilities to his palatial home have been shut off because he cannot pay his bills. I am not the only one for whom he will not open the door. I am the least of his worries. I doubt I even cross his mind.*
>
> *I had no grand fortune. I had modest prospects of comfortable years ahead to begin with. But that is nothing to cling to at a time like this. When presented with an opportunity for bold action that will allow me to make some contribution to my fellow men and still provide for my family in a way I believe will serve them well for years to come, I give thanks to God and say a resounding yes to both callings. How can I do otherwise?*

He laid down his pen on the kitchen table, where he'd been writing while nursing a late evening cup of tea. Missouri came in from her thinking bench and stood at the window to continue her evening vigil.

"He'll come," Cliff said.

"It's late."

"Not so late."

"I didn't mean to disturb your journaling."

"You didn't." Cliff capped his pen and closed the journal.

"Mama needs to understand that Loren and I are going to be together," Missy said.

Clifford nodded. "You have my blessing."

Tears filled her eyes. "Thank you, Papa."

"You're not so different than when your mother and I started out. She'll come around."

"Do you really think so?"

"I'm in your corner, Missouri. Right now everything feels untrue. No jobs, no money. Your mother's nerves clanging about every little change. You're old enough to remember she hasn't always been like this."

"Doesn't she know she can trust you?"

"I certainly like to think so."

"Then what changed?"

Clifford drew in a slow breath. "Sometimes other things get in the way. Things we can't control. Things we never imagined would happen that mean the old answers won't work no matter how badly we want them to."

"Well, I trust you, Papa. I don't know what the answers are for our family, but I know you won't stop looking for them."

Clifford smiled. "I do enjoy our little talks, Missouri."

"Me too."

He picked up the journal. "I think I'd like you to have this."

"Your journal? That's private."

Cliff shrugged one shoulder. "I suppose. But I haven't written anything in it I'm ashamed for you to read, even if some of it may be new to you. You share my heart in a way your sisters don't. It's only half full. Why don't you take it from here?"

"But what will you write in?"

"Maybe I'll start another someday. Or maybe my writing days have come to a close. My life is taking some unexpected changes, but yours is just starting." Cliff held the journal toward Missy.

Tentatively, she took it. "I don't know what to say."

"Just receive it and carry on." Cliff glanced out the window. "Looks like he's home. You can go to bed and rest easy now."

"Thank you, Papa."

"In the morning, ask him to wait for me around the corner. We can go out to the relief camp together and see if we can find news of our other men."

She nodded, and they both went upstairs.

Loren had on fresh clothes the following day. The trousers fit his leaner frame better than his own had after the last few weeks, though Missy was doing what she could to fatten him up again now.

"Tell me you've left your money clip at home," Loren said.

Clifford nodded, and they began to walk. It was a long way to Riverfront Park, where the camp was, but they both had more time than money, even for a streetcar.

"I have some news," Loren said.

"Oh?" Clifford looked at him.

"The People's Tabernacle is going to make an announcement today."

Clifford's stomach sank. "It's not good news, is it?"

"I heard Parson Tom talking about it yesterday. Their committee has made a firm decision. They can no longer keep trying to feed all the single men who have flooded the city."

"I don't know how they've managed as long as they have."

"They feel they must return to focusing on serving the poor who are permanent residents of Denver, especially women and children. There just aren't enough donations to go around."

"This will be devastating to the camp," Cliff said.

"I'm so grateful that you've taken me in," Loren said. "Obviously I would hate to have to leave Denver, or even Colorado, right now. I'm going to try again to see if I can get one of the jobs the city is offering."

"They must have four or five men applying for every job they have."

"I'm still going to try."

"If it helps, I'm happy to be a reference. But Loren—"

"Yes?"

Clifford shook his head. "Never mind." It was better if no one knew until arrangements were certain.

At the camp they found piles of lumber. Clifford stopped one of the camp organizers.

"What's all this? Are we building more permanent structures than the tents after all?"

"Rafts," the man said.

"Rafts?"

"The city is providing the lumber. The men can build rafts and put off into the river."

Clifford blinked, awaiting a more reasonable explanation. When none came, he said, "Put off into the South Platte River without provision or destination? Where will they go?"

"The current will take them." The man mopped sweat off his forehead. "They can't stay here. We don't know if we'll even have a meal for them tomorrow or the day after."

That evening Clifford found Missy writing in the journal—or trying to—as once again she waited to be sure Loren had come home for the night.

"I don't know how to get started," she said.

"It will come to you when you're ready."

"I read what you wrote. I felt nosy at first, but you wouldn't give me the journal and not expect me to read it."

"That's right."

"You worked so hard for so long, Papa. I'm sorry everything fell apart. None of it was your fault."

"The drop in silver prices wasn't, and I can't help what President Cleveland intends to do even though he knows it will only make the catastrophe worse in the western states. But there are some decisions I wish I could take back."

"Mama was very quiet at dinner tonight."

Clifford nodded. "Everything is out of her control. I think she realizes none of this is suddenly going to improve."

"Have you no employment prospects at all, Papa?"

Clifford reached for the inner pocket of the suit jacket he still wore most of the time when he left the house, to appease Georgina, and touched the envelope of papers.

"I have put together an unconventional plan." He resisted the urge to remove the papers and say more. "It won't be long now."

CHAPTER TWENTY-THREE

I wasn't there, but my dad said it was bad. Very bad." After her morning run, Jillian pulled a brush through her tangled hair while she spoke to Nia using the speaker feature on her cell phone. "I feel like I'm prepared to work harder at thinking before I speak, but I can't control what state of mind her own mother puts her in."

"Has Nolan thought about checking with the police or Child Protective Services to see if there have been previous complaints?"

"I think he plans to. My guess is neighbors have complained about noise, but if the police get there and don't see anyone hurt, what will happen?"

"Sadly, nothing," Nia said. "I had a student in Denver in a similar home situation. But he showed no signs of physical abuse. He had secure shelter, food, and clothes. They dropped him at school on time every morning. He didn't always come in, because, like Tisha, he had bigger things on his mind. But they got him there."

"I guess we never know what someone is going through." Jillian grabbed a band and attacked the task of taming her hair enough to get it off her neck for the hottest hours of the day.

"Unfortunately, being nasty to your kid is not illegal," Nia said. "And in Colorado, parents can use reasonable and appropriate force to discipline a child."

"But what is reasonable and appropriate?"

"That question only becomes relevant if a case gets in front of a jury."

"In other words, it has to be pretty bad."

"Right. Just listen to her, Jills."

"It seems like no one else does. Except my dad." Jillian moved from the powder room into the kitchen. She had time to make a fortifying caffeine beverage before Tisha's arrival. "Somehow Brittany and

Peggy manage to put on their manners to work in the shops."

"But they're never all that happy about it, if you pay attention," Nia said. "It's like they work in the stores because they've always worked in the stores, not because they enjoy interacting with people. Seems to me the family has been unhappy a long time, all the way back to that diary fragment at the Heritage Society."

Jillian's movements froze. "The one in the display case in the front room?"

"Yep."

"I haven't thought of that in years. Georgina Brandt, wasn't it?"

"That's the one."

"That's what Tisha meant when she told me her family used to be rich. The Brandts. But no one has ever figured out why one random diary page surfaced. It's not much of a story."

"Well, there you go," Nia said. "Now there's a girl who needs to know the whole story and a genealogist who can help her sort it out."

The doorbell rang.

"She's here," Jillian said. "Gotta go."

Tisha wore a change of clothes since yesterday, so she'd made it home at some point, Jillian presumed. The defiance in her features, which had softened slightly after a day of building with Nolan, had reset beneath haggard shades, suggesting she hadn't slept much.

"Great! You have your raspberry soda." Jillian infused sparkle to her greeting. "Ready to work!"

Tisha simply nodded and shuffled into the house.

"I looked at the bookshelves last night," Jillian said. "They look terrific!"

"We still have to finish the second one. Nolan said maybe Saturday, or Friday afternoon if he has time. You can't put any weight on those shelves yet."

"Thanks for the warning. I got out the file boxes I bought, so we can put those together. Do you feel ready to get back to labeling so we can box everything up?"

"Nolan will be glad to have the table back."

Was that a half smile on Tisha's face?

Jillian sipped her coffee. "I believe the two of you might be colluding, but since it seems to be friendly conspiring, I will let it pass."

"They're not the same, you know. Colluding and conspiring. Separate legal definitions."

Jillian chuckled. "My dad would be proud of you for pointing that out. I'll look up the distinction and be more careful."

"You're all right, because it is possible to be doing both at the same time."

"How about we avoid anything involving nuances of deceit and go straight for positive cooperation?"

Tisha met Jillian's gaze, but her eyes had flattened again. "I can do that."

Jillian felt like sentencing herself to a fifteen-mile punitive run. She'd taken the banter a jive too far. Reading Tisha—well, she still wasn't very good at it.

"Well, let's get started." Jillian nodded toward the sideboard. "The label maker is there."

"Do you still want separate blue and red folders?"

"Yes, please. It's important for our research to know what came from the original folders and what comes from other sources. Plus, for the families we eventually find, they might like to have those original documents. I want to be confident I know right where they are, even if I've scanned them."

"That makes sense."

"Have you ever used a scanner?"

"A couple times at school."

"I have a pretty good one. You're going to become an expert at adjusting settings for the best image."

"I don't know about that."

"Until yesterday, you didn't know you could use a power drill."

Tisha almost laughed.

"I have a nine thirty video call with my client Raúl. I will leave you to carry on."

"You're not going to check my every move?" Tisha cocked her head, suspicious.

"I have to be on this call," Jillian said. "Raúl relies on me, and I don't want to lose his business. I expect it's going to take thirty or forty minutes. So I'm depending on you to do the best work you can labeling and stacking the folders, getting them ready for boxes to go on the shelves you built with your own hands."

"I had some help with the shelves."

"Shhh. Don't let my dad hear you say that. He tends to let that sort of thing go to his head."

Jillian exhaled as she went around the corner and set up for her video call. She might well spend her evening going through the work Tisha did while unsupervised because the girl's head swam with the emotions of her home conflicts. On the other hand, if Nolan's efforts at making the Duffy home a safe space—and Jillian's apology—were bearing any fruit, Tisha might surprise her with more accurate work. Jillian likely wouldn't know until she double-checked everything later, away from the impulse to chastise and correct.

Forty minutes later, her heart sank at the sight of an idle label maker not even within easy reach and very few blue and red completed folders. Instead, several previously organized stacks were unclipped and the contents spread atop other piles. Jillian sucked in her lips for a few seconds before speaking.

"Tisha?"

The pink head lifted. "These stories are awful."

Jillian slid her feet forward a couple of yards, waiting for words to come to her. The table was a disaster—and Tisha? What just happened?

"Have you read these?" Tisha said. "I mean, really read them?"

Jillian nodded, resisting the urge to sort pages she could see were intermingled. "That's how the mess ended up on the table in the first place."

"I suppose the babies never knew the difference—if they went to good homes. We don't know where they ended up, though if they had decent mothers to begin with, they didn't deserve what happened. But some of these kids were separated from their parents and then separated from their brothers and sisters too. And they were old enough to remember having another family than wherever they ended up. That is so unfair."

Righteous indignation. Yes!

Jillian sat in a chair beside Tisha and looked at the papers on the table and in her lap.

"Before, you asked me to look at names," Tisha said. "Spelling. Ages. Whether there were siblings. Whether the papers mentioned cities."

"Yes. All that will help in the searches as we eventually build a database."

"But don't you see? That's like trying to answer questions on a book you haven't read. The students who do that fail the quizzes. You have to know the whole story for any of it to make sense."

Click.

The explanation Jillian gave the previous week hadn't fallen into place. Maybe she hadn't had time to consider how to approach introducing the project, and maybe Tisha hadn't had opportunity to clear her mind—and attitude—to care. Whatever had gone wrong was shifting today, right now, even at the risk of the piles losing order yet again.

"What in the world did they tell those kids about why suddenly they had new parents?" Tisha tapped a page.

"That's a very good question." Gingerly, Jillian moved a few sheets from a chair so she could sit down. For now she kept the pages safe in her lap.

"I read one file where they took children from a woman who didn't have a husband. So what? They wrote some ridiculous platitudinous thing about how every child deserves a father. Well, as much as I'd like to know who my father is—and that's a lot—I never said I didn't care who my mother was."

"Of course not." Jillian blinked at Tisha. Did Nolan realize how close to home this work was going to hit for her when he suggested it?

"Children are people too, you know."

"I do know."

Tisha picked up another stack from the table. "Here's one where a woman who was babysitting a family with twin baby girls stole one of them. She knew she could get money for that 'extra' baby. Extra baby. That's what they called her. It's right there in the notes. What kind of people would write down words like that? Maclovia, if that was really her name. Who knows what happened to her?"

"I remember that one." Jillian took the file from Tisha. "A name like that sticks in your head."

"They even put where they got her from specifically so there could be absolutely no chance they would adopt her out to a family in that county, because, after all, the twins were identical, and that would be a dead giveaway."

"That's going to be a huge clue." Jillian scanned the file for more information. "She was born in 1939, so there's a chance she's still alive."

"But her parents aren't."

"Not likely. Her twin could be, though, and their other siblings. The notes say there were other children in the home. They probably lived their whole lives wondering what happened to their baby sister."

"She has a right to know," Tisha said. "We have to find her."

We.

Jillian nodded. "We'll put this at the top of the list. There are some good leads in the file. Place. Date. A unique name. If she was taken as an infant, there's a good chance she was born in the town she was taken from. Since she was born before the 1940 census, which is the last census we have public access to, we have that as a starting point."

"Is that how this works?"

"It's one avenue. The records we have are from June 1940, so there's at least some chance she would be listed in the census with her birth family in April when the census was taken. Whoever took her would not have been able to alter that. Depending on the state, sometimes birth records are public. I have paid subscriptions to various databases. We keep looking until we find the piece of the puzzle that starts opening up the whole picture."

"But how do we know if the names or birth dates in the original files are true?"

"We don't."

Tisha's shoulders sank. "This isn't right."

"No, it's not. That's why it's so important to do whatever we can and why we have to be so careful with the information we do have."

"We have to find that twin. Can I work on this?"

Jillian's chest was about to burst open. "Of course you can. You can even make your own photocopy of everything in the file so you can mark it up and write on it. Keep notes on the ideas you have, and we'll talk about them."

"What color should I use?"

"Color?"

"For my own folder."

Jillian unleashed her smile. "I'll get you a green folder from my office. How's that? Then we'll know it's yours, and it won't get mixed up."

"Thank you." Tisha stood up and began straightening papers. "I'll clean this up and get back to labels. I'll make sure everything is right."

"You can read anything you want to, Tisha. I have a feeling that if you put your mind to it, you'll have a good eye for what we need to look for in some of these cases. Two minds are better than one."

"Not when one of them is mine."

Jillian reached out, stilled Tisha's hands, and looked in her face. "Especially when one of them is yours."

"Don't placate me." Tisha wiggled her hands out from under Jillian's. "I keep telling you."

Jillian nodded. "I'll be right back." She ducked out to her office and returned three minutes later with a canvas bag. She pulled out its contents.

"That's a laptop," Tisha said.

"It's a little old and sluggish, but it'll do the job." Jillian bent over to plug it in. "You have Wi-Fi at your house?"

Tisha nodded. "No cable, but Grandma Ora loves her Netflix, so she pays for the Wi-Fi out of her Social Security."

"That'll do it, then. I'm going to show you a few sites and how to use them. Spend as much time as you want looking for Maclovia's family. Keep track of your hours. I'll sign off on them."

CHAPTER TWENTY-FOUR

Denver, Colorado
Tuesday, August 15, 1893

If Georgina had her druthers, the family carriage would be painted green with yellow tires. Once she had seen an illustration in a magazine of one like that, with a hard roof and sides and an elevated seat for a driver. Theirs had never been so fancy. When they agreed to purchase a carriage after they found themselves owning a home with a stable—rare enough for the neighborhood—that was also large enough to accommodate a carriage, Clifford gently impressed on Georgina the reality of their budget. The carriage would be efficient and one she could handle on her own. Certainly there would be no hired driver or livery colors. So the open carriage, in an ordinary black color, had sides that came only halfway up and a soft roof. Two benches were a tight fit for two parents and their three grown daughters in corseted garb.

But today it would have to do.

"Clifford, where in the world are you taking us?" Georgina wanted to know.

He urged the horses a little faster before the incline ahead steepened. "Seemed like a nice day for a family adventure."

"Clifford Brandt, it's an ordinary Tuesday, and you know it."

"But we were all available today," Cliff said, "and the summer has been stressful. We could use an adventure before Lity starts back to school in a few weeks."

"I like adventure," Lity said.

"That's my girl." Cliff glanced over his shoulder at his youngest, squeezed in between her sisters, and winked. Lity tried to return the wink but only twitched both eyes instead. At sixteen she was still thin and girlish. He would miss these days once the last of his children took on the appearance of an adult.

"I especially like the mountains," Lity said. "We're going to the mountains, aren't we, Papa?"

There was no denying it. They were well to the west of Denver now, and the horses were beginning to strain with the weight of the entire family in the carriage as the road wound upward.

"Did one of our mines strike gold?" Corah asked. "I hope it was the Decorah Runner!"

"No, Corah, we're not going to any of the mines," Clifford said. "Not today."

"It's a lovely day," Georgina said, "and the mountains are beautiful, of course. No doubt it will be cooler there. But if we were going to make a day of it, you should have let me pack a picnic basket."

"No fear," Clifford said. "I've made arrangements."

"What sort of arrangements?"

"Let's all go into an adventure with an open mind."

He drove a few more miles.

"I know where we are," Missouri said. "We just made the turn toward Canyon Mines."

"You always did make good marks in geography," Cliff said.

"Really?" Lity said. "Canyon Mines? I've never even seen the Fidelity Wink. Are you sure we can't see the mines?"

"I'm sure. Not today. But we'll have an opportunity soon, I promise."

"Maybe the Fidelity Wink will be the one that has gold. Are you going to try to find gold, Papa?"

"We'll see."

"Clifford, why are we going to Canyon Mines?" Suspicion oozed through Georgina's tone.

"I've always loved this town." He chose his words with care. "I hope you will find it as delightful as I do."

He turned into the main street that ran through the little town. A few of the businesses had shuttered since the mines in the area closed, but most persisted. Not all of the tiny mountain towns would survive the demise of silver, but Cliff was optimistic for Canyon Mines. Or perhaps he needed to believe it would offer him optimism he no longer found in Denver. What he was doing had its risks.

But it would be right in the end. Here the Brandts would find themselves again.

Cliff brought the team to rest in front of a small mercantile and set the brake on the carriage.

"Clifford?" Georgina gave him a quizzical look. "What kind of picnic spot is this?"

"I said I'd made arrangements," he said, "not a picnic."

She tilted her head, unconvinced.

Loren Wade stepped out of the mercantile, wearing a shop apron.

"Loren!" Missouri pushed past her sisters to disembark and jumped down to the sidewalk. "How did you get here?"

The rest of the family exited the carriage as well.

"Yes, Clifford, how did that man get here?" Georgina asked.

"I took the train," Loren said.

Georgina's fingers on Cliff's arm made a vise. "Did you give that man train fare?"

"He is not 'that man,' Georgina. He's Loren. He was a trusted employee, and you can see our daughter is fond of him."

"What have you done?"

"Let's all go inside."

Inside, Cliff waited for his family to take in their surroundings.

"This store isn't open," Georgina said. "It's the middle of the day, and the shelves are reasonably stocked for a town this size. Why aren't there any customers?"

"But that man is wearing an apron," Lity said.

"His name is Loren," Missouri said. "Get used to using it, please."

"It's all right, Missy," Loren said.

"No, it's not. But—what are you doing here? Did you get a job in Canyon Mines?"

"I guess you could say so."

"Someone is trusting you to run the store?"

"I was just cleaning up. The store hasn't been open the last few weeks while it has come under new ownership."

"How fortunate for you to find this job," Missy said. "I know you love the mountains more than city life."

Georgina cleared her throat. "I have the sense that more explanation is forthcoming."

"As always, you are astute," Clifford said. "I'm the one who hired Loren to work here."

"Clifford?"

"Missouri," Cliff said, "you'll be glad to hear there are some small living quarters on the second floor where Loren can stay. He doesn't seem to mind being next to a storage space. It's quite an improvement over a stable full of hay and horses."

"Papa, thank you! But I don't think I understand."

"Whatever happens to us, we are all in it together," Clifford said. "So I'm going to be straightforward with all of you."

The girls' faces paled. Georgina's hardened.

"No one can actually afford to buy and sell real estate right now," Clifford explained. "That takes cash or enough credit to get a loan—which requires a bank with cash. You might as well all know that in another two weeks, I would have owed one of the few open banks in Denver a large payment on our home. I've already explained this to your mother. Given the events of the last few months, that was going to be beyond my means. However, I have been aware for some time that the owner of this store wished to move to Denver for family reasons. Wisely, he has been saving for this eventuality for quite some time while doing a thriving business among the silver miners."

"Get to the point, Clifford," Georgina said.

"We were going to lose the house, Georgie. We couldn't make the payment, and there is no market to sell the house, either. When approached with the opportunity, I made a non-cash transaction that benefits both us and the former owner of this mercantile."

"You traded our family home for. . .this collection of dust?" Georgina's face, rather than turning white, as the girls' had, was a deep red.

"And a house," Clifford said. "It's not as large as what we had in Denver—"

"*Had?* We just left our home a couple of hours ago. Surely you can't mean this arrangement is final already."

"It is." Cliff was firm. "We'll have a stable livelihood going forward.

One day the mines may turn around as well. There is no hope for Mr. Tabor, but our mines are on a small enough scale and we're not so over-extended that we can't try again someday. And yes, girls, we might find gold beneath the silver. Others have. We need to be in the mountains to do that. Canyon Mines has always been a town for miners—supplying them, educating their children more and more, growing with them as they are ready for permanent homes. We'll be here for all of that again someday."

"But our *home*, Clifford!" Georgina's features crunched.

He plowed ahead. He'd thought this through, and it was better to just get it all out. "I made a cash contribution to the People's Tabernacle yesterday so they can continue to offer some support to miners who are still looking for a way out of Denver. We will be fine here in Canyon Mines. We have the house, the shop, the stock, and enough liquidity to order more items once we decide what we need to carry. It may be a more modest life, but it's all free and clear. We have each other, and we can make a go of it. Loren can help with the heavy work. The girls can learn to run the store. Georgina, with everything you know about dry goods, textiles, and fashions, the women of Canyon Mines will love you."

"You want me to be a small-town shopkeeper."

"We're in it together, Georgie."

"I like it." Lity ran two fingers along the length of a shelf of knick-knacks. "Will I go to school here?"

"Yes, you will. They have a small but fine high school. I made thorough inquiries. The principal used to teach in Denver. The art teacher is a painter of some local renown."

"A painter!" Lity's eyes glowed. "Can I have art lessons?"

"You want me to be a shop girl?" Corah grimaced, a mirror of her mother. Of the three girls, Decorah was the one Clifford could count on to parrot Georgina.

"You'll catch on quickly," he said. "In time I believe you'll all see the wisdom."

"You will undo this mess right this minute," Georgina said.

Clifford crossed the aisle to take his wife's trembling hands. It wasn't easy for him to put her in this state, but she would never have agreed. When the house was put up for auction—and it would have been—where would they be?

"There is no going back, Georgie," he said. "Only forward. Let me take you to the new house. It has a spectacular view, right along the little waterway that runs through town. It has basic furnishings, so we don't have to worry about whether all our furniture will fit the rooms."

"You're asking me to live with someone else's furniture?" She drew back.

"Loren and I will go back and arrange for some of our things to be shipped by train, but we won't need everything. The new owners likely will want most of it, or the charities can surely use it. I think I can find a buyer for the carriage. We all know how to ride a horse, though Canyon Mines is small enough that we probably won't need to. In any event, a wagon will be more practical for the store. We can offer deliveries—Loren's idea."

"Will you teach me to drive the wagon?" Lity asked.

Clifford winked and smiled. "Of course."

They rode to the new house in silence because Georgina could not abide any chatter. The girls and Loren, who had trotted the few blocks on foot to meet them there, explored the rooms, leaving Clifford and Georgina alone in the parlor. He approached her and leaned his forehead against hers to wait for the calming and softening that always came when they stood this way.

But it did not come.

"Georgie."

"Don't Georgie me," she whispered. "Not this time."

CHAPTER TWENTY-FIVE

Nolan dropped his briefcase onto a stool at the breakfast bar.

"I tried to keep supper warm." Jillian pulled a glass dish from the oven. "But twenty past seven is later than I expected. I'm afraid I no longer recommend this pasta."

"I hoped to be here an hour ago," Nolan said. "It's been one thing after another all day, starting with that seven o'clock breakfast meeting."

"You look beat."

"I am."

"And your briefcase looks especially fat."

"It is." Nolan stuck a fork into the pasta for one bite. "I don't have time to eat anyway. One more meeting to go."

"What's going on?"

"Crowder mediation in ten minutes."

"What? You're trying that again after Tuesday's smashing success?"

"Choice of words, please, Jillian." Nolan loosened his tie. "I have to try. I'm glad you and Tisha seem to be on better footing, but what good will the alternative sentencing hours do her if nothing changes at home?"

"It's impressive you'd get Brittany and Tisha to agree to another meeting."

"Peggy and Ora too."

"Ora? Really?"

"Tisha wouldn't come without her. Somebody she can count on to be on her side, I think. It has taken some persuading all around. I even had my assistant fielding calls when I was tied up."

"Clark is letting you use the Cage again?"

Nolan laughed softly and shook his head. "After he overheard the commotion the last time? Hardly." Also, since Nolan had been unsuccessful at getting Joanna to be truthful with her uncle, at the moment Clark had a dubious opinion of Nolan's mediation skills.

"Where, then?" Jillian asked.

"Nia has agreed to let us use the library at the Inn."

"What about the guests?"

"No guests tonight. Full slate for the weekend but nobody tonight. And she and Leo will be on hand in the parlor if things get out of hand."

"Like ready to dial 911?"

"I hope it won't come to that."

"Shall I make you another dinner that's less dried-up crusty in nature?"

"I'll pick something up when everything's over."

The Inn was only half a mile away, but Nolan took his truck so he'd be on time. The library at the front of the Inn was arranged just as he'd asked. Two champagne-colored tufted Victorian chairs were in their customary spots on either side of a round table, and Nia had situated three padded chairs from the dining room in a manner that made the room feel like a cozy circle.

No sides. That was the point.

In fact, Nolan made sure to drape his suit jacket over one of the Victorian chairs to break up the temptation for any two people to come in together and automatically drift to the "power" chairs in a sort of alliance.

Tisha came in first with the great-grandmother Nolan hadn't met before.

"You must be Ora." He extended a handshake.

"Nice to meet you."

He didn't know Ora's precise age, but she seemed to be a young great-grandmother. She must have been a young mother herself when she had Peggy.

Ora. Peggy. Brittany. All teenagers or barely out of their teens when they gave birth. Was Tisha headed down the same road? The boyfriend definitely had seemed older to Nolan. He might even have already graduated high school.

As Peggy came in next, Tisha scooted two of the dining room chairs closer together and sat beside Ora. Peggy chose the other tufted chair, leaving the third dining room chair for Brittany, who arrived late with the excuse that she had trouble closing Candles & Cards on time.

That could well be true.

Or she could just not be in any hurry for what the evening would bring.

Tisha scooted an inch closer to Ora.

"Thank you all for coming," Nolan said as he took his own seat. "You all care about Tisha, and my daughter and I certainly have come to appreciate that she's a remarkable young woman, so I hope we can work together for Tisha's best interests."

He scanned the four faces around the circle. Having them all together like this certainly made it easy to see the family resemblance.

"The other day," he said, "Brittany was talking about how important it was that you are all part of the historic Brandt family of Canyon Mines. I thought it might be useful to return to that topic and help Tisha better understand this part of her family tree."

"I didn't say I wanted to do that," Tisha said.

"Bear with me, please," Nolan said.

"Are there any magic timers this time?" Brittany asked.

"Everyone has agreed to one hour," Nolan said, "with the proviso that if it becomes untenable, I will close the session sooner. Do you all still agree?"

Everyone nodded.

"We all also agreed not to talk over one another. Correct?"

More nods, slightly more reluctant.

"When I meet with families in conflict, my goal is always that they'll learn something that helps them understand each other better. I think in your case, with four generations here, the Brandts may be a great place to start."

Brittany gestured to Ora. "Well, my grandmother is here this time. She knows a lot more than the rest of us."

Ora waved a hand. "Oh, it's just family stories."

Nolan said, "My daughter the genealogist would say those are the best kind."

"I wouldn't know where to start."

"Tell the stories you used to tell me when I was little," Brittany said, "about your grandmother on the Brandt side."

Tisha stiffened slightly.

"I know you don't understand why the Brandts are so important to your mother, Tisha," Nolan said, "but that's one of the things we're going to learn together."

Tisha nodded and chewed her gum a little harder. At least she didn't smack it.

"My grandmother was Decorah Brandt," Ora said. "They called her Corah. I suppose my name was a form of hers, but she never approved of the shortening."

"So Decorah's family were the Brandts of the Brandt Building on Main Street," Nolan said.

Ora nodded. "They had a mercantile. She married rather late for a woman in her time. She was already past thirty. But the store was in trouble, and a man who was interested in investing was also interested in her. Axel Emery. He wouldn't invest in the store if she wouldn't marry him, though."

"So she did," Nolan said.

"Yep. It turned out he was more interested in the store than he was in her, but she found that out too late. It wasn't a happy marital arrangement, but they did have two daughters."

"He wanted a son, though," Brittany said. "Isn't that what you always told me?"

"It's what Grandmother Decorah always told me. In the end, they lost the store anyway, at the start of the Great Depression. Axel abandoned her after more than twenty mostly miserable years. The rumor was that he found another younger wife and finally had a son, but I don't know if that's true."

"But Decorah stayed in Canyon Mines?" Nolan asked.

"She had two barely grown daughters—my mother and her older sister—no store, no husband, no money. Eventually she lost the house as well because of unpaid back property taxes that she had no idea Axel hadn't been paying for years. She never had a kind thing to say about that man. She never had a kind thing to say about anybody, actually. Not even her own daughters."

Peggy spoke for the first time. "My mother was glad to get out from under the heavy tongue of her own mother, who learned well from Decorah."

Ora shrugged. "Darlene. She never approved of the man I married. Thought I married too young."

"If you hadn't married when you did," Peggy said, "you wouldn't have had me, and none of us would be here now. Nineteen years old, ten months married, and a mother. No going back from that. Maybe we're all just a string of mistakes."

Nolan held up a hand. "No one said that."

"Of course not," Peggy said. "The real mistake was Decorah's—marrying that man to save the store. All he really wanted was title to the house and store. That's what happened in those days. But if she hadn't, we *really* wouldn't be here."

"You are *not* a string of mistakes," Nolan said.

"Well, he died anyway," Ora said. "My mother never forgave him for wooing me, and then she never forgave him for leaving me a young widow and Peggy without a father."

"Is that where the Crowder name comes from?" Nolan asked.

Ora nodded. "Micah Crowder. Even if only three years."

"You never married again?"

"I had offers. But no."

"I wonder if you know why you chose not to marry again."

"I do. Because I hated myself. Who would truly want me? Maybe Micah wouldn't have stayed, either."

"Ma! What are you saying?" Peggy said.

"I'm sorry it took me as long as it did to rinse their filth out of the way I spoke to my own child and grandchild, but I'm hoping to do better by Tisha."

"Ma," Peggy said, softening.

"It's true," Ora said. "We all know it. Sometimes I open my mouth and Darlene is talking. Tisha deserves better."

Tisha's eyes brimmed.

"Was Micah's death your fault?" Nolan asked.

"Of course not!" Ora said.

"I didn't think so. Then there is no reason for anyone to carry the weight of Darlene's lies all these years later, is there?"

"What are you talking about?" Brittany spat out.

" 'We're all Brandts,' you told me the other night," Nolan said. "You have to go all the way back to Decorah Brandt, before she was married, to find some pride in a family name. Yet it doesn't sound as if even Ora remembers much about Decorah herself to like."

Brittany mumbled, "I never thought of it that way."

"Yet Micah Crowder made you happy. Right, Ora?"

"He did. I was very young, but he did. I would do it all again if he would have me again."

Placidity cradled the room. Nolan let it do its work, seeping out of released sighs and swaddling tentative exchanged glances until they took hold, enfolding generations.

"And so you are Brandts," he said, "but also Crowders, with no cause for shame."

"I have a question," Tisha said.

"Yes?" Nolan looked at her.

"The Brandts lost the store because Decorah married Axel Emery and then the Depression happened. But how did we get the store to begin with? Isn't it a big thing to have your name on a building?"

"Oh that," Ora said. "The mercantile had been there a long time, during the mining years. Decorah's father bought it. No—he traded for it. My grandmother used to tell some cockamamie story about how they had a nice home in Denver, but he wanted to live here. He was broke or something when his mines gave out."

"Wait," Tisha said, "he had a store *and* mines?"

"Apparently."

"That doesn't sound broke to me. What happened? Something must have happened."

"I can't tell you, honey. I was twelve when Grandmother Decorah died. My mother never had any use for the old stories. My father left us when I was six, and after that she was as bitter as Decorah was. Probably before. Maybe it's what drove him off. I can't say."

Nolan mentally ticked off the generations. Brittany. Peggy. Ora. Darlene. Decorah. In all those years, five women had only a handful of happy married years between them—and Ora's marriage had been in the shadow of her mother's disapproval.

"There has to be a way to find out more of the story," Tisha said.

"The story is you should be proud you're a Brandt," Brittany said.

"And a Crowder," Nolan said.

"And I'm something else," Tisha said quietly. "I still want to know more."

Nolan nodded. "This is a good example. We've all been wrapped up in what Ora shared. She knows quite a bit about where she comes from, with some gaps. Tisha feels like she has a lot of gaps—half of herself is a gap."

Tisha was nodding heavily.

"I think she's old enough to handle answers," Nolan said. "I'm not saying we have to hear the answers tonight. But, Brittany, I'd like you to seriously consider answering some basic questions. If we need to have a counselor present for the conversation, I'm happy to help arrange that."

Brittany clamped her mouth shut and stared at the ceiling and then at the bookcases and then at a painting on the wall.

"You don't have to decide anything tonight," Nolan said. "I'm just asking you, on Tisha's behalf, to consider how she feels about this question and how you can help her navigate the journey by coming alongside rather than putting up obstacles in her way."

Brittany cleared her throat awkwardly and glanced at Peggy.

"You don't have to be so dramatic," Brittany said.

Nolan waited.

"Just a college boy I met at a concert at Red Rocks. I went with friends." Brittany's tone was hushed, halting.

Tisha slid forward in her chair.

"He was a little older—you all know I was still in high school—but we hit it off and saw each other on and off for a few months. He had a car, so it wasn't hard. Sometimes he was waiting for me after school."

"I want to meet him," Tisha said. "I want you to tell me everything you remember about him."

Brittany shook her head. "None of that is a good idea."

"I'm old enough. You heard Nolan."

Brittany leaned forward, elbows on knees, head in hands. "Letitia. Why are you doing this?"

"Mom, please."

"Don't get your hopes up," Brittany said. "Believe it or not, I'm trying to protect you."

"From what? Don't I deserve to know?"

"From getting hurt."

"How can I be more hurt than I feel now by not knowing?"

"You can get involved with a man who disappoints you, like the rest of us have done. Haven't you been paying attention at all?"

"Micah Crowder didn't disappoint Grandma Ora." Tisha was unrelenting. "He died. That's not anyone's fault."

Brittany exhaled. "Tisha."

"How do you know where my father is if he's such a disappointment?"

"It's the twenty-first century, even in Canyon Mines."

"Then it won't be hard for me to find him, either."

"But it would be a mistake." Brittany's edge sliced just as hard as it often did.

"You don't know that." Tisha's pitch crept higher with every exchange.

Nolan intervened. "How about this? I'll act as the go-between and approach Tisha's father. A buffer, a cushion, so if there is the possibility Tisha will be hurt, it won't be so direct."

Peggy clucked disapproval, and Brittany glanced at her.

"If it will get Tisha to shut up and straighten up her life," Brittany said, looking at Nolan but not her daughter, "then maybe it will be worth it. But when she gets hurt, and she will, don't say I didn't warn you."

"Can I at least know his name?" Tisha sat on the very edge of her seat.

"Wouldn't it be better to let Nolan do his thing first?"

"I just want to know his name." Her eyes shone, pleading.

"Tisha," Nolan said, "if your mother gives you his name, I need your promise that you will not go off half-cocked and do something impulsive. The agreement is I make the first contact—and it might be the only contact. Understand?"

Tisha trembled and nodded.

"Jayden," Brittany whispered. "His name is Jayden Casky."

"Jayden Casky," Tisha whispered.

"Good," Nolan said. "Thank you, Brittany. I'll get the information you have about where he is separately, as we discussed. I have one last question for all of you."

Tisha slid back in her chair.

"The diary page the Heritage Society has," Nolan said. "What do you know about it?"

"I've heard of it, but I've never even been to the museum," Tisha said. "We're related to it, right?"

"Georgina Brandt," Ora said. "That's who they think wrote it."

"Who is she, again?" Tisha asked.

"Decorah's mother."

Tisha thought and ticked off the generations on her fingers. "So my great-great-great-great-grandmother."

"That's right," Ora said. "Her husband is the one who traded for the store."

"What does the diary page say?" Tisha asked.

The other women looked around and shrugged.

"I don't remember exactly. Some grumbling," Peggy said. "I don't think she much liked living in Canyon Mines."

"Now I want to see it," Tisha said.

"It's right there in the museum," Brittany said. "Hop on your bike and go anytime."

"It's the kind of thing Jillian would put in one of her folders," Tisha said. "An original source document."

Nolan grinned. "Exactly."

CHAPTER TWENTY-SIX

*C*he bella cosa na jurnata 'e sole, n'aria serena doppo na tempesta!"

Nolan sang at full volume as he tapped down the front stairs and strode through the living room. It was a beautiful day to be singing about a sunny day, no matter the language.

"Look at these boxes. Red, blue, red, blue. It's almost as if you two have a system."

Tisha tilted her head and eyed Jillian. "Does he do this often?"

"The singing, or observing the obvious?" Jillian squatted to add a label to the front of a box.

"Once again I am mocked for my talents," Nolan said. "Just for that, I am going to make you both sandwiches and demand a lunch break."

"My grandma Ora would say your dad has a screw loose," Tisha said.

"Some days he's lucky if he has one single screw that's not loose."

"I know where he keeps his power drill. I can fix that."

Jillian and Tisha snorted.

"I can still hear you," Nolan called over his shoulder. "Now you're getting double lettuce and mayo *plus* mustard on the sandwiches."

Nolan lined up six slices of multigrain bread from Ben's Bakery, which Jillian assured him had been baked just yesterday, spread the mayo and mustard, stacked the lettuce and thinly sliced chicken before setting the top of the sandwiches and cutting them all in half. After arranging them on plates adorned with red grapes and green apple slices, he called in Jillian and Tisha.

"Normally I would make a four-course hot luncheon on Friday," he said, "but because of the mocking, this is all you get."

"Hush," Jillian said. "May you always find nourishment for your body at the table. May sustenance for your spirit rise and fill you with each dawn. And may life always feed you with the light of joy along the way."

They picked up their sandwiches.

"I thought after lunch we could wander down to the Heritage Society, if you have time, Tisha," Nolan said.

"The diary?" Her eyes brightened.

"It shouldn't take too long."

"Do you have time?"

"I do if you do."

"Mind if I tag along?" Jillian asked.

"No problem." Tisha dropped a grape in her mouth.

They ate and decided to walk into town. By the time they arrived at the Heritage Society, the director was returning from her own lunch break.

"Marilyn! Just the person we were hoping to see." Nolan held the door open for everyone.

"What's on your mind, Nolan?" Marilyn asked.

"I don't know if you've ever had the pleasure of meeting this young lady, but she is a direct descendant of Georgina Brandt and has never seen the famed diary fragment. I'm pleased to introduce Tisha Crowder."

"My goodness. A Brandt woman in our museum. By all means, you should see the page. Let me grab some keys. Follow me."

Marilyn led the way to a display case on one side of the main room of the museum that featured Canyon Mines historical items from the late nineteenth century.

"Normally we only allow people to see it through the glass," Marilyn said. "As you can imagine, it's fragile. But because of your connection to the Brandt family, I'll get it out and let you have a closer look. But no touching, please."

"Absolutely not." Nolan crossed his hands behind his back and winked at Tisha.

Marilyn stepped behind the case to unlock it, then slid a door open and lifted out the small shelf the diary page sat on.

"Fancy handwriting," Tisha said. "None of my friends write anything in cursive. I mean, I guess we learned how in like the third grade, but who really needs to know how to do that anymore?"

"Elegant penmanship was an art in the days of your ancestors," Marilyn said, "but it was also considered a reflection of character and discipline. Mrs. Brandt would have been of an age to learn penmanship in the Spencerian method, which emphasized order and precision."

"I wouldn't want her to see anything I wrote," Tisha said, "but I bet I can type faster with my thumbs than she could."

"That's certainly one perspective," Nolan said.

"It's ragged at the edges." Tisha pointed without touching. "Like it was torn out of a book."

"It probably was," Marilyn said. "That's why we refer to it as a diary 'page' or 'fragment.' It seems to be a diary entry of some sort, but we don't have the whole diary."

"Then how did you get this one page?" Jillian asked.

"It came from Stephanos at Motherlode Books."

"From the Brandt Building?" Nolan said.

Marilyn nodded. "He was doing some remodeling to update the two small apartments on the second story some years back—you know, where Joanna Maddon is living in one of them."

"Right," Nolan said.

"She's got that puppy. Just looking for trouble if you ask me."

Nolan laughed. "Do you think Stephanos really doesn't know?"

"I'm not sure, but it's not my business. Anyway, this fragment of a diary was caught between layers of the flooring when they took it all apart to do the job right. There it was, a bit dusty but perfectly readable."

"How are you sure Georgina Brandt wrote it?" Jillian asked.

"It's signed with the initials G. B., and we have enough other documents from the history of the store—correspondence, sales records— to match the handwriting easily enough. She worked in the store for quite a long time, so we're certain."

"Am I remembering correctly that she and her husband are buried in the town cemetery?" Jillian asked. "Somehow that fact just floated to the front of my brain."

"You are correct," Marilyn said. "Their daughter Decorah was laid to rest there as well."

Tisha sighed. "Well, I'm staring at this fancy writing, and it reminds me of trying to read a copy of the Declaration of Independence in my history book. It's a little too fancy and slanty and loopy. What is she saying?"

Nolan leaned in and began to read.

"October 23, 1894. This is the end. Clifford, I hope you're pleased with what you wrought for those miners in Denver we don't even know. I doubt you're even getting proper credit for any good you might have accomplished, but I can't say you have much to show for yourself here. If I know you, your donation was anonymous. Our name on the building here? A perpetual embarrassment if you ask me. What were you thinking hiring that stone mason? That it would please me? Well, it doesn't. What were you thinking in any of this? If we were as compromised as you claimed, why dispense funds to an engraver?

The money's gone, and now the girls are gone. You've made sure I'm left in misery. So I'm making sure no one will ever write in this silly book again. G. B."

"She was one bitter lady," Tisha murmured.

Nolan nodded. *Georgina. And Decorah. And Darlene. And Ora. And Peggy. And Brittany. All of them.*

"Kind of sounds like my mom," Tisha whispered.

Nolan squeezed her shoulder.

"I'm not sure I want people to know I'm related to that."

"That's not you," Nolan said. "That's six generations back. People know that."

"Still, they can connect the dots." Tisha peered at Marilyn. "Why would you display something like that? It's not flattering to Canyon Mines. It's trash ugly."

"It's still a piece of our town history," Marilyn said. "It's one of the oldest things we have in the museum, and it was found in a unique way, preserved in a remarkable manner through the decades."

"Can I take a picture?"

"Of course."

Tisha aimed her phone's camera and snapped a couple of shots. "I may never look at them again, but at least I'll have the photos. Clifford must have done something really generous in Denver, but Georgina sure didn't like it."

"Thank you, Marilyn," Nolan said.

Nolan, Jillian, and Tisha stepped out into the sunlight again.

"Motherlode Books carries a small booklet about the history of the Brandt Building," Nolan said. "Why don't we go by and pick up a copy?"

They wound their way back toward the Brandt Building. Tisha paused outside and raised her fingers to trace over the engraved name.

"This made Georgina so mad," she said. "After everything I found out about Decorah Brandt and her mother, I still don't understand what the big deal is about being Brandts. Whatever that Clifford dude did in Denver didn't count for much here."

"The building was in the family for nearly forty years before the Depression," Nolan said. "A lot of people lost their businesses in the Depression. They wouldn't have been the only ones."

"I guess. But if Decorah only married to save the store to begin with, was it worth it—just to claim being a Brandt?"

Inside the bookstore, off to one side, a loud sneeze greeted them, and they all looked to see the tight cluster. Joanna Maddon sneezed a second time and then a third. Stephanos, who owned the building and the bookstore, shook his head in disbelief as she knelt and buried her head in the coat of a Great Pyrenees that looked like it was part Labrador—with maybe some mastiff mixed in.

Jillian laughed. "Where in the world did she find such a creature?"

"He's adorable," Tisha said.

Joanna sneezed, stood, and handed a leash to Dave Rossi. "His name is Wriggly. He likes to snuggle, and he'll keep wriggling until he feels just right in your lap. He's the best."

Four-year-old Nadia's eyes were enormous. "Grandpa Rossi, is this really going to be our puppy?"

"Yes, sweetheart, I've found my puppy."

Nolan chuckled. "He'll be big as half a horse when he's grown, but he'll be everything a little girl could ask for."

"How come I never had a puppy?" Jillian asked.

"You never asked for one."

"Daddy, can I have a puppy?"

"No."

Clark Addison looked over, saw them, and rolled his eyes.

Nolan leaned his head toward Jillian. "I guess I won't have to worry about following up on that particular family mediation." Maybe something he'd said had mattered after all.

Joanna sneezed. Three times.

Her eyes were puppy-dog sad at the prospect of surrendering the animal. If she was going to try again with a puppy, she would have to ask Stephanos's permission, look for a hypoallergenic breed, find something far smaller, and come up with a better plan for housebreaking it.

"At least the truth is out," Nolan said. "Nobody has to dance around the question of being a snitch, and Jo can get back to work and enjoy her new apartment all on the up-and-up."

"Were the apartments always there?" Tisha asked.

"Let's find the booklet and see what it says."

Stephanos sold Nolan a copy, and he handed it to Tisha, who opened it to flip through it as they walked up Main Street toward home.

"Tisha, what are you up to this afternoon?" Nolan asked.

"The Maclovia case." She popped a fresh piece of gum in her mouth and turned a page in the booklet.

"Maclovia case?"

"Tisha is on the hunt for a missing twin," Jillian said. "One of the St. Louis files."

Tisha tapped the booklet. "This shows where the graves are in the cemetery."

"Hang on to it," Nolan said. "The cemetery is a big place. That will come in handy."

"Wait a minute." Tisha's steps stopped. "According to this, Clifford died in 1893."

"Yes?"

Tisha pulled out her phone and scrolled for a photo. "The diary page in the museum is dated October 1894. Georgina was writing more than a year after he died. She says, 'This is the end' and 'The money is gone and the girls are gone.' What girls? Decorah didn't go anywhere. I knew there was more to the story."

"More daughters?" Jillian said. "Doesn't the booklet say?"

Tisha flipped pages. "Nope. It's mostly about the building. Who owned it first. Then the Brandts took over the mercantile in 1893. Georgina and Decorah ran it after Clifford's death. Then it was closed for a while in the 1930s. Ever since then it's been various businesses. The library for a while after a flood. A furniture store. A yarn and fabric store. Even a pet store. Then it became Motherlode Books in 1997. It's still called the Brandt Building because Clifford put his name on it." She threw her head back and laughed. "And made his wife mad. That's hilarious."

"Mm," Jillian said. "I'll have to see what I can dig up when I get a chance."

"I can ask my grandma Ora if she knows."

Back at the house, they entered through the kitchen. Tisha headed straight for the dining room.

"I'm going to turn on the laptop. I have some questions for you on the Maclovia case."

"I'll be right in," Jillian said. "Just want to check my email."

Nolan wagged one eyebrow at his daughter and drew in a deep, satisfied breath.

"What?" Jillian said.

"Four days ago you were ready to throw in the towel with her. Now she has the 'Maclovia case.' "

"Turns out the child knows how to read."

A text chimed into Jillian's phone, and she extracted it from her shorts pocket. "Drew. Min's daughter is coming for a few days at the ranch. He says he can be here midday tomorrow and stay a night or two. You don't mind, do you, Dad? If he comes again?"

"Will I get to cook with him?"

"The two of you can make me an exquisite dinner on Sunday. How's that?"

"Text the man back. Tell him to bring his own chef's hat."

CHAPTER TWENTY-SEVEN

Canyon Mines, Colorado
Monday, September 25, 1893

Outside the store, Clifford inhaled the nippy fall mountain air. The day would warm as the hours progressed. In some years snow might blow through the Colorado mountains in late September, but the threat was not serious. Even a month from now storms were likely to be fleeting. After that Georgina and the girls might face the adjustments that came with living in a small mountain town rather than Denver, which was at a lower elevation during the winter.

There was still time.

Georgina would come around to the charms of Canyon Mines and the possibilities of the house here once they began turning enough profit for her to have funds to work with and put her own touch on it.

An arm slipped around Clifford's elbow, and he glanced at Missouri.

"A beautiful day, Papa," she said. "I'm so glad our store has such a happy view."

"I am as well."

"If the train was on time, Loren should be here soon with the wagon and the new stock."

Clifford nodded. "He has a good head for business, your young man." Missouri and Loren clearly were headed for the altar. Canyon Mines had a beautiful church just a couple of blocks over. Perhaps they would take their vows there.

Missy smiled. "I'm glad you approve of him."

"Your mother will too."

"Will she?"

"Give her time. She's had a lot to adjust to."

"She won't come near the store. She won't speak to Loren. She barely speaks to you."

Clifford winced. "I'm working on that last bit. Then the rest will come. The store is already proving its potential. Customers are curious about our changes, and we're getting steady traffic. As long as we carry the basics, people will need us. I hope we can create an event where your mother can show off her knowledge of textiles and style to the women of Canyon Mines."

Behind them, the shop's door opened.

"Are you coming back in?" Decorah asked.

"Of course." Clifford turned. "Just about time to open, after all."

"Mama says she doesn't know why we bother," Corah said. "This place will never compare properly to McNamara's."

"Why should it compare to McNamara's?" Irritation rattled through Missy's voice. "We're open with our name on the sign, and McNamara's is closed, and if it reopens it will have another name."

Corah huffed. "How long are you going to need me? Mama says she doesn't understand why I can't help her more at home."

"Mama knows good and well Loren is bringing a wagon of new stock from the train." Missy threw a glare in her sister's direction. "We all need to work together to get everything priced and on the shelves as fast as we can."

"What's the point? Mama says we're just going to lose our shirt in this wilderness and you'll ruin your life with that miner."

"Decorah!" Missouri's tone slashed with a razor's edge.

"Please, girls," Clifford said. "This is a place of business, and while we're here we will put on a united front to our customers. Is that understood?"

They nodded, not meeting his eyes—nor each other's.

"I'm going to turn the sign to OPEN. Decorah, you'll work the counter. When Loren gets here, the rest of us will work on stocking, and you can call for help when you need it."

"Yes, Papa," Corah muttered.

He drew in a long, slow breath and eased it out as the three of them walked into the store and Corah echoed everything Georgina said. Missouri was not the only one for whom this habit was wearying. He had to figure out how to reach Georgina and make her happy again—without returning to Denver and bankruptcy. The house was gone. Lack of means remained an obstacle for most people. Even if he wanted to sell the store and house and return to the city, finding buyers would be difficult with cash still in short supply. Nothing was substantially different than it had been two months ago, except the Brandts were not on the edge of bankruptcy.

It wasn't long before townspeople began trickling in for flour, rice, potatoes, coffee beans, soap, butter, ribbons, rope. Clifford shifted items around to make room for the fresh fruit, bolts of cloth, buttons, collars, and small rugs he expected Loren to arrive with. When Loren pulled the wagon around back, he and Clifford sifted through what they would put on the store floor immediately and what they would heft up to the second-floor storage space for the time being. Decorah was more than happy to be released when their task was finished. The hours of the day passed swiftly in busyness until Lity's cheery voice rang through the door after school.

"I stopped by the post office for the mail," Lity said. "It's so tiny and adorable. Not at all like going to the post office in Denver. Did you know the post office used to be here in our store?"

Clifford smiled. Some days it seemed like Lity saved up all her words until she got out of school, and then the logjam broke. "I did know. They only moved it out about eighteen months ago."

"Maybe they'll move it back!" Her dark eyes widened. "That was before everything, right? Canyon Mines has fewer people now. Do they really need a separate post office? Wouldn't it be fun to have the post office here again?"

"Did we have any mail?" He held out a hand.

Her face turned serious as she handed him two envelopes. "These look like invoices." Then she brightened. "But I got a letter from Kittie."

"That's nice. You must miss her."

"She's only in Denver, not New York. I'll see her again. And I've made new friends."

Lity, the adventurous, resilient daughter.

"Can I work today, Papa?"

"Have you got studies you need to complete?"

She scowled. "Can't I do that later?"

Clifford put a hand on her shoulder. "You know your mother's policy. Studies first. How about I walk you home?" He wanted to check on Georgina anyway. Even when Decorah was at home, Georgie spent too much time alone and largely idle.

Lity chattered for the few minutes it took to walk home and then disappeared with her books to the room she and Missouri shared. Neither of them could abide the thought of sharing with Corah, so how the sisters would double up in a smaller house had been an easy choice. Georgina sat in the parlor with a volume in her lap. It was a pose. She'd been reading the same book in the same chair every afternoon for weeks. Clifford steeled himself for today's barbs.

He kissed her cheek. At least she did not recoil from that gesture even if she had no generous words to offer him anymore.

"Corah tells me you are spending our money on stock for that store you're playing with." Georgina turned a page without looking up.

"Georgie, I've told you many times, we were certain to lose the house in Denver. There was no position for me there that would have sustained us in that location. I did the best I could for the family."

"And I've told you many times that would be a more believable explanation if you had been making more credible choices with the money we did have."

"You should see the store now, Georgina. It's cleaned up well. People like it. They would like it even more if you were there. I'm certain of it. You could handle ordering all the textiles. Perhaps give a lecture on decorating."

For a moment she tilted her head. Then she hardened again. "Are you going back to that place?"

"Loren and Missy have it well in hand. I thought I might go for a ride and a constitutional before supper."

"You'll ruin your boots."

Clifford left quietly. Georgina found fault in every decision he made, down to where he left the sugar bowl when he offered to make her a cup of tea. An hour or two of physical exertion would do him good. He had plenty of time to be back for supper. Here in the mountains it had proven more practical to keep and feed both horses after all. They were surefooted beasts that transitioned well from a carriage to a wagon to transport supplies from the train depot to the shop but also make deliveries to some of the outlying areas, an extra incentive for customers to purchase from the mercantile. That service had created a small and growing line of revenue.

The horse took the path from Canyon Mines westward in familiar rhythm, having known it for years on excursions from Denver. When he was ready to exert himself, Clifford tied the animal to a tree and mentally planned a hike that might take him forty-five minutes or so, leaving him sufficient time to descend to town and clean up for the evening meal. The Missouri Rise was within reach on foot with a bit of ambition. With a little extra huffing, which he was willing to muster, he could manage. Already the path others had used in the past was growing over with the rhythms of spring, summer, and early fall with the cessation of mining activity on the mountain, but he knew the way. Whether on horseback or foot, the landmarks were there, and Clifford found the clearing. Until now, since arriving in Canyon Mines to keep shop, he hadn't allowed himself to think of anything else. If the shop did not succeed, all else was of no consequence. Fidelity pestered him about the Fidelity Wink at least once a week. For her it was curiosity, but eventually the family conversation would come around to what Clifford intended to do with the mines. The others were farther out, but the Missouri Rise was a reasonable trek at this point in the day.

The sign was still there, only three months after the visit when he shut down the operation and threw his men out of work, along with the last cars of ore the crew had brought up. Thieves did not even bother with it. Cliff had no reason to go to the Missouri Rise now other than wistful remembrance of better times, not just for himself but for all those men in Denver. Perhaps he could at least give this mine to Loren and Missouri—a wedding present. Likely it would be years before they would know if the silver market would recover enough to open it again or to save enough money to explore the mine for other minerals, as some mine owners were considering in their properties. Cliff doubted there was gold, but there might be copper, lead, or zinc manganese. No matter what, it would take more capital to operate a mine than either he or Loren had now. Mortgaging the store or house, which were both free and clear in the trade, was out of the question. Clifford wouldn't take that risk again. But sometime in the future Loren might make a go of it. If Loren was a successful mine owner, Georgina might accept him, and he would give Missouri the life Georgina believed her daughter deserved.

A crate tucked out of sight at the opening to the mine, between a straggle of rocks and a half-filled ore cart, still held a couple of oversuits and hats and candles. On impulse, Clifford donned the gear. He might never do this again—enter a mine he still held title to. Striking a flint, he lit the candle and carried it past the barricades warning wanderers of danger should they enter the cave-like opening. It was not his intention to go far, just down one tunnel and perhaps squat at the top of a ladder and remember the cold and damp that crawled up his spine with each foot of descent into a shaft. The ladders were fifty or a hundred feet tall and hanging in sheer blackness. Even with a flint in his pocket just in case, his tiny candle would not take him far under the circumstances.

Clifford chose a tunnel and found the opening where the ladder hung, hearing in his mind the sounds of picks and hammers and ore carts and voices of men calling safety warnings to each other. He shifted position and climbed down three rungs, then four, five, and six and paused there, breathing in memories he did not expect to form ever again. Instead, he would hear the shop's bell jangle and the cash register door shut hard and the wagon full of new stock pulling up to the rear door. Perhaps grandchildren would giggle in the aisles, and he would be ready with striped lollipops.

Cliff smiled at that thought and began to climb upward.

He missed a rung.

Dropped his candle.

Lurched.

Lost his grip on the ladder.

November 4, 1893. Everything changed that day in September. All of us could have been happy here. Should have been. The shop makes enough profit to see the potential Papa saw, and the house is well-built even if it is smaller than what we had become used to. Papa didn't have the hammer of bankruptcy coming down on his head, and he chose thoughtfully in bringing Mama's favorite furnishings here. Why was gratefulness so difficult? If it hadn't been, perhaps he would not have gone.

Mama didn't seem to care at all that Papa hadn't come home for hours that day, that he missed supper when he promised to be home, that he wasn't home when she retired. And I can't seem to stop writing about it. Somehow he sacrificed and gave what he could to the charities in Denver for the miners who will never know their benefactor and also managed to take care of us. He filled the pages of this book, and all the others, with his own heart for doing both. And my heart breaks that he is gone from us so suddenly after making sure we will be all right.

I see in Loren's face every day that he will never forget what it was like to go looking for Papa in the dead of night, find the mare, and realize he had gone down in the Missouri Rise. He strapped Papa's crumpled, broken body to himself and carried him out of that place and brought him home.

We will never want to mine it now. Not ever. Not for all the riches in the world.

Missouri closed the journal as her mother approached.

"You should throw that thing out," Georgina said. "All of them. If your father paid more attention to the real world, he'd still be alive, and we wouldn't be in this destitute place."

"Mama, please."

"I never could depend on him."

"That's not true. He took good care of all of us." Even now he was taking care of them. The store was doing well. Financially, they would be fine.

"I guess you'll have to learn the hard way, Missouri. You just can't depend on a man. They leave you in the lurch every time."

CHAPTER TWENTY-EIGHT

Jillian wiped up the last errant drop of coffee from around the machines, lined up a practiced aim across the breakfast bar, and tossed the sponge into the sink.

"So the second set of shelves will be finished today?"

"That's the plan." Nolan drained his mug, opened the dishwasher, and found space for it.

The doorbell rang.

"There she is, right on time." Jillian turned to answer the front door. "Racking up the hours. What happens if she finishes all her required hours before the summer is over?"

"A positive dilemma, I'd say." Nolan headed up the back stairs. "Send her right up."

"Oh good, you're here," Tisha said when Jillian opened the door. "I found some information on Maclovia. I think it could be something."

Jillian nodded. "Let's see what you have." It had only been two full days and three nights since she launched Tisha on the project of looking for the missing twin's family, and they'd both been busy with other tasks. It seemed unlikely Tisha had reached a true turning point yet, but the last thing Jillian would do now was dismiss Tisha's enthusiasm.

Tisha blew a bubble and smacked it, a habit Jillian had come to accept as more telling of nerves than defiance. Still, she hoped it might resolve sooner rather than later. The dining room table was blessedly clear, with papers sorted, folders labeled, and boxes readied for the shelves upstairs. Tisha confidently set up the dated laptop Jillian had loaned her and opened her green folder.

"I don't have a way to print at home," she said, "but I took lots of notes and made diagrams, and I can show you the website pages where I found information. I bookmarked them just like you showed me.

And I took screen grabs and stored the links in the folders you helped me set up."

"Sounds like you're doing everything right."

"I'm really trying to."

"That's good."

"I stayed up like all night last night. Literally. I did not sleep."

"Tisha, you have to sleep."

"No, I don't. I'd rather find Maclovia. I'm young. I have the rest of my life to sleep. So according to the original documents from St. Louis," Tisha said, "Maclovia was born in 1939. You would think that would be a really unusual name."

"Yes, I would, but sometimes I am surprised."

"I figured it was a made-up name, but Google says it's not."

"Even if it was made up," Jillian cautioned, "the question would be whether her parents made it up or the people who stole her made it up."

"Like you said. The census. The counties around St. Louis. Southern and central Illinois. Perhaps eastern Kansas."

"You found something?"

Tisha clicked a bookmark and a webpage opened. An infant named Maclovia with a birthdate identical to a sister named Ernestine was listed among several other children of two married parents in a rural area of Missouri.

"That's her, right?" Tisha said.

Jillian nodded. "Yes, it absolutely could be. A twin named Maclovia in the right year. Good job! But we don't know what happened to her after her illegal adoption, so we still have work to do."

"They wouldn't keep that name. It wouldn't be like adopting a girl named Mary, who would blend right in. A Maclovia would stick right out if someone was looking for her."

"Almost certainly."

"But something sort of similar, maybe. Clover. What if the new parents were told the adoption agency was calling her Clover and liked it? It's sort of cute."

"It's possible," Jillian said. "But we don't really know. There are going to be a lot of 'what ifs' in this work, Tisha. Adopting parents like to name their children themselves, especially infants. We have to be cautious about what ideas we get attached to."

"But some ideas are going to pay off, right?"

"Technically, yes, obviously." Jillian hesitated to let Tisha's hopes keep rising unrealistically.

"Please, just listen. I was up all night checking every possible combination."

"Combination of what?"

"Everything I could think of. All the things you told me to look for. Every variation I could think of. Combinations of variations." Tisha's brown eyes pleaded with wells of earnestness Jillian hadn't seen in them before.

"All right. Show me."

Tisha began spreading sheets from her green folder around, and Jillian leaned in to look at them as she listened to Tisha's explanation. She asked questions. Tisha had answers. Thirty minutes later, Jillian conceded it was possible. Far from certain, but possible.

Maclovia *might* have become Clover, or Clover *might* have become Chloe. And Clover *might* have been renamed with something else still in the "purple" family. Mauve? Lavender?

Tisha produced the marriage record from publicly available vital records in Illinois of a Chloe Lavender Richardson and Thomas Louis Depue. The birth date was right, but how many baby girls in the Midwest were born on that date? A birthday alone didn't mean anything, but in combination with her theory of how an adoptive name might have evolved—it was at least possible.

Property records indicated several moves around Illinois and Indiana.

Thomas Depue had died.

A Facebook profile Chloe obviously wasn't using, likely set up by some other family member a long time ago to try to include her in social media, also showed the same birthday but without a year. However, it had enough links to trace to a son about Nolan's age who looked like he'd be fairly easy to contact.

"Eli Depue," Jillian said. "We'll want to find a phone number, if possible. In my experience I get the best response that way. We can try reverse white pages for starters."

Tisha pulled out another sheet that revealed ten digits in elegant shapes that would have made Georgina Brandt proud. "Can I call him?"

Jillian held up a hand. "You've done solid work, Tisha, but I'm afraid I'll have to make the call. These conversations can be delicate and take experience."

The girl's face fell.

"I'm sorry," Jillian said. "If it pans out, you will absolutely get all the credit."

"Okay," Tisha muttered, eyes downcast.

"Even if this is Maclovia, and she really did become Chloe Lavender, it's only one side of the puzzle. If she or someone from her family is willing to give us DNA, we also need something to match it with—someone else related to the original family she was taken from."

Tisha perked up. "I can work on that? Finding someone?"

"Yes, you may. You have the names of other siblings right there in the census. We can see if we can trace them down a generation or two and see if there are family stories of a missing aunt, and then we'll know we're onto something. The Maclovia and Ernestine you found had brothers, which is a big help, because their names are less likely to change than sisters who might marry and take their husbands' names."

Tisha nodded, eager once again. "Right. Women in my family don't tend to get married, but other people do."

"Tisha," Jillian said, "you did good work. I mean it. If I found this kind of lead myself, I would definitely keep poking around to see if it solidified, so I'm going to follow up. But we have to be careful. We can be wrong because we don't have a lot of information we can verify yet. Or even if we're right, people may say no to getting involved, and we still can't verify it. Other things could go wrong."

Tisha rubbed one eye. "Yeah. I get it. But still. It's like that story you told me about how you found Sophie's family and they were happy. Maybe it'll be like that."

"Maybe."

Nolan rapped on the bannister from the landing. "I thought we were building shelves today."

Tisha looked up. "We are. I just had some questions. And I have one more."

"What's that?" Jillian said.

"How can I find out exactly where Clifford Brandt's mines were? Maybe I could hike out to see where they were."

"That's tricky," Jillian said.

"Agreed." Nolan came down the stairs and crossed the living room into the dining room. "But the one person in this town who knows the most about mines is Leo Dunston."

"The man at the Inn at Hidden Run?" Tisha said. "Where we were the other night?"

"That's him. In that very room, as a matter of fact. He has a couple of shelves of books about mining history in the region. Maybe he can help us—after lunch. Let's get these shelves up."

"Cool." Tisha nodded. "Then we can all take a hike and find my family history."

"Jillian," Nolan said, "why don't you give Leo a heads-up?"

She nodded. Her list of calls seemed to grow with every idea Tisha had.

Eli Depue.

Leo.

And Drew. She'd hoped to have him to herself this afternoon, but Tisha had swung from one extreme to another in her attitude. Defiant, disinterested, and distracted had morphed into enthusiastic, engaged, and enquiring.

Leo likely wouldn't know where Clifford's mines were, but he would relish being asked. And Drew was always game for being outdoors.

In her office, Jillian dug into what little they knew about Clifford Brandt, making notes on a narrow-ruled yellow legal pad.

Moved from Denver 1893.

Owned the mercantile.

Owned mines.

Lost the mines?

Father of Decorah and possibly others.

Act of generosity in Denver toward miners. Georgina disapproved.

Died 1893. Cause of death?

She tapped the space bar of her computer to wake it up and opened an academic search engine to do some serious probing for information on Clifford Brandt. After an hour, though, she hadn't found much. He worked for Horace Tabor, who was widely known to have lost his fortune in the 1893 economic recession that hit the Colorado mining industry especially hard because the US government ceased purchasing vast quantities of silver on a monthly basis after making gold the sole currency standard. It was reasonable to surmise Clifford Brandt also lost his livelihood in the industry. In a few newspaper clippings, he was also associated with social ministries of the People's Tabernacle, a large church in Denver that cared for the poor on an ongoing basis and organized additional efforts to provide for thousands of unemployed miners. An especially generous gift, known as the Belonging Bequest, was designated to help former miners who wished to leave Denver for other parts of the country do so with adequate food, clothing, and cash to reach destinations where they could be reunited with family members or establish themselves in locations with more promising employment than Denver could offer after the collapse of silver mining.

She found no mention of Brandt's family members or what became of them after he left Denver.

It wasn't much, but Jillian printed off the pages she found and slid them into a green folder to give to Tisha. Certainly this was a Brandt who was far from bitter and angry.

Eli Depue didn't answer his phone—likely because her number was not one he recognized—and Jillian left a calm, organized message of a sort she had become accustomed to leaving strangers in her line of work.

Leo launched into a lecture on mining on the phone, which was only cut short by Nia taking his phone away from him and assuring Jillian they'd be ready for the post-lunch visit.

And Drew. Sweet Drew. Accommodating Drew. Of course he would meet them at the Inn and gladly go for a mountain hike if that's where the afternoon's agenda took them.

"A registry? Not exactly," Leo said, when they gathered in his library later to see what was on his shelves. He reached for a sheet of paper and jotted a website. "Try this, and you might find what you're looking for if you know the name of the mine."

"But I don't," Tisha said, "just the name of the owner."

"In that case"—Leo pulled a slim binder off a shelf—"I downloaded this document from the Denver Public Library site. It's a sort of index of the owners of the mines that also gives the names of the mines."

Tisha eagerly flipped the pages. "There are hundreds."

"Just look for Clear Creek County," Jillian suggested.

She nodded and kept flipping. "I don't see his name."

"Are you sure this is everything?" Nolan asked.

"I didn't create it," Leo said, "but it came from the Denver Public Library and covers the whole state."

"Then why isn't Clifford Brandt on it?"

"There could be several reasons. Maybe he gave up and abandoned his claim very early. That happened with unpatented mines."

"What's an unpatented mine?" Tisha asked.

"It means the owner essentially leased the land from the federal government and only owned the minerals that came out of it—if there were any. If the mine was a bust, or the mine owner couldn't afford to keep going, they simply walked away."

"Could someone else make a claim?"

"Theoretically, once it was declared abandoned," Leo said. "Then there's the reality that most mines started as claims by individuals on fairly small pieces of land that they scraped together the money for. But a mining magnate like Dumont or Tabor would buy up the small claims, which might or might not pay off for individuals, and put together larger parcels that would be more economical to mine and get the ore milled. The magnate would have a better shot at being profitable than the little guys. And if they started making money, then outside companies would be interested in gobbling up huge parcels. Now those guys would be more interested in actually owning land."

"Kind of like how a start-up without a lot of money can't really compete with what Google and Facebook and Amazon have become?" Tisha asked.

Leo pointed at her but looked at Nolan. "Now, she's quick. Some things about business never change."

"So the start-up guy's name gets completely lost when he gets bought out," Tisha said.

"Later listings, from when the mine was actually yielding, would show the owner of record at the time."

"But how am I ever going to find what I'm looking for?"

Leo pulled several tomes off his shelves and dumped them in Tisha's arms. "You can learn a lot about nineteenth-century mining from these books."

"Leo," Nia said, immediately relieving Tisha of the volumes, "she's not trying to learn a lot about nineteenth-century mining. She wonders if she can find the mines her ancestor might have owned around 1893 right near here somewhere."

Leo tapped his chin, thinking. "Well, there's always the picture books."

"Hey!" Tisha said. "I'm not in second grade."

"Not that kind of picture books." Leo pulled another book down and opened it. "Historical photographs. They often have captions. The information isn't consistent, of course. It depends on the book and what the author or editor decided was important, or what information was available, where they got the photos from. But you never know."

Tisha hunched over the book. "The Red Elephant Mine?"

"True thing, as you see."

"What kind of name is that?"

Leo shrugged. "There's no rhyme or reason to the names. Mostly sentimental."

"Wouldn't Brandt Mine Number One be more efficient?"

"To you maybe."

Leo handed a couple of other books with photographs to Jillian and Nolan, and they all flipped pages.

"New Era Mine," Jillian said.

"Central Mine at Silver Dale," Nolan read. "At least that's a location."

"The Busy Bee. The Danville. The Conley," Tisha read. "Those were all something called Cragmor mines."

"In the Colorado Springs Coalfield," Leo said.

"Not around here, then." She turned a page. "The Lost Pin."

"Near Delta. Western side of the mountains."

"Also not exactly around here."

"Missouri Rise," Jillian murmured. "That could be anything. A ridge somewhere."

"That's a nice picture, though, don't you think?" Leo said. "I always thought so."

"I would agree," Jillian said.

"Money Musk Mine," Tisha read. "No location. No owner. Fidelity Wink. But there's not even a photo of that. Just a mention in a caption about some tunnel. This all feels a little hopeless."

"Maybe you won't find it today. You can come back."

"I might have to."

"Anytime," Nia said.

Nolan gasped.

"Dad, don't toy with us," Jillian said.

"I'm not," Nolan said. "I turned a couple of pages, and there's a caption below an old mountain cabin that says it's near the Decorah Runner and served as a boardinghouse for the workers."

"That has to be Clifford Brandt's mine." Tisha seized the book. "But there's no picture of the mine, and it doesn't even say where the cabin is."

"Granted, not the most helpful," Nolan said, "but a probable connection."

"Do you really think so?"

"I do."

Jillian winced. She wanted to give Tisha hope as much as anyone, but they didn't know for sure the mine's name meant anything.

"My head is spinning." Tisha stared at the photo and caption before snapping an image with her phone.

The Inn's door opened, and there was Drew, effulgence standing in the foyer. Or perhaps Jillian was the only one who saw his brightness. She went to greet him.

"Are we still going for a hike?" With an arm around her, he addressed the group.

Tisha shrugged. "Sure. Maybe it will help to just get in the mood somehow."

"Go on the trail Jillian and I took for her birthday hike," Nia said. "There's some good mining scenery. Just don't let her talk you into any shortcuts. My legs still haven't forgiven me."

CHAPTER TWENTY-NINE

Jillian raised her eyes over the top of her laptop, open on the table in the kitchen nook, to the view of Nolan and Drew in their white aprons and chef hats.

"*La donna è mobile qual piuma al vento,*" Nolan sang.

"*Muta d'accento, e di pensier,*" Drew responded.

Both of them grinned at her, their knives flying over the island strewn with vegetables.

Jillian refused to do more than flinch one side of her mouth. Those two thought they were so hilarious. Verdi's *Rigoletto*. When she asked Drew not to encourage her father's antics, Drew looked at her as if he didn't know what she was talking about and switched operas. In truth they were adorable together. Nolan had been singing his whole life out of love for music, only melding it with cooking after her mother died and he discovered that food could be an art form as well. Drew was a professionally trained musician whose father insisted he also be trained in a skill that could generate income if performing concerts didn't pan out. Together they were an irresistible and admirable whirlwind of passion for everything they did. But if she said any of that aloud, her father would take the whole game up six more notches, and it really would be over the top.

"You know the words," Nolan said. "Sing with us."

"I will not," she said. "You are singing about a fickle woman, and I will not support the stereotype."

"I don't think I've ever heard you sing," Drew said.

"I assure you, it's better that way." If you were going to date someone with a trained operatic voice who could sing in six languages, Jillian figured, it was better not to chase him off in the first few months by letting him hear you massacre the simplest of tunes. Better to first make sure he was solidly attached to other, more certain qualities you had to offer. When it came to music enjoyment, she was right there with the two of them. When it came to performance, she was happy to let Nolan stand in her stead.

"All those piano lessons," Nolan said, "and your mother and I never thought to add voice lessons during your formative years."

Jillian rolled her eyes at the dramatic swirl with which her father moved an empty mixing bowl to the sink. "I thought you two decided we would have a nice salad for dinner tonight."

"We are having salad," Nolan said. "Quinoa salad."

"And fig caprese salad," Drew said.

"And peaches and shaved fennel salad," Nolan said. "With red pepper, of course."

"Of course." Drew nodded. "And tomato-watermelon salad with turmeric oil."

"And may I say I find your concept of a smashed cucumber salad intriguing, rather than sliced."

"It augments the cucumber's ability to absorb the flavors of the lemon and celery salt."

"If I may interrupt," Jillian said, "what you have in your hands right now, Drew, looks suspiciously like some sort of patty, not a salad."

"Veggie burgers from scratch. Almost a salad. Ready to throw on the grill."

"This is a lot of food!"

Drew shrugged. "The veggie patties will keep up to three days. You will thank me after I'm gone."

"But for dessert?" Nolan wiggled that one eyebrow in the way Jillian would never be able to move hers.

"Chocolate–salted caramel swirl meringues. You will master them in no time, my friend."

Jillian furrowed her brow at her laptop screen.

"What's the matter, Silly Jilly?" Nolan said.

She blinked, enlarged the block of text she'd just found, and read it again.

"Jillian?" Drew said.

"I've been poking around archives of Denver newspapers some

more," she said, "looking for references to Clifford Brandt. Honestly, there hasn't been much. I was just hoping for anything I could give Tisha. All I've found were a few references to the fact that he worked for Horace Tabor and minor civic activities. Then I switched to looking for Georgina, which turned up more in the society pages."

"And?" Nolan said. "Don't keep us waiting."

"They had three daughters." Jillian raised her gaze to look her father square in the eyes. "Missouri, Decorah, and Fidelity."

"The mines." Nolan dropped his stirring spoon. "Well, I'll be."

Jillian nodded.

"Missouri Rise. Decorah Runner. Fidelity Wink," Nolan said. "They were all mentioned in the captions in Leo's books."

"Just not in the same book. So we didn't string them together."

"If he had three daughters and named his mines after them," Drew said, "why aren't their names known around here?"

"That's a good question," Jillian said. "Maybe Decorah is the only one who lived in Canyon Mines."

"You're going to keep digging, aren't you?"

Jillian flicked her eyes up at him. "Salad away, you two." She was already clicking into new screens.

The sounds of cooking—and singing—resumed. The quickest task Jillian could do was run the other daughters' names through any public records for Clear Creek County. Colorado's state archives, though admittedly incomplete in the early decades, went back to 1890. If the Brandts—at least some of them—came to Canyon Mines in 1893, she had a reasonable chance of catching the name of a married daughter in the old records.

Missouri Brandt.

"Bingo."

Drew wiped his hands on a dish towel and came around to the table. "What did you find?"

"Missouri Brandt married Loren Wade right here in Canyon Mines late in November 1893."

"Who is Loren Wade?"

"No clue. But now we have more to trace Missouri with." Jillian typed in Fidelity Brandt. "No hit on the third daughter."

"So she didn't marry here."

Jillian shook her head. "Nowhere in the state." She navigated to another website and entered first one name and then the other. "They're both buried in Tennessee. Different cemeteries in two different counties. Looks like Fidelity has a married name. Most likely she married in Tennessee."

"And Loren Wade?"

Jillian clicked again. "Also in Tennessee. Looks like he's adjacent to Missouri."

Drew leaned over her shoulder to peer at the dates. "They made it all the way through the Depression and then some."

"Let me check one more thing." Jillian wanted to know more about Fidelity's married name. She didn't expect what filled her screen.

"An artist." Drew scanned the screen along with Jillian. "Of some regional renown in her time."

Jillian's head pivoted toward the small reproduction hanging in the corner of the kitchen—the one Tisha claimed to have the original for in her attic.

The clatter of Jillian's phone ringing startled them both, and she snatched it up off the table. "Tisha's guy."

She hustled out of the kitchen and into the quietness of her office.

"Thank you for calling back."

"I promised I would." Eli Depue's solid bass voice sounded resolute in a way that unsettled Jillian. "After discussing the matter with my mother, I'm calling to say that we can't help you."

"Can I answer more questions for you?"

"No, that's not necessary. Mother feels that even if the outrageous theory is true, she's had a good life and has no wish to disturb it at this point."

"May I ask if she has an original birth certificate? Is there any chance at all she was adopted?"

"It would make no difference to her. She always felt loved by the parents she grew up with and certainly learned to pass love on to her own children and grandchildren. A DNA test will not change that."

"I see." Jillian maintained a professional tone. "And what about you? Are you curious to know if you are related to descendants of the other twin sister?"

"I don't think so," Eli said. "I'm not going to hurt my mother over this. It wouldn't change my life, either. My sisters and I had a lovely family. We still do."

"Have you also discussed this opportunity with your sisters?"

"Again, in deference to my mother, I've chosen not to do that, and I would ask you to respect her wishes as well."

"I understand. If you change your mind, you know how to reach me." She'd keep his contact information in her file.

"No offense, Ms. Parisi-Duffy, but it's my opinion that the genealogy rage is overrated. We each make our own way in the world. Certainly my mother has. Pretending to find affiliation with a group of strangers because of some event eighty years ago has no real point."

Jillian swallowed. "Thank you for your time."

She blew out her breath as she returned to the kitchen.

Nolan ceased his rapid chopping of tomatoes. "That doesn't sound good."

"It's not," she said, slumping back into her chair. "The family Tisha found is not interested. So even if we find the other twin, it won't matter. We can't find out if this is Maclovia."

"Tisha's going to take this hard."

"Yep."

"Someone from the original family might have DNA out on record with one of the companies," Drew said. "So many people do. That's how you found my fourth cousins."

"You found them," Jillian said. "All I did was say the results were valid. But you're right. We might still have something to work with that could lead us back to Eli Depue."

"Tisha's waiting to hear," Nolan said.

"Yep."

"The sooner, the better."

"Yep." Jillian sent a text, suggesting Tisha meet her at the park beside the school grounds for an update. It was still midafternoon.

She could meet Tisha, flush the dread of her reaction out of her own system, and be back in plenty of time to enjoy a bevy of salads.

A text message chimed back in response.

"What does she say?" Nolan asked.

"She'll be at the park in twenty minutes."

"Do you want me to come along?"

"Or me?" Drew said.

Both offers were tempting. Nolan was much better at difficult moments than she was, and Tisha might need calming. And Drew was calming to Jillian.

Jillian drew in a long breath and exhaled. "I've got it. Thank you both."

She reached the park ahead of Tisha. On a warm Sunday afternoon, families with children took advantage of the playground while older kids tossed Frisbees. A group of young adults was spreading out a picnic on the tables under the small pavilion while a couple of the men poked at the coals in the grill, a platter of burgers ready to go on. Jillian staked out space on a bench midway along the path from the parking lot to the playground where she could easily see the arrival of the bright green bicycle from any of several directions.

Tisha pedaled in from the back side of the athletic fields. Jillian waved her over and offered a water bottle.

"It's mixed news," Jillian said.

Tisha's guard flashed up, a block of distrust set in her jaw as she balanced the unopened water down on the bench between them. "What does that mean?"

"It means," Jillian said, "that you did a phenomenal job of tracking Maclovia and producing contact information for her son. But we can't control how people respond on the other end."

Silent, Tisha stared at her feet.

"Rejection happens sometimes," Jillian said softly. "This is not the first time I've seen it in my line of work."

"Well, it's stupid." Tisha raised a glare. "People should want to know who they came from."

Jillian waited a few seconds before speaking. "It's hard to say one *should* applies to all people."

"Now you're taking her side."

Whose side? Were they still talking about Maclovia?

"I'm sorry, Tisha." Jillian laid a tentative hand on Tisha's shoulder. "For now, at least, Chloe Depue is not interested in disturbing her life to find out if she is the lost Maclovia, and out of respect for her wishes, her son doesn't want any further contact, either. I think if we tracked down his sisters—which probably wouldn't be hard to do—things could get unpleasant."

"They don't even get a say?" The words burst out of Tisha, and she threw off Jillian's touch. "He's calling all the shots just because I found him first?"

"For now."

"But the sisters don't even know. Now there's a big secret in their family. And I put it there."

"No. You didn't put it there. It was always there. What happened to Maclovia was always there."

"But now Eli knows. If I had a brother, and I found out he knew something like this and didn't tell me, I wouldn't be very happy."

"I wouldn't be, either."

"There must be something we can do." Tisha slapped the bench.

"We look for the twin who wasn't stolen." Jillian thrummed her thumbs against her thighs. "That's what we do. Then perhaps we approach Maclovia's family with another opportunity. We'll have more information—maybe even photos of the other family. Something to draw in their interest. DNA to compare to. We can try again."

Tisha kicked up loose dirt with the toe of her flip-flop. "I don't like it, but I guess there's not much I can do. As usual, I have no control over anything."

Jillian's heart heaved as she tried to rescue the conversation.

"I have other news," she said. "Better news."

"Yeah?"

"That picture Leo had of the Missouri Rise mine was a Brandt mine. So was the mention of the Fidelity Wink."

Tisha gave Jillian her eyes now. "How do you know that?"

"I found his other daughters."

"Missouri and Fidelity?"

"Right."

"Weird names. All of them."

"Unusual by our standards, yes."

"You're sure?"

"I am." Jillian nodded emphatically. "Maybe Leo can help find one of those specific mines now that we're sure Clifford Brandt owned them. They can't be too far from here, and he must have owned them around 1890."

"Maybe." Tisha shrugged.

"And something else," Jillian said. "Fidelity Brandt Longthorne was an artist. I wonder if she painted that picture in your attic and that's why your family has it."

Tisha's mouth opened slightly as she thought. "That pickax on the front of the house and that painting are the two things Grandma Ora always says are her two oldest memories. It's wacko that we hang the pickax but not the painting. In a stupid sort of way, it makes a statement about our family."

Jillian said nothing.

"Why Tennessee?" Tisha said.

"I don't know yet," Jillian said. "One part of my brain said maybe I should try to figure that out for you, like I do for other people. Another part said maybe you'd like to figure that out yourself. It turns out you might have a knack for this."

"Well, it's no power tool," Tisha said, "but I guess I could try. If I need a consultation, I could always work off your fee by helping with the St. Louis files."

"Yes, you could," Jillian said, her thumbs still knocking against her legs but her stomach feeling calmer.

"Can I ask you about something else?"

"Of course."

"Has Nolan talked to my father yet?"

Jillian's thumbs stilled. "Not yet."

CHAPTER THIRTY

Either Brittany Crowder maintained at least occasional contact with her daughter's father, or she was a skilled internet stalker who could be useful to Jillian's line of work. Her standard of living didn't suggest she'd been receiving child support for the last fifteen years. She lived with her mother and grandmother in a smallish rented home in a neighborhood that had never seen very good days. A competent shop clerk, currently she held the title of assistant manager, but the staff of Candles & Cards was small and transitory. The owner had to trust someone with a second set of keys, making an occasional bank deposit, and knowing how to call a vendor and check on an order. Nolan didn't see any sign that Brittany was going to break out into a new profession or income bracket. Her next job, just like her last, was likely to be in another of the shops. She would make the change because someone offered her a shift she preferred, promised weekends off, or could pay another dollar an hour.

Nolan lacked grounds to poke around town and ask specific questions, but having seen Brittany's volatility up close, he couldn't help wondering if it contributed to changing jobs every couple of years.

Brittany had followed through on providing contact information for Jayden Casky. Her life may seem like it stalled after she became pregnant and dropped out of high school, but his seemed unaffected. He was thirty-five years old, held a PhD, and taught in the education department at the university in Greeley.

A hundred miles away.

If Tisha knew, she'd be hitchhiking before the summer was over. And she'd know soon. She had his name, and it was sure to turn up easily enough in an internet search attached to his academic bio. Even if it didn't, Jillian had given Tisha access to subscription-only websites that could provide Tisha easier information than she would have had otherwise. At the time, that had seemed like the right thing to do to build trust. Now it seemed like a thin, faint line waiting to be rubbed out with a giant pink eraser in the grip of an angry, impulsive child.

In his office Monday morning, Nolan laid Brittany's note flat on his desk. It was printed in clear, block capital letters, with a heavy imprint on the paper, as if she was afraid any other kind of writing would leave room for error in interpreting her meaning.

I AM DOING THIS UNDER FORCE, BUT HERE IT IS.

Still, the information was there. Name. Where he worked. Office phone number. Work email. Cell phone number. Home address. When Brittany said she knew where he was, she wasn't just taunting Tisha in the moment. She really did.

Nolan swiveled his chair to his computer and navigated to the university website. One click through to the education department tab and another to faculty soon had Nolan looking at the face of the man Brittany claimed was Tisha's father. The likeness was not immediate, but it was strong enough to believe she hadn't chosen a random name. Brown eyes, hooded in the same way. The square of the chin. One more click led to a full list of Casky's education, professional experience, and topics of research interest. Social studies. Teacher preparation. He was well published for an academic still fairly early in his career.

Poking around didn't yield office hours, but a class schedule was easy enough to find and make a reasonable guess about when he might be in his office. He didn't have a class right now.

How Brittany had his home address and cell phone number was a mystery, but Nolan would let that be for now. Hopefully he wouldn't need to use personal information he couldn't verify was acquired by above-board methods. He picked up his office phone and dialed the university phone number for Dr. Casky. After the third ring, Nolan was prepared to hang up. He'd rather try repeatedly, even if he got an administrative assistant at first, than leave a cold-call phone message on a university line where he didn't know who might retrieve it.

Just at the start of the fourth ring, a baritone voice said, "Casky here."

"Dr. Jayden Casky?"

"Yes, that's right. Who's calling, please?"

"My name is Nolan Duffy. I'm an attorney in Denver, but more important, I live in Canyon Mines and I'm acquainted with Brittany Crowder."

"Who?"

The pitch of his voice had hitched. He was covering. Nolan had heard enough people bluffing over the course of his career to know when someone was buying time.

"Brittany Crowder. I understand you met her first when you were in college in Denver."

"I met a lot of girls in college. Didn't you?"

"Brittany wasn't in college. She was in high school."

Pause. "Oh. Right."

"Brittany's daughter is fifteen now and would very much like to meet her father."

"What? Me? No. I'm sure you're mistaken."

"Are you saying it's impossible?"

"Well, no, not strictly speaking. More to the point, how is this any of your business?"

"The family has asked me to contact you on their behalf. Brittany is the one who told me how I could find you."

"She knew?"

"Does that surprise you?"

"It doesn't matter," Casky said. "As to your request, I think it would be inappropriate."

"Why is that, if I may ask?" Nolan wasn't going to let him off that easily.

"This child is not anybody I know. I have only your word that she is connected to me, and you have only Brittany's word. You're an attorney. Surely you recognize hearsay when you see it."

"Might you be willing to talk to Brittany?"

"Mr. Duffy, I think our conversation is over. Please don't call this number again."

The call ended.

"Well, Tisha," Nolan said aloud in his empty office as he set the handset in its cradle, "I do believe we just found your father."

He got up and stuck his head out of his office to see if his assistant was at her desk. "Have I got anything today that absolutely can't be moved?"

She opened his calendar on her computer and ticktocked her head. "Probably not. I haven't put anything new on since this morning. No clients. A few internal things I could get you excused from."

"Then please make my apologies, or reschedule, or stuff my briefcase for me to deal with things from home tomorrow. We can do video calls or whatever."

"What's up?"

"That alternative sentencing case. I need a few hours. I'll try to get back this afternoon, if I can."

"You got it."

Nolan checked the university website one more time to find the room assignment of Casky's office and get a quick glance at a campus map to find the building. Then he was in his car and headed north. If he had to sit outside Casky's office and smile blandly at an administrative assistant, who would become more motivated to track down Casky the longer Nolan sat there looking patiently determined, he would. He could always play the card of amiably offering to call Jayden's cell directly, suggesting a friendship that didn't exist. Just in case, he created a contact for Casky in his phone with the information Brittany had provided.

Now who was the stalker?

Nolan got lucky. A student, rather than a wizened veteran, was on duty at the desk.

"He shouldn't be more than fifteen or twenty minutes," she said. "Then he has office hours, but he doesn't have any appointments scheduled. It should be no problem. Would you like some coffee?"

"Just black, thank you." Nolan settled in.

"Dr. Casky, this gentleman is here to see you," the young woman said sixteen minutes later as the man matching the photo Nolan had viewed ninety minutes ago unlocked his office.

Nolan stood and smiled. "It's a private matter."

Casky stiffened, no doubt recognizing his voice. He wasn't going to make a fuss, though. "Come on in."

Nolan followed Casky into the office. Casky closed the door.

"I specifically told you not to call here again."

"I didn't call," Nolan said. "I drove."

"I think my meaning was clear." His irritation also clear, Casky rounded the desk and sat in the high-back brown leather chair on the other side.

"May I?" Nolan gestured toward an empty side chair.

Jayden nodded.

"I'm not normally so intrusive," Nolan said, "and I suspect you're not normally so curt. The circumstance is unusual."

Another slight nod.

"Tisha Crowder is a remarkable girl but a confused girl. One of her deepest wishes is not so difficult to understand. She sees other children with their fathers. Coming to school programs. Playing in the park. Going out to breakfast on Saturday mornings. Even if their parents aren't married, her friends know who their fathers are. Even if there is a custody agreement, there is some arrangement for the children to know their fathers, spend time with them. Tisha has grown up in a household of women who, for the most part, haven't known their fathers. I think she is right to wonder why this is and to think she deserves better."

"That's quite a speech, Mr. Duffy. One that you should give to this girl's father, now that you've practiced on me."

Nolan steepled his fingers. "Well, now, you see, in my line of work, I give more speeches than you might imagine, and I can quite humbly say that far and away, I generally hit the mark the first time."

"Is that right?"

"As a matter of fact, it is." Nolan sat back in the chair, one ankle propped on the opposite knee. "I've only just met you, but my guess is that being a college professor suits you and you're on a tenure track. You're building a nice life. A life of learning and expanding not only your mind but the minds of hundreds of young people who come through your classrooms. There's always at least a little bit of curiosity and selflessness in a serving profession like teaching. But it has its rewards."

"It's my life, Mr. Duffy. I've worked hard to be where I am."

"Of course you have. You had certain opportunities, and you were able to make the best of them because no responsibilities weighed you down or held you back."

Silence.

"Like a baby, you mean," Jayden finally said.

"She's a teenager now, not so much younger than some of your students. She could apply to enroll here in another couple of years. You have the opportunity to get to know her, answer questions, provide a stable influence."

"Anyone who has achieved the age of fifteen has already formed her core values. Research has established this. Whatever Letitia has the ability to become, the resources are already within her."

Nolan tilted his head. "You just called her Letitia."

"That's her name, isn't it?"

"I never told you it was. You knew there was a child. This is why Brittany knew where you were."

Jayden pushed back from his desk and swiveled a quarter turn. "I met Brittany at a concert with some friends. She kept in touch with one of the girls who was there with my group."

"So this girl knew Brittany was having your baby."

"She knew Brittany had *a* baby. But Brittany told her to make sure and tell me the baby's name was Letitia."

"Does that name mean something to you?"

"My grandmother's name. I used to say that if I ever had a daughter I'd like to give her a classy, old-fashioned name like Letitia. And Brittany would say she'd have to bring it into the twenty-first century."

"Tisha."

Jayden nodded.

"Do you have other daughters?"

Jayden shook his head. "Two small sons."

"And they're part of the lovely life you're building that doesn't have room for Letitia?"

"My wife. I've worked too hard to get over past mistakes. I knew her before I ever met Brittany. We were on and off for years, and I kept scrambling things up. Flirting too much. Drinking too much. Cutting too many classes. But she was always the one. Eventually I grew up. Fortunately, she was willing to give me one more chance. We're happy, Mr. Duffy."

"Brittany even has your home address and cell phone," Nolan said. "Have you spoken to her?"

Jayden's head wagged emphatically. "Not once since we broke up."

"Then how?"

Jayden thought for a moment. "She's probably still in touch with Katelynn, from college. She married one of my fraternity brothers. It wouldn't be hard for Katelynn to have the information." Jayden put his head in his hand. "I suppose Katelynn must have figured it out years ago."

"As soon as Katelynn told you the baby's name was Letitia, you knew she was yours."

Jayden exhaled.

"Your daughter knows your name now," Nolan said.

Jayden flinched upright. "She cannot come here. I don't want to talk to her."

"She has no interest in causing pain. She just wants to know who you are."

"She cannot come. You tell her. She should just go on with her life."

"She'll come someday, Jayden. She has your name, and she's smart. By virtue of your work, you won't be difficult to find once she starts trying."

"So you stop her from trying."

"Agreeing to meet her now—with me present—can remove some

of the shock factor that might come later if she turns up on campus or at your house."

"I am telling you in the firmest manner possible to tell Letitia in the firmest manner possible that she should not come to meet me. She should not even apply to this university. Is that clear?"

Nolan turned his palms up. "It's clear to me, but I don't make decisions for another person who is not my child and will be a legal adult in less than three years. She's fifteen now and gets around on a bicycle because she likes her independence. That won't last much longer. She'll start driving and take her mother's car, with or without permission. Or she'll hitch a ride to west Denver and Uber the rest of the way. Or maybe her older boyfriend will be the one to drive her. Once she turns eighteen, she's a free agent. And this is a public university. Anyone can apply. Unless you plan to dismantle your careful, comfortable tenure track professorial life and disappear with your wife and two little sons, Tisha *will* come looking for you. Your daughter is a force to be reckoned with. I'd like to help you both."

Jayden stood. "You should go. I have a lecture to prep for."

Before he left, Nolan slid his business card across the desk. "You'll need this when you're ready. Don't waste too much time."

CHAPTER THIRTY-ONE

Jillian knocked on the doorframe of her dad's office on Tuesday morning.

He looked up. "She's here?"

She nodded. "I'm sorry her own mother was right all these years."

"When Brittany gave his daughter his grandmother's name and he still stayed away, she knew for certain what she was to him."

"And what the baby would never be."

Nolan stood. "But I have to tell Tisha the truth."

Ten minutes later, Tisha's thin frame was taut and her face ashen as she sat on her hands at the edge of the center cushion of the navy sofa.

"He really doesn't want to talk to me? Not even once? Not even to meet me? To see what I look like?"

"That's what he says." Nolan leaned toward her from the ottoman, his knees against hers.

"There's a chance it's not what he means, right?"

"I'm being honest with you, Tisha. I believe it is what he means, at least for now. But people do change their minds."

"It's just like Maclovia." Tisha slumped into the couch. "Go get another family. Throw away the old one like trash. That's what he thinks of me. A piece of trash not worth having in his life."

"I'm so sorry," Jillian said from where she stood at the edge of the room. "You're not trash. He doesn't know what he's missing."

Tisha huffed. "I wish you would stop saying things like that."

Jillian held her breath, afraid to say anything.

"It's just not helpful," Tisha said. "It doesn't make me feel better to hear lies. My whole family is trash. Nobody has ever wanted them. And now nobody wants me. My own father is not even curious to know whether I look like him."

"You do," Nolan said softly. "Around the eyes and your chin."

Tisha's eyes filled, and she dragged the back of one hand through them. "Well, it doesn't matter. I want him, but he doesn't want me. And grown-ups get what they want."

"I gave him my card," Nolan said, "for when he changes his mind."

"But he won't." Tisha pushed up off the couch. "We all have work to do. Jillian, what do you want me to work on scanning today?"

"We don't have to worry about that," Jillian said.

"I want to. It's better if I'm busy."

Jillian felt like she'd eaten Legos for breakfast and couldn't dislodge them from her throat. She made clearing noises. "How far have you gotten with the stack you're working on?"

"Almost finished. Three more folders, but there's not much in one of them."

"Okay. I'll go up and bring down the next batch of priorities."

"Whatever." Tisha smacked her gum and went into the dining room, where Jillian had set up her best scanner at the end of the table that had become Tisha's usual workspace.

"I could use some coffee," Nolan said.

"Me too," Jillian said. "Tisha, are you sure you don't want to try an iced coffee? I could whip it up. No trouble."

Tisha flicked her eyes up for a quarter of a second. "Disgusting."

The tortoise was back in her shell, nursing her old distraction. Jillian would have to double-check later to see if she'd labeled the scans according to the system they'd settled on and placed them appropriately in folders in the computer.

Jillian followed Nolan into the kitchen. They stood side by side at the coffee machines, holding mugs and pushing buttons.

"I suppose there was no way that could have gone well," Jillian finally said.

"Short of my saying I'd arranged for a visit with Jayden Casky, no."

"What are we going to do, Dad?"

"Give her some space for now." Nolan tested the temperature of his beverage. "If she wants to work, let her work."

"And if she takes off?"

"I don't think she will."

Jillian's more complex latte was ready now, and they walked together through the dining room and living room toward the front stairs. Tisha had earbuds plugged into her phone, but a folder was open on the table and the scanner and laptop were operating. She didn't look up.

Nolan turned toward his office, situated right above Jillian's, and she headed for the large guest room now outfitted with shelves to hold the St. Louis boxes. She set her coffee on an end table while she slid a couple of boxes off the shelves and assessed what might be the most fruitful use of Tisha's time, both to accomplish the next step in a long series of repetitive tasks but also to help her feel she was doing something significant—and of course to get Jillian launched on cases that might have the strongest trails to solve.

Thirty minutes later, Jillian's mug was empty, and she had an armful of files that made sense for Tisha to focus on next. She took them downstairs, ready to swap for the stack Tisha was surely finished with by now.

The laptop was open, the unfinished file folder still spread on the table, and the scanner still powered up, but Tisha wasn't there.

"Tisha?" Jillian set down the new stack of files and padded into the kitchen. No Tisha. She left her mug in the sink and stepped into the hall. The powder room door was open. No Tisha there or in the office. "Tisha?"

No answer.

Jillian stuck her head out the back door. No Tisha.

She looked out the front door. No bicycle. Her stomach sank and she called up the stairs.

"Dad! She bolted."

Nolan came immediately. "A note?"

Jillian hustled back to the dining room table and then to the desk in her office. "Nothing."

"Did she sign out her hours?"

Jillian found the record sheet. "Nope. No entry at all for today, even though she was here on time."

"I don't like how this feels. I'll call her."

Jillian followed Nolan back up the stairs to where he'd left his cell phone on his desk and paced while he waited for her to answer.

"Nothing," he said. "I'll try texting."

"What if she does something now and throws away everything you're trying to do for her?"

"Just me?" Nolan glanced up from his phone. "Face it, Silly Jilly. You are on this train now too."

"I am," she admitted. "Even Drew is. He was great with her over the weekend. He baked cookies with her yesterday before he left. Do you know she had never baked homemade cookies in her life? He had to correct that situation immediately."

"He's a gem, that one."

Jillian could not disagree. "Any response?"

"No signs of life on the other end of her phone."

"Dad, you don't think—"

He cut her off. "No, I do not think she would hurt herself. Poor choice of words. But I do know where the boyfriend lives."

"Boyfriend? There's a boyfriend?"

"I'm not sure how serious it is, but there is someone she goes to when Brittany doesn't want her around."

"Even 'not serious' can be dangerous. That's why Brittany has Tisha. Don't tell me he looks older."

"He looks older."

"I asked you not to tell me that."

"It'll only take a few minutes to drive over there and see if we spot her bike." Nolan dropped his phone in a pocket. "Get your shoes. Let's go."

The bike wasn't along the fence where Nolan had found it on his previous visit to this address, and snooping a little harder didn't turn up any evidence she was there. In fact, the house seemed unoccupied—no lights, no television, no footsteps in response to a doorbell, no wildly barking dog.

"She might have gone home," Jillian said.

"It's possible." Nolan set the pace back to his truck. "She's still not answering my text. We might as well look."

"It bothers me that she didn't take the laptop," Jillian said. "She's hardly had it out of her sight since I gave it to her almost a week ago."

They drove over Eastbridge and into the Crowder neighborhood. At least the home gave off no crashing noises, but the bicycle wasn't in sight. Brittany's car was there, though. Tentatively, they exited the truck and knocked.

Nolan glanced at the pickax on the front of the house. "Interesting decor."

Brittany opened the door and looked at them through the screen.

"Hi," Jillian said. "We're looking for Tisha."

"I thought she was working for you today." Brittany pushed hair out of her face. "I was just glad for some peace and quiet on my day off."

"She was working," Jillian said, "but we may have had a little mix-up about the schedule. If she's not here, we won't bother you."

"Wait a minute. She's been jabbering nonstop about Jayden, and now you lost my kid. What did you do?"

"I did talk to Jayden," Nolan said, "and the news was not good."

"It's her own fault," Brittany said. "I told her not to get her hopes up. She never thinks that her own mother might actually know what's good for her."

The evidence has been a little thin. Jillian mustered a small smile. "If she comes home, we'd love to hear from her."

"She'll turn up eventually. She always does." Brittany closed the door.

"Well," Jillian said. "There's that."

"I haven't plied out of her the names of any other friends," Nolan said. "Have you?"

Jillian shook her head as they shuffled back to the truck. Then abruptly she snapped her spine straight.

"What is it, Silly Jilly?"

"The trail. The one we all hiked together on Saturday."

"She insisted on climbing that pile of rocks."

"Because I told her that Nia had mentioned it dated back to the mining days," Jillian said, "when people dug up the mountain without any care for what it did to the environment."

"And she wanted to go off trail and look for a grate covering an old mine entrance because maybe it was a Brandt mine."

"Even though you suggested she should talk to Tony Rizzo about his mining museum and the tours he gives."

"I've heard Tony's tour a thousand times," Nolan said. "I know his mine is not old enough to be a Brandt mine. That's what I told her. But anything Leo doesn't know about these old mines, Tony might."

Jillian raised her eyes to the attic window with the yellow curtain and the outdated air-conditioning unit. "I think she really believes there is a Brandt mine up in the hills."

"But we found no evidence—"

"Dad, I practically told her I thought Fidelity Brandt painted the original of that picture hanging in our kitchen. She has the original in her attic."

"Even if that's true, it's just a landscape."

"Is it? Coincidence that it's the view from a rock pile where there might be a lost mine in the area?"

"We're going for a hike, aren't we?" Nolan jangled his keys.

"Only if we see her bike somewhere. Most of the trail is not bike friendly. She can't have ridden out. Not on that bike."

They drove out west, past Tony Rizzo's old mine and into the tangle of trails circling in the hills above it, dipping into several small parking lots at the trailheads.

"There!" Jillian pointed. "If she wants to camouflage her bicycle, she really needs a different color."

"Let's hope she's not too far ahead of us." Nolan put the truck in PARK.

"Oh, she is." Jillian slammed the passenger door closed. Tisha could have had as much as a thirty-minute head start leaving the house, and they'd whittled away time looking in the wrong places. "Keep up, old man."

Jillian set a jogging pace she could easily sustain even on an incline, choosing the priority of reaching Tisha. She'd feel better if she had the girl in sight. Then she could think about waiting for her father. It dawned on her that she was in shorts and tennis shoes, but that he wore jeans and, before leaving the house, had quickly slid his feet into shoes meant only for a quick errand or two, not hiking a trail or scaling a rock pile. They'd both left the house without water bottles in the middle of July. Periodically, she glanced over her shoulder to judge his progress, but she was more concerned with what lay ahead.

Sure enough, Tisha had found a relatively flat sunny spot among the boulders, about two-thirds of the way up, and situated herself. Jillian shielded her eyes and looked up before beginning the climb. At least it wasn't a sheer rock face.

"Why are you here?" Tisha called to her.

"Because you're supposed to be at work and I'm worried." Jillian found footing and pushed higher.

"I'm way ahead in my hours, and you know it."

"That's not what I'm worried about." Even in tennis shoes, the hard edges of the rocks dug into Jillian's feet. Somehow Tisha had made the climb in her usual flip-flops. Somehow she did everything in those flip-flops.

"You should know by now you're wasting your energy," Tisha said.

Jillian kept climbing. "I'm coming anyway."

Tisha said nothing more. At least she kept still, and Jillian hadn't found her clambering around looking for a hidden mine entrance. Finally, Jillian lowered herself onto a flat space near Tisha. The hot rock burned the back sides of her thighs, and immediately she pulled her knees up to her chin.

"You've had a lot of bad news," Jillian said.

"And you're going to try to give me advice about how to handle it. Thanks for nothing."

"Advice? No. I don't have a clue what you should do."

"Such a big help."

"I'm sure my dad wants to help in every way he can. If Jayden Casky isn't ready, well, maybe more time will make a difference."

"He's had fifteen years."

"You are not wrong." Jillian glanced down the path, hoping for reinforcement. "Your mom was not that much older than you are now when she got pregnant. Even college boys are not the greatest at stepping up."

"She could have made him."

"Legally, she could have taken steps to get child support, and it looks like she didn't."

"Money doesn't buy love."

"Maybe we should give your mom credit for knowing that. Maybe she didn't want the money if it didn't come with love for the baby too."

Tisha side-eyed Jillian. "Are you just making this stuff up?"

"Maybe. How am I doing?"

"Could be worse." Tisha repositioned her feet. "So I'm supposed to give up on ever knowing my father."

"I didn't say that."

They fell into silence. Sweat soaked the back of Jillian's T-shirt.

"You know what this is, right?" Tisha finally said.

"I wondered if you might recognize it."

"I got the painting out last night. I kept thinking about how you said maybe Fidelity painted it."

"Is it the same picture?"

Tisha nodded. "And it's this view. The mines, a piece of the rock pile, the canyon, the mountains, Fidelity being a painter. Too many coincidences."

"If Fidelity made that painting," Jillian said, "why does your family keep it stuck away in the attic?"

Tisha huffed. "Why does my family do anything? That seems to be a question dating back to Clifford and Georgina."

"An astute observation."

Tisha stood up, finding her balance among the stones. "I'm out of here."

"What are you doing?" Jillian shifted to her feet as well.

"Leaving."

"My dad will be here soon."

"The two of you can have a nice chat about me behind my back."

"That's not what we do."

"Isn't it?" Tisha glared for a couple of seconds before scoffing and beginning her descent. "You don't understand. No one who has known her dad all her life can possibly understand."

Jillian followed, but Tisha was nimbler on the rocks, making Jillian feel old and cautious. By the time she was back on the main trail, she wasn't even sure which direction Tisha had darted off in.

Nolan approached, slightly breathless.

"Did you see her?" Jillian asked.

"How does somebody run that fast on a trail in that kind of footwear?" He shook his head.

"Which direction?"

"Back to her bike, I think. She wouldn't stop for me. What did you say to her?"

"What did *I* say? Dad, don't go there."

"Sorry. That came out wrong."

"Just when I think I'm making progress with her, everything falls apart again."

"Tisha Crowder processes in her own way."

"Dad, tell me I was never like that when I was a teenager in pain."

"You processed in your way too, Jilly," Nolan said softly.

She linked her arm through his. "But I had you."

"We had each other."

They began winding their way back down the trail toward the car.

"She's way ahead of us," Jillian said. "We won't catch her at this rate."

"Maybe we shouldn't try. Give her space."

"I'm parched."

"We'll get something as soon as we're back in town."

CHAPTER THIRTY-TWO

Canyon Mines, Colorado
Tuesday, December 12, 1893

Can't you at least stay for Christmas?" Lity's eyes filled, and her warm exhale clung to the cold air for an instant before surrendering and dissipating, and with it her hope. "Our first Christmas here—and without Papa. And now without you. How will we stand it?"

How will I stand it? That was the true question Missouri heard tremble in her sister's words. Fidelity was a tender seventeen. Fatherless. Essentially motherless now. Adventurous within a certain frame of safety but not yet brave enough to do something brash like leaving the family home, frail as it was, without a sure plan for independence. And she shouldn't. Missouri would not encourage such a choice. In fact, quite the opposite.

Missouri choked on her own choice. "Mama has accepted the store now. She's learned how to work there as well as any of us. It will be all right."

"She still hates it."

"It's a first step."

They stood on the porch of the house their father had expected to live in for many more years, shivering against a blast of winter air funneling through the narrow high mountain valley that cradled Canyon Mines. She would miss this. Only four months, and already it felt like a place she might have called home for a long time.

If only. Missouri wrapped her arms around her midsection, reminding herself that where she was going would be warmer, and her sisters would need the thickest cloak she was leaving behind more than she would.

"Mama hates Papa for dying even more than she hated him for taking us out of Denver," Lity said.

"*Hate* is a strong word, Lity."

"Do you have a better one?"

Missouri rubbed her gloved hands together. She did not have a better word. "She's hurt, and she doesn't know what to do with her pain."

"Shouldn't we help her? Instead of leaving."

"I don't know how to help her, Lity. Loren has been nothing but good to me—to our family and to Papa—but Mama is determined to hate the man I love and wants me to hate him."

"So you do think it's hate."

Missouri sighed. "Only for lack of the right word. My leaving might actually help her because she won't look at me and Loren every day and. . .I don't know. . .blame us for what happened." At the end, Papa had floundered in his attempts to abate Mama's descent from occasional to constant anxiety and finally suspicion and bitterness. Somehow he was supposed to have exempted the Brandt family from the effects of silver's collapse and a national recession. Missouri had read her father's journals. What he'd given away was generous, but it would never have saved their home, not without substantial employment to carry them forward.

"Leaving will help? That doesn't make sense." Lity's bottom lip slipped out into a pout.

"None of this makes sense."

The front door swung open and Decorah stomped out. "I thought you would be gone by now—or have you changed your mind and decided to do the sensible thing and stay with your family instead of running off with a man you barely know?"

"Don't start, Decorah," Missouri said.

"Do you have any idea what you're doing to Mama? Marrying that man the way you did?"

Missouri held her tongue. *That man* was her husband now. Her loyalties were clear. The minister at the Lutheran church three blocks from the mercantile was a regular customer and had been happy to perform a private ceremony. Lity had been there, along with the witnesses. But Mama wouldn't come, and of course Corah did whatever

Mama did. Missy doubted she would ever have a mind of her own. Would she ever find love, or would Mama spoil that for her too?

"Tennessee?" Corah said. "Why don't you just go to Leadville or Colorado Springs or back to Denver. I hear most of the homeless men are gone now."

"Loren has cousins in Tennessee," Missouri said. "They've invited him to go into business with them. You know that. You were there when we explained it to Mama. We made the decision together."

"Cousins." Corah scoffed. "You have *sisters* here. And a *mother*."

"Go inside, Corah," Lity said. "You'll catch your death out here without a wrap."

Corah glared at Lity, but she was shaking with the cold, so she did withdraw into the house.

"You can't leave me here." Lity's voice hitched. "With them."

Missouri glanced down the street. Loren would be there any moment with their meager belongings and the train tickets. She had come to the house one last time only to see Fidelity.

"It's your best chance to finish high school without losing credits," Missy said. "So many girls don't get that chance, and you're so close. Finishing will give you opportunities you might not have if you don't finish. The principal has already said you're doing very well and you'll have enough credits to graduate next December, a full semester ahead of schedule."

"It's still a whole year! And then what?"

"A lot of things can change in a year, Lity." Missouri's chest burned. Leaving behind her baby sister was the hardest part of this plan. "You love the store, and you've made friends here in Canyon Mines. You can work after school and all next summer. And in a year? Maybe the store is where you'll want to stay. You could live above it. You wouldn't have to live at the house."

"And if not?" Lity's voice shrank.

"I've already given you the address where you can write to me in Tennessee." Missouri unfolded her arms from beneath her shawl and offered a package to Lity. "And you can always describe for me what you've done with these."

Lity sniffled as she pulled the string to release the wrapping. She smiled past her pain. "More shades of green paint."

"You always seem to be running out."

"It's the views. There's so much green to capture."

Missouri took both her sister's hands. "I left something else for you in our room."

"What is it?"

"Look under your mattress at the foot of the bed."

"Papa's journals?" Lity's eyes widened. "That's where you used to keep them on your bed."

"They're yours now. They belong here in Canyon Mines. I wrote something for you, and after that it's up to you to write what's on your heart."

"I wouldn't know what to write. That's why I paint."

"It will come to you."

Lity ran a finger across her dripping nose. "Here's Loren."

He was driving a borrowed cart. The owner would meet them at the train station to reclaim it.

"I've always liked Loren," Lity said, "from the first day he came to the back door in Denver."

"Thank you." Missouri whispered hoarsely into Lity's ear as she pulled her into a tight embrace. "That means the world to me. It really does."

She kissed Lity's cheek and left her sobbing, freezing, on the front porch as she climbed into the cart beside Loren. Never would she forget this scene.

December 12, 1893

Dearest Fidelity,

My pen—Papa's pen—quivers as I write because I know this day will bring our parting, and our family has endured enough parting in the last few months. Even when we have sat across the dining room table from each other, we have parted. Yet I know I cannot stay. Every day our mother speaks poison about the man to whom I have bound my heart and future. She speaks poison about our Papa to whom she bound her own future. And I can no longer live with this bitter poison.

Our Papa was a dear man. He was not a man of tremendous wealth, but he was a man of tremendous generosity. I always want to remember him that way, and I hope you will too.

Loren is a dear man as well. I hope and pray that our parting now will not mean that this is the last opportunity for you to know the strength and goodness of this man who is my husband, and I hope and pray that someday you will know love like I know—and love like our mother once had and has forgotten.

I know that "home" right now is a hard place even for a spirit as cheerful as yours. When you have finished school, leave if you must. You will be old enough to make your own choice. Come to me then, if you wish. We will always have a place for you. Always.

Please, Lity, do not lose yourself in the poison as Corah has. And pray every day, as I do, morning and evening, for Mama to come back to herself.

All my love,
Missouri

CHAPTER THIRTY-THREE

Nolan and Jillian came out of the Canary Cage gulping tall cold drinks.

"How pitiful is it that twice in one day we have woefully underestimated how to handle the way a kid on a bike takes bad news?" Jillian took a long draft of her raspberry Italian cream soda.

"She would be pleased with your choice of beverage."

"It seemed the least I could do."

"I really think she'll be all right, Jilly. We all hoped Jayden would make a different decision, and of course it's hitting Tisha hard, but when we think about the coping mechanisms she's had to develop to come as far as she has—"

"Like shoplifting?"

"Not her best, I grant you, but her whole life is ragged. She could be in far more trouble. I'm not throwing the baby out with the bathwater because we have this one setback."

"I hope you're right, Dad."

They sauntered in the direction of where they'd left the truck parked.

Jillian grabbed Nolan's arm. "Do you see what I see?"

"I see a girl with pink hair getting off a green bike in front of Motherlode Books," he said. "Please tell me I'm not hallucinating because I'm dehydrated with heatstroke."

"Please tell me two people having the same hallucination is not even a thing."

They picked up their pace, waving their hands at a couple of cars approaching the intersection. They had to get across the street. Tisha lifted the front wheel of her bike into the rack in front of the bookstore to park it and then went inside. Jillian and Nolan weren't more than two minutes behind her.

Tisha was at a spinner rack at the rear of the store with Dave Rossi.

Dave glanced up at Jillian and Nolan. "I'll be right with you."

Tisha exhaled. "Really? Now you're here?" She looked at Dave. "Are they supposed to bring drinks in here?"

"Technically, no," he said.

Jillian snatched Nolan's drink, found the nearest trash can, and dropped both half-empty cups in. "Problem solved."

"Looks that way," Dave said. "You folks come in for something in particular?"

"We'll have what she's having." Nolan nodded toward Tisha.

"You are really off your game," Tisha said.

"You're both interested in journals as well?" Dave asked.

"Journals?" Jillian said.

"Did you think the new guy at the bookstore was dealing drugs to teenagers or something?" Tisha said.

"No!" Jillian waved both hands, fingers splayed. "Absolutely not. I thought no such thing about either of you."

"That's a relief," Dave said. "I would have a hard time explaining that to my daughter. She'd never let me see Nadia again—or my dog, who stays with them some of the time while I'm working. Selling books, not drugs."

"So, journals," Jillian said.

"We have a nice selection," Dave said, "and they're thirty percent off. Some people like to have a special pen to use with their journals, so we've got some of those as well."

"Journals?" Nolan said.

"Am I not explaining this right?" Dave said. "This entire rack is journals. Big ones, little ones, leather ones, cutesy ones, lined ones, unlined ones. Tisha came in asking about journals, so I'm showing her what we have. We also have pens."

Nolan and Jillian laughed

"You are perfectly clear," Jillian said.

"These two are a little wacko today," Tisha said. "I've had a couple of hard days, and they think—well, I don't actually know what they think. Maybe that I'm made out of glass, which I assure you I'm not.

Or that I'm going to start throwing golf balls at people's heads or smash windshields with a baseball bat or run away from home or buy drugs from some old dude I hardly know."

"But you're not going to do any of those things, are you?" Dave said.

"Let's just say I'm not going to do any of those things right now." Tisha turned back to the rack. "In the first place, you don't sell golf balls. Or bats. I just thought I would see if I had enough money for a journal."

"A journal," Nolan said.

Tisha looked over her shoulder at Nolan, scowling, before shifting her gaze to Jillian. "Is he all right?"

Jillian stepped toward the girl. "Out on the trail, up on the rocks, you were pretty upset."

"I was just trying to work things out."

"You shot off pretty fast."

Tisha shrugged one shoulder. "Biking helps. By the time I got back to town, I had decided to start a diary. Maybe that will help too."

"That actually sounds like a solid idea," Nolan said.

"You don't have to sound so surprised." Tisha gave the rack a slow spin.

"Tisha Crowder," Nolan said, laughing, "nothing about you can surprise me."

"Not sure how to take that," she muttered. "But anyway, I'm going to start a diary. A real one. Not like Georgina's two pages torn out of somebody else's, but my own, from start to finish."

Joanna poked her head around the end of an aisle. "How's my puppy?"

"Wriggly is doing very well," Dave said. "I'm sure he'd love to see you. Let's arrange a visit."

"I'll take plenty of allergy medication first."

"Good thought."

"Does Clark know you're here?" Nolan said. "Are you sure you're supposed to be on a break?"

"Very funny," Joanna said. "I actually have the whole afternoon off. Legit. That happens sometimes."

"I suppose so."

"I heard you talking about journals and diaries," Joanna said to Tisha. "Do you like old ones?"

"What do you mean? Like old-fashioned covers?"

"No, actual old diaries."

"Somebody else's diaries?" Jillian's radar turned on.

Joanna nodded. "I have a small box up in my apartment. It was just there, in the closet, when I moved in. I left it alone because it doesn't actually belong to me, but I don't really know what to do with it, either."

"You found it in this building?" Jillian said.

"That's right."

"The Brandt Building."

"I guess. There are several. They're not very big. They all have dates from 1892 and 1893. Maybe a little bit from 1894? I haven't tried to read them all, because that's not really my thing, but maybe someone else is interested."

Tisha's eyes were enormous. Jillian's heart rate kicked into high gear.

"A lot of people have lived in these apartments over time," Jillian said, "but of course journals that old would be interesting to see."

"Then let's go see them." Joanna led the way through the back of the store. "There's a stairway out here. Stephanos says it's not original, but it's rickety enough that I'm not sure I believe him."

Everyone but Dave traipsed up the creaking steps. Inside Joanna's compact apartment, the rooms and fixtures had been modernized, but the bones of the exposed beams and supports captured the nineteenth-century construction of the building. A small kitchen, living room, bath, and one bedroom made for cozy living.

"Supposedly I got the storage side of the old upstairs," Joanna said. "The other apartment is a little larger because it was always living quarters. At least that's what they tell me."

"This is cool." Tisha marveled, soaking up what she saw.

"There's this little closet in the entry." Joanna tugged on a door.

"It's not much, but it holds a few coats and has a couple of shelves up top. That's where I found the box. I have a feeling somebody stuck it up there ages ago and no one has ever known what to do with it, so they just leave it. Maybe they didn't even see it when they remodeled, because who cares about the closet?"

Joanna pulled a small stool from the bottom of the closet, stood on it, and reached for the box, not even the size of a shoebox. Tisha was ready when she handed it down. It held four slim volumes.

"One person must have started them." Joanna tucked away the stool. "But I flipped through the last one and noticed several different handwritings. The name in the front says Clifford Brandt, but later it seems like someone named Missouri took over. Then she gave it to Fidelity. Those are strange names, don't you think?"

Jillian, Nolan, and Tisha laughed.

"Well, the names aren't *that* funny," Joanna said. "Just old-fashioned, I guess."

"The Brandt Building," Jillian said. "*This* building. Clifford Brandt. Missouri and Fidelity were two of his daughters. The third one was Decorah, who was Tisha's great-great-great-grandmother."

"No way!" Joanna's jaw dropped. "See, I've only been in town a few months. I don't know all this stuff."

"I'm only learning it myself." Tisha took the box to Joanna's love seat and extracted the final journal and carefully turned to the back. "I wonder."

"I do too," Jillian said.

Tisha pulled up the image of Georgina's torn diary page on her phone. "I think it matches!"

Jillian leaned in. "You might be right. We'll have to take this down to the Heritage Society to know for sure, but the tear looks like it could have come from this journal."

Tisha flipped back to earlier in the book.

June 28, 1893. The day has come. On the surface, this will look like an ordinary excursion to Canyon Mines, where I can stay in a decent hotel while I do business I never imagined a

few months ago. But it's unavoidable. For now, and probably
for good, I have to shut down my own mines. Is my equip-
ment worth anything? That's hard to say. Who needs ore carts
when there is no market for the ore? I suppose the carts could
haul other freight if the railroad could be persuaded. One
step at a time. I see no hope for silver to recover—certainly I
cannot hold on long enough to find out."

"Very sad," Nolan said.

"May I see?" Jillian asked, and Tisha handed her the volume. Jillian gingerly turned the yellowed pages filled with black ink.

"July 27, 1893. Violence is worsening. One can feel it in the
streets. I have not told Georgina how close Missouri and I
were to being caught up in the Arata business, and I will
not. She would not be able to cope. Who can cope? That is the
question, is it not? No money. No jobs. Only uncertainty and
stress and impossible choices. 'The LORD is my rock, and my
fortress, and my deliverer; my God, my strength, in whom I
will trust.' Psalm 18:2."

She turned to another entry.

"August 9, 1893. I have received word from Parson Tom that
my donation, as feeble as it feels to me, is considerable enough to
do substantial good. I have his assurance that he will be able to
channel it in the manner I have designated to allow men who
choose to return to their loved ones to do so with dignity, well
fed and well kept and traveling in comfort. It is my wish that
no man fall into the arms of those who love him looking as poor
in body as he may feel in spirit, but that he may have a bit to
tide him over until he stands on his feet again. If I can share
with some of the destitute miners the same dignity that I myself
preserve even as I also reconcile the changes in my financial
standing, I will feel that I have heard and answered the voice

of my Maker to do unto the least of these."

Nolan took the book now and turned a few pages with care. "This is where it looks like someone else took over.

> *"August 21, 1893. Reading what Papa has written in this volume overwhelms me. Such a mild-mannered man who thinks not only of his own gain but for the situation of so many others. He has done his best by us—by Mama, whether she can see it or not, by my sisters and me, by my sweet Loren, by miners he knew to call by name and many others he did not. When I look through my papa's eyes, I see that he saw people whom God dearly loves and for whom God calls us to sacrifice even as Christ sacrifices for us. I know he will give his blessing for my nuptials to Loren. Mama needs some time still. Life will be different here in Canyon Mines, but it can still be a life rich in love."*

Tisha reached for the journal again. "I want to see the end, where the last person wrote." She turned a few pages. "I see here where Missouri gave the journal to Fidelity and where Fidelity started to write. Here's the last entry.

> *"October 3, 1894. I've made up my mind. I know Missouri will encourage me to persevere. My high school graduation is only a few weeks away in December. I will be eighteen and have a diploma. I realize many young women do not have this opportunity. But I cannot wait. Truly I cannot. Missouri is not here. She doesn't understand that Mama and Corah get worse by the day. Their words bite into me, taking pieces of me with every conversation. If I stay, there will be nothing left of me to get on a train to Tennessee once I have that diploma in hand. So I'm going now. I've saved enough money for the fare, and I've made up my mind."*

Tisha looked up. "That's the end. Missouri and Fidelity really left. Decorah stayed."

Joanna cleared her throat softly. "Obviously, the journals should be yours."

Jillian took the journal again, holding the old brown leather by the edges.

"But how did the journals survive?" Tisha asked, looking at the image on her phone again. "Georgina said she made sure no one would ever write in them. I thought she destroyed the journal her page came from."

"That's a great question." Jillian opened the back of the journal again, inspecting the tear. "Wait, there's something here. Jo, turn on that lamp."

"What is it?" Tisha asked.

They huddled over the volume in brighter light.

"There are pencil markings inside the back cover," Jillian said. "So faint with age! Let's see.

"Papa, why did you go? I've always missed you. I could never let Mama burn all that was left of you. Love always, your little Decorah Runner."

"Oh my goodness," Nolan said.

"But Grandma Ora said Decorah was such a grumpy person," Tisha said.

"At least in this one moment, she wasn't."

"It's almost enough to give a person hope." Tisha closed the journal with a hush and held it against her chest.

Jillian met her eyes and nodded.

"I want to read them all, start to finish," Tisha said. "But then I might give them to the Heritage Society so people in this town can see that my family were not all a bunch of cranks."

"That would be your choice to make," Nolan said. "You'd be in control."

"What I want to control right now is whether to buy a brown journal or a black journal."

CHAPTER THIRTY-FOUR

I'LL JUST BE A LITTLE LATE, the text said. NEED TO DO SOMETHING.

Jillian settled in with a third cup of coffee and tried not to guess what Tisha's words meant. Instead, she decided to straighten up the dining room table.

Again.

Her dad was probably dying to throw one of his impromptu dinner parties, the kind where he didn't decide until two o'clock in the afternoon what the menu would be and assigned Jillian to round up the guests. But as soon as she got the table cleared of one stage of the St. Louis files, another phase of the project took over. When Tisha bolted for the trail the day before, she hadn't made any effort to tidy her workspace. Certainly it had been an eventful day. Nolan and Jillian both had put in a long evening of work, trying to catch up on hours of neglect during the day, though it had been nearly impossible to concentrate on anything after finding those journals. Jillian hadn't even looked at any of the scans Tisha had done while she was in a funk of disappointment, to see if they were right.

For now Jillian abandoned the straightening effort, beyond separating the files she knew Tisha hadn't touched. She'd have to let Tisha tell her what was what among the papers spread out around the scanner.

When she arrived. A little late.

Whatever that meant.

Jillian took her coffee to her office, checked her email, answered a phone call, starred the items on her to-do list to prioritize for the day, and carried her empty mug to the sink to rinse it out.

Forty minutes.

Jillian resisted the urge to make another cup of coffee, but she gave in to the temptation to wander out to the front porch and glance down the street for a flash of spinning green. Her vigilance was rewarded. Now she wished she had a beverage in her hands so she could casually drop into the wicker rocker or the swing and pretend she was simply taking a break. Making a show of admiring the mountain view sufficed.

Tisha parked her bike. "Did you think I wasn't coming?"

"Not at all. You said a little late. So I did a few other things."

"Is Nolan home?"

"He's in Denver on Wednesdays."

"I forgot." Tisha took a canvas bag off the handlebars and ascended the stairs. "I wanted to finish something so you could read it. I started my diary."

"Diaries are supposed to be private."

"I know. And mine will be too, after this. But you guys have seen plenty of my family's dirty laundry in the last couple of weeks, so nothing I write will shock you. I think you might actually like this." Tisha handed the new brown leather diary to Jillian and sat on the top step.

"Are you sure you want me to read this?"

"Yes. But please don't make me read it to you, and don't even think about reading it out loud. I don't want to hear how stupid it sounds."

"I'm sure it doesn't sound stupid."

"How many times do I have to tell you? Stop placating me. It might sound stupid. It also felt, I don't know, real, to write it. I guess Nolan would say I was in control of something. My own words. My own thoughts. Anyway, you read—silently—and I'm just going to sit here."

"It would be my honor." Jillian opened the journal.

> *Dear Missouri and Fidelity.*
> *You are long ago and far away, as they say. Did they say that when you were around? I don't suppose you could have imagined me and my pink hair and the way I run around with my legs showing. And I mean practically all of my legs. Maybe you can. Maybe you had rebellious granddaughters like me, who did whatever they had to do to stay cool in the summer.*

I hear it can be pretty hot and humid in Tennessee. We don't know the meaning of humid around here. I guess you know that.

I was up all night imagining you. I found the diaries you left behind when you escaped. They were in the Brandt Building all this time. Can you believe it? Escaped. I don't think there's really a better word for it. I could politely say you moved or you followed your dream or you made life choices. But I read the diaries, so I know the real reasons you made the life choices to go far away from this place.

I also know Decorah stayed here, because she's the reason I'm here. Well, not the whole reason. A few other people made life choices too that had something to do with why I'm here, but a lot of it has to do with Decorah and Georgina staying here. The funniest part is that your dad (may he rest in peace) chose this place, but your mom and your sister were the two people who wanted to be in Canyon Mines the least. That's according to what they said. But they never left. So I'm not sure what I believe about that. Couldn't they sell the store and the house, once times were better, and find a place in Denver again? Maybe not Denver. That could be embarrassing for someone like Georgina, I suppose. Everyone would know she'd been banished from her big society house. But what about Chicago? Or San Francisco? Or lots of places where people wouldn't know they'd once been wealthier?

Maybe as mad as Georgina was at what Clifford did, and it seems like she was really, really steamed for a really, really long time, she couldn't leave him here alone. That's my theory. Missouri, what you wrote about how Loren carried your father's broken body up out of the mine and brought him home wrecked me. Straight up wrecked me. I have to say, I was sobbing half the night. True fact. That scene is straight out of a movie. But I'm very experienced with the truth that you can be very mad at someone, even a lot of the time, but that doesn't mean you don't love the person.

And maybe if Georgina couldn't leave, then neither could Decorah. Leaving them here alone, without any of their children, was just too big a thought to bear. I honestly think that's a possibility. And where would she go, because we're talking truth here, aren't we? It's not like the two of you gave her an open invitation. She was half of what you were escaping.

(I have to say, you three have very strange names. I wish somebody had explained that in the journals. Although these days, people are named things like Dakota and Apple and North, so who am I to say?)

I guess an important thing to say here is that Decorah became my grandma's grandma. I don't know if she even ever told you she had a family. Did you stay in touch at all? She married Axel Emery. It would have been nice if they'd been happy. Maybe things would have turned out differently down the line. Their number two daughter, Darlene, married Dudley Winfield, but he didn't stick around long. I guess you'd say Dudley was a dud! Darlene's daughter, Ora, married Micah Crowder. She really loved him, but he died very young. Her daughter Peggy (Margaret, if you're formal) didn't bother tying the knot. (Maybe after the family track record, she didn't see the point, but I think she could be wrong on that question.) Peggy just had Brittany, who discovered I was on the way before she discovered she'd made a mistake with the guy. I'm not going to do that.

So here I am. The women in our family who stayed in Canyon Mines don't have a great track record with men. Or happiness. I'm kind of getting a better grip on why. I'm thinking I might like to hold out for the right guy and give marriage a try, if I ever get myself straightened out. That comes first.

I'm not going to be like the Brandt women I know. I'm telling you that here and now. Despite learning really well how to keep a grudge, I am facing facts about why some things happen, why some things do actually matter, and that I don't have to give up on absolutely everything.

*Because now I know Clifford is in my family tree.
Nobody's perfect, but he seems like he was very sincere. And
kind. And generous. And hardworking. And spiritual. And
somebody I would like to know and can be proud to be related
to. And I don't say that very often. True fact. Ask anybody
who knows me.*

*And Loren seems like a cool dude too. He stood by you and
you stood by him, Missouri. And his heart was big enough
for Fidelity. Not every man takes in pieces of his wife's crazy
family.*

*Fidelity, you were so brave! Everybody had an idea
what you should do, as if coloring inside the lines would solve
everything. But you weren't a color-inside-the-lines person
any more than I am. You were a be-happy person!*

*And you know what? That's what I want to be. A
be-happy person. True fact. Not a pretend-to-be-happy
person, not a look-happy person, but a person who is actually
happy.*

*I don't have a great start. True fact. (I have to stop writ-
ing that, because I don't want to scratch stuff out the first time
I write in a diary.) But that doesn't mean I'm stuck where
I've always been or where the women in my family have
been. Not sleeping a single minute last night was worth it if
I can just hang on to that one thing. I'm not stuck. And I will
be happy.*

*So Missouri and Fidelity, thanks for the journal. I am
here. And I am going to be fine.*

Letitia (Brandt) Crowder

*P.S. The Brandt Building is so cool now. You would love it.
Not only did I find your journal there, but I bought my journal there.*

Jillian sniffed. She'd been meaning for weeks to bring a fresh box of tissues out to the little end table on the porch.

"You're not crying," Tisha said. "Tell me you're not crying."

"Who, me?" Jillian sniffed again. "Letitia Crowder, you are going to be fine."

"Don't I know it."

"I was considering finding out what it would take to color my dark hair pink," Jillian said.

"I know the answer." Tisha smiled slyly. "Courage. Pure stubborn courage."

"In that case, I've come to the right person for advice."

AUTHOR'S NOTE

This book is about finding that place where you understand you belong and know acceptance. God created us to belong—ultimately to Him but also to one another in the process.

I think one reason genealogy is fascinating to many people is a sense of connection. Even if we don't know these people from generations past or because our family trees have wonky branches somewhere, we can stand beneath them, the way we stand under towering oaks or cedars or pines and appreciate that they're much older than we are and connect us to something significant outside the small part of the world we've experienced.

And somehow we *belong* among those branches.

When we meet someone whose last name is the same as our mother's maiden name, we perk up. Who knows? Maybe we're distantly related. Or we say, "My father's family came from that area," because who knows? Maybe there's a connection.

Given the population of any state or of the United States or the world, the odds of randomly meeting someone who is your mother's distant cousin or knew your father's family are remote, yet we always think it would be remarkable if it happened.

We seek connection and belonging.

We are free agents. On one hand, we choose more than we realize. Who to be friends with. Whether to go to college and where. Whether to move to another area for employment or stay close to family. Whether to buy, sell, or build a house, run for the school board, volunteer with a community group, learn to perform stand-up comedy, date, marry, or a hundred other decisions that shape our lives.

On the other hand, some experiences and circumstances shape our lives whether we choose them or not. Whether we grow up in want. Whether we experience trauma or serious illness. Whether we benefit from or struggle against racial and economic biases. Whether we had an adult or a friend who cared at critical times in our lives. Whether we had a decent third-grade teacher! Often social, financial, educational, and relational forces shape us in unseen ways and influence the possibilities available to us at the moments when we are ripe to make choices for better or for worse.

One of the best choices we all can learn to make is what we do with our words. The unseen consequences shed not only in our lives but into the buds and branches still forming on the family tree. Perhaps this is the most important choice of all.

As usual, the historical portion of this story is a blend of fact and fiction. The Brandts are a fictional family, but I have endeavored to render the world in which they lived in the summer of 1893 faithfully. Several western states, Colorado in particular, rose up in ways in which their economies depended on the natural resources available in the wide expanse of their miles. Colorado had great stores of silver, and the US government was buying vast quantities as fast as they could be unearthed, while the national currency was backed by both silver and gold. Once the movement to move to a single gold standard, more popular in the East, won out, the collapse of silver mining magnified for Colorado the effects of the economic recession that settled on the entire country in 1893.

Horace Tabor is a historical figure who lived a colorful life with two marriages, became wealthy by gambling audaciously on mining in various parts of Colorado, and was also philanthropic. When silver collapsed, Tabor lost his financial empire virtually overnight, resorting to low-wage menial labor for a few years before being appointed postmaster for the city of Denver the year before his death. He never recovered his wealth. The nature of Clifford Brandt's work for Tabor in this story is purely fictional.

The social services crisis portrayed in Denver in the summer of 1893, along with the mob scene culminating in the murder of Daniel Arata, were real. I drew information for these scenes from newspaper accounts and scholarly research. Denver's proximity to the mountains meant that at the time the industry failed, thousands of men did, in fact, abruptly need assistance—overwhelming the largely faith-based social services network in place operated by two large churches which was already providing a variety of services. Once word got out that Denver was organizing to help miners, even more men from other parts of the state headed for the capital as well.

As I read through the available literature, it struck me that the city made some good decisions—like providing temporary jobs and temporary shelter for some men—and some well-intentioned but dubious decisions—like putting homeless men on rafts to float down the river and be someone else's problem when the money was running out. But this mix of decision quality is often true in times of regional and national crises.

Crises also occur when we don't make the best decisions with our words. We see them happen on social media all the time, but the truth is that most of us hear moments that make us wince even in the circles of our real-life family and friends. Sometimes these thoughtless words come out of our own mouths, if we're honest.

I want to express particular thanks to my friend Jack, who read my story about stolen children, *In the Cradle Lies*, and shared the story of twins Maclovia and Ernestine in his family tree. It's a saga, beginning in the 1930s, of one baby taken with no memory of her first family and the loved ones left with a gaping hole who sought her for generations—because of a longing for connection and belonging.

My hope is that *What You Said to Me* will help all of us understand the power of words. We know what they feel like when we receive them, and because of that we will choose to give the best of ourselves in the words we speak to one another and create space for others to connect and belong.

Olivia Newport
May 2020